Lan didn't reply with words. She reached up and pulled Emma down onto her lap then kissed her.

"I guess you do want me to finish," Emma gasped then returned the kiss.

"How about you? Do you want anything from me?" Lan asked as she ran her hands through Emma's hair, fluffing it out then letting it fall in soft cascades.

Emma looked longingly into Lan's eyes. She didn't have to say a word. The thoughts were already being shared. This moment had been coming since that first cool autumn evening when Emma roared into the parking lot and caught Lan in her headlights. It had only been a matter of time before their fight to remain mere professional associates crumbled into a passionate explosion of desire. At the same precise moment, they each were asking themselves the identical question. Why had they waited so long? With thorough kisses and inquisitive hands, the dance of intimacy had begun.

Visit

Bella Books

at

BellaBooks.com

or call our toll-free number

1-800-729-4992

Shared Winds

KENNA WHITE

Bella
BOOKS

2004

Printed in the United States of America on acid-free paper
First Edition

Editor: Anna Chinappi
Cover designer: Sandy Knowles

ISBN 1-59493-006-6

This book is dedicated to Ann,
for her fresh, sincere, and honest love
that opened my eyes to life.

Acknowledgments

A special thanks to Dustan and Irene for their unconditional love and support. Without them, this book would not have been possible. A thank you to Townie for her solid friendship through the years. To Jamie for her understanding and encouragement, as I found myself and wrote it down. To Tara for her humor when I most desperately needed it. And to Ellen DeGeneres for the *Puppy Episode*, thank you from the bottom of my heart.

Chapter 1

The 150-horsepower Mercury outboard flung a huge rooster tail behind the fiberglass boat. The plume of water seemed to pursue the craft across the lake. As she tightened her grip on the steering wheel, Lan Harding urged the throttle wide open. After several seconds of wind-driven exhilaration she throttled back, let the boat settle into the wake, and listened to the uniform churn of the engine. She smiled with satisfaction as she ran her fingers through her wind-blown auburn hair. Lan raised herself onto the back of the driver's seat as she guided the boat into the cove. Her tanned face was absent of any makeup. She was thirty-eight but could pass for someone in her twenties. Her eyes were her strongest feature, dark, expressive, with tendencies toward a greenish cast when she stood in the sunlight. She was thinner now than when she was captain of her high school basketball team, but her leg muscles were still well defined under her faded jeans. She considered her breasts, though small, ample for someone nearly six feet tall.

She gave a thumbs up to the man standing on the dock. His shoulder-length graying hair was held back from his deeply wrinkled face with a piece of leather lacing. The left sleeve of his flannel shirt was turned back to reveal a dirtied plaster cast covering his forearm. His greasy hands were big and weathered. He nodded and waved Lan toward the dock. He waited at the head of the boat slip for Lan to ease into position, a maneuver she could do almost without looking.

"RPM's good and no hesitation Max," Lan reported as she tossed up the bowline. "You have this one in good shape."

Lan cut the engine and tossed Max the keys, then stepped onto the wooden dock, her long legs taking the awkward step easily.

"That contractor, Quinn Bishop, called and left a message," Max announced in his deep but quiet voice. He rested one foot on the bow of the boat to steady it as the wake rolled through the slip.

"Good. Thought I'd never find an available contractor. When is he coming by?" Lan asked hopefully. "I've been calling him for three weeks now. You'd think he'd want the business." Lan looked up the hill at the storm-ravaged marina and shook her head plaintively. "How much longer do I have to wait?" she asked rhetorically.

Max busied himself with the boat's bow cleat. His eyes narrowed with crow's feet webbed out from the corners as if he was forcing his concentration downward and away from Lan's questions. Max wasn't much of a small talker, but it wasn't like him to be evasive or indifferent.

"What?" she asked after studying him for a long moment. "Max?"

"Hell, Lan," he muttered between his teeth. "He ain't coming. Said he was too backed up to come by, what with all the storm damage and bigger contracts. Said he didn't have the manpower. Stretched too thin as it was."

Lan was silent for an uncomfortably long time then took a deep breath. Her eyes searched the shimmering morning waters of Oklahoma's Grand Lake of the Cherokees. Now it was her turn to narrow her eyes and squint off into distant concentration.

"Said maybe late summer or next fall he might have time to come by and take a look," Max continued, lowering his eyes, almost ashamed of the news he had been reporting. "Sorry, kid." Max walked to the end of the dock and joined her in searching the lake waters for whatever relief it might offer.

"That was the last one, Max," Lan replied in a low voice.

He did not respond as he stood beside her, the deep creases of age wrinkling his face.

"Well," she said squaring her shoulders. "Guess I will have to look a little harder 'cause I'm not giving up on my marina. Shared Winds *is* staying open." Her smooth cheek became a rippled knot of clenched jaw muscles.

Lan turned on her heels and strode off toward the marina office. One of the flooring planks creaked and fell through with a splash as if to agree with Lan's determination. A bird, startled by the commotion, left its nest from high up in the dock rafters and flew out toward the open water. Lan took this as a good sign. The spirits were watching her. She walked the obstacle coarse of missing planks and twisted posts along the wooden boardwalk and headed up the sidewalk. The large A-frame building with its huge log timbers and glass front, was set into a clearing of thick woods that ran down to the rocky shore. A wooden deck wrapped around both sides and across the front of the building providing a breathtaking view of the sunrise over the lake. But now it looked splintered and twisted with gaps like a witch's smile.

Shared Winds had been conceived and born of Lan's image of the perfect lake business. Coupled with her master's degree in business administration and the years she spent working for inept marina owners, she knew she could create an environmentally responsible yet efficient and viable business. When she heard about an old marina that was closing because of its deteriorating condition and slumping sales, she mortgaged everything she could and scraped together enough to make a down payment. The biggest selling factor was the location. It was in a shaded cove, with room to expand, a freshwater spring feeding into the lake, and a view to die for. These were all the ingredients she needed to let her dreams take flight. But now, through the early morning mist, it looked like it had been chewed on by a mad dog.

Lan spent the rest of the day checking construction companies as far away as Kansas City, Fayetteville, and Wichita only to come away with rejection and disappointment. She tried answering a few e-mails and letters about when the marina would be back to full speed. Half a dozen potential boaters trickled in but those hoping to do some fall fishing grumbled their frustration about the unusable boat ramp and took their boats and gas money elsewhere to launch.

The September storm with tornado-force winds still rolled over and over in her mind. The wind-whipped hail lashing the roof, the boats bouncing and crashing helplessly against the docks, rental cabins toppled like a house of cards, scraps of asphalt shingles littering the campground, tree branches exploding through the picture windows, then the angry waterspout taking dead aim on the helpless marina.

When the wind, rain, and hail had wreaked its havoc and moved on, Lan, Max, the other employees, and guests were left to stumble through the shredded wreckage stunned and helpless. Max was taken to the hospital in Grove with a broken arm. A few minor injuries were tended to before Lan helped the shocked campers gather their scattered possessions and limp home. With only her numbed instincts to guide her, she searched the remains of her forty-two-acre marina and campground for bits and pieces of salvageable debris. A farmer near Ketchum, some twenty-five miles away, called to report a splintered sign floating in his pond that read Shared Winds Campgrounds. Several sections of dock railing were found washed ashore on Two Tree Island. The most humbling sight for Lan had been the huge slab of concrete that had once been the boat ramp. It had been smashed like an eggshell when the wind uprooted the tall trees that grew along either side. Now boats could be neither loaded or unloaded at Shared Winds, sending business around the point to one of the other marinas, business she hoped would one day find its way back to her cove.

Lan's dream of building the finest marina on the lake had been dissolved in one freak storm. Eight years of work and reinvesting every penny into the business now seemed perilously close to vanishing. The long days of work and lonely nights after the storm, waiting to rebuild, hoping the insurance would cover most of the damage, left Lan plenty of time to think. And now the bitter memory of Rachel's death could not have chosen a worse time to resurface.

Lan leaned back in her desk chair and closed her eyes, her hands clasped behind her head, surrendering to the memory of Rachel's soft smile. The thought of her lover's long raven hair, the way her jeans hugged her hips, their three wonderful years together, even the last tumultuous year as Rachel became increasingly more distant, left Lan painfully hollow.

Lan had hired Rachel to work in the ship's store, something she seemed perfect for. Within six months, Rachel had flirted her way into Lan's heart and her bed. For Lan, love was definitely blind. Rachel's occasional affairs and random indiscretions didn't soften the shock of her death.

She heaved a deep resolute sigh. If Rachel had been anywhere else but on that stretch of road, on that foggy night, she would still be here, yelling at Lan to get busy and find a contractor instead of being bogged down in frustration.

Lan was so deep into her thoughts she hadn't heard Max tapping his cast against the doorjamb.

"You need me anymore tonight, kid?" he asked from the doorway.

Lan came crashing back to reality. "Um, don't think so," she said trying to look busy. "Might as well cut out early."

"Early?" he replied with a chuckle. "It's quarter past seven. I'm starving. Sure miss the snack bar. I've locked up the pump house and gearboxes. I'm leaving the rest up to you."

"Okay," she nodded. "See you tomorrow, Max."

"Damn! You are someplace else tonight. Don't you remember? It is Duninvdi, month of the Harvest moon. This weekend is the Pow-Wow in Tahlequah. I told you about it three months ago."

Lan took a deep breath and slowly nodded. She hated it when he caught her daydreaming.

"Is that this weekend? Sorry. I guess I've been a little distracted these days. But don't worry about it. I can handle things here. After all, I am the boss," she added, gesturing toward the pile of papers on her desk.

"That's what worries me," he replied with a wink. "Well, if you need me, you know where I'll be."

"Just what I need, a sixty-eight-year-old full-blooded Cherokee, in warpaint and feathers, running up and down the dock, whooping and hollering, scaring the fish. As if things weren't bad enough already." Lan pushed papers around on her desk, trying to hide a grin.

"Might not hurt you to come along with us. You may not be full-blooded, but there's enough Cherokee in you. Maybe you need to return to your roots a little."

"Who, me? No thanks. I have plenty right here to keep me busy. And I've told you, my heritage is *my* business, no one else's." Her eyes narrowed slightly, a trait she demonstrated when she felt cornered or needed to hide her feelings. She accepted her Native American heritage as inner strength but preferred to handle it without fanfare.

Max picked up a tiny leather pouch from Lan's desk and let the beaded string fall through his broad fingers.

"Let your heritage work for you. There are great powers all around you. Reach out to them, let them help. The spirits of your ancestors have not abandoned you. Let your inner strength guide your steps, Allana."

Max used her given name like a parent used a child's full name to get her attention and to make a point. He tossed the medicine bag toward her. She caught it with one hand, holding it tightly in her fist.

"I know," she replied as its sweet aroma floated over her senses. She slipped the medicine bag around her neck and let it drop inside her shirt.

"Now," she ordered impishly. "I have work to do so get out of here. And remember those three motors we fished out of the cove last week. I expect them to be purring just like new in no time. So not too much firewater."

"See you next week," he replied turning to leave.

"Have a good time, my friend," she muttered after hearing the front door slam.

It was well after nine o'clock before Lan turned off her desk lamp and locked the front door. She was tired. She was hungry. And she was in no mood to deal with the car speeding up the road toward her. Before she reached the door of her Jeep Wrangler, the car screeched to a stop, the big sedan's headlights freezing her with a blinding glare. Lan squinted and raised her hand to protect her eyes.

"Excuse me." A soft female voice came from behind the headlights. "Are you Miss Harding?"

Lan stared into the glaring lights, looking for the face behind the voice.

"Yes," she answered over the noise of the car engine. "Who wants to know?"

"Bishop Construction," replied the woman. "Can I talk to you?"

"Bishop's, eh?" Lan clenched her jaw and swallowed back the urge to blurt out a string of obscenities. She reached for her door handle. If Bishop Construction thought they could send some secretary out to smooth ruffled feathers and convince her to wait a year for some half-hearted bid on her urgently needed repairs, they had another think coming.

"Please!" the woman pleaded as she stepped out of her car and slammed the door. She reached through the open window and switched off the headlights, leaving the amber glow of the parklights between her and Lan. "Could you give me a few minutes?"

Her blonde hair shimmered in the moonlight. Her lips curled to a cautious smile as she studied Lan's face. The long points of her shirt collar extended over the lapels of her suit jacket like arrows marking her seemingly perfect breasts. The top two buttons of her shirt were open revealing the top of her cleavage.

Lan caught herself staring at this remarkable creature, wondering if the parts she couldn't see were as angelic as the parts she could see. It had been a long time since she caught herself ogling over some woman's features. She forced her eyes downward, hoping her rude gawking had gone unnoticed. Even if this was an available candidate, she had neither the time nor energy to start a new relationship. She felt almost disloyal somehow, to Rachel and to Shared Winds.

"I got the message. Quinn Bishop isn't interested in bidding on the repairs to Shared Winds. No problem. I'll have someone down from Kansas City next week. There are lots of contractors out there." Lan hated lying. It was the one thing she hated more than anything else. Her word was her bond, her promise to herself, her way of life. But this woman didn't know that. "You go back and tell your boss Lan Harding can manage just fine without him."

"I'm sure you can," the woman replied reassuringly. She crossed her arms and leaned against her car. "I just thought that phone call was poor business practice. I wanted to say we are sorry for any inconvenience we might have caused. Bishop's usually doesn't treat our clients with such light regard. But you will have to admit things have been a little, well, shall we say unusual. We have four counties with damages nearing ninety-six million dollars, two thousand houses, businesses, commercial sites, state and local government buildings, roads and bridges, all needing their repairs done ASAP. The construction companies who want to keep their government contracts are having to prioritize."

"I have a business to run. If I lock my door and wait until next summer or maybe next fall to begin repairs, I might as well leave the door locked forever. It took me two weeks just to get the power back on and the gas pump repaired. I can't afford to let a full season go by without revenue. I need the income from that boat dock, ramp, and campground to keep my doors open. I don't plan on being one of the businesses that fold up and disappear in the night because this storm wiped out my marina. Shared Winds is going to stay open, if I have to get a hammer and do it myself."

Lan took a deep breath and fixed the woman with a determined stare. She hadn't meant to hop up on her soapbox. A sheepish look crawled across her face.

"Geez, I sound like Scarlet O'Hara," Lan said with a chuckle. " 'As God is my witness' . . ." She raised her hand to the sky in an overly dramatic pose.

" 'I will never be hungry again,' " they both announced in unison, then smiled at each other.

"I'm sorry. I shouldn't take this out on you. It isn't your fault. You're just following orders." Lan half expected the woman to climb back into her car and leave her alone. The other half was glad when she didn't.

"We all take orders from someone." The woman leaned forward and extended her hand. "Emma Bishop. Glad to meet you, Miss Harding. Quinn Bishop is my father."

Lan took her hand and shook it slowly, letting this news sink in.

"Well, well. Sorry about that tirade." Lan continued to shake Emma's hand. The evening was cool but this Emma Bishop's hand was delicate, warm, and comforting.

"Don't worry about it," Emma said reassuringly. "I understand."

"I can't let go of this." Lan gestured with her head toward the marina. "This is a dream I can't let die." Her voice trailed off.

"Hey, I know all about dreams," Emma insisted. Her calm and steady voice echoed through the still night air. "We all have dreams."

Emma went to the trunk of her car and took out a large flashlight. Without waiting for Lan to lead the way, she walked down the hill toward the dock. The spot from the flashlight darted along, capturing broken windows, downed trees, and piles of debris sorted by type. Lan shook her head and reluctantly followed along, taking long strides to catch up. Grotesque shapes and shadows followed the two women and their single flashlight beam as they meandered toward the remnants of the boat dock.

"What are you doing?" Lan asked, studying the woman's profile against the moonlight.

"I want to see how much damage you have. You don't mind if I look around, do you? Get an idea of what you have left to work with." Emma studied the twisted metal roofing, crumbled concrete, and missing sections of dock flooring.

"I don't mind, but don't you think the middle of the night isn't exactly the best time for examining storm damage? Watch your step. You can fall through on that walkway."

"Oops," Emma gasped as her foot found a hole in the flooring. "I see what you mean."

Lan reached out, grabbed her by the arm as she began to stumble, and pulled her close. She could feel Emma's bicep tighten at the touch. Emma stiffened and pushed away from Lan. Their faces met in frozen communication.

"What are you doing?" Emma snapped, both surprised and annoyed.

"I don't need someone falling through my boat dock right now," Lan replied protectively. "If you want to sightsee, why not come back in the daylight?" Lan released Emma's arm and headed for the parking lot.

"Just how badly do you need a contractor, Miss Harding?" Emma asked sharply, her flashlight trained on Lan's retreat.

Lan stopped in her tracks but didn't turn around. "Am I supposed to beg? Is that what this is all about?" Lan turned around and straightened her posture.

"No," Emma added quickly. "I'm not asking you to beg. I'm asking you"—Emma took a deep breath before finishing—"for help." There was a long silence neither woman cared to fill. "Actually, you will help me, and I will help you." Emma had climbed the hill and passed Lan on her way to her car. "Let's say tomorrow, ten o'clock?" Emma dropped the flashlight into her trunk and slammed the lid. She opened the car door and waited for Lan's reply. She knew she had raised her interest and like a mischievous child, she reveled in the turmoil she had created in Lan's mind.

Lan nodded, curiosity written in big letters across her face. "Okay. Ten o'clock. I'll be here."

Emma slammed the car door and started the engine. She nodded a polite smile and pulled away.

Lan watched until the taillights turned onto the highway and disappeared. She knew she wasn't going to sleep much tonight.

Chapter 2

Lan couldn't understand why she had spent so much time choosing what to wear. The usual jeans and whatever shirt touched her hand first didn't seem right this morning. After several failed trips to the bathroom mirror, she became disgusted with this unnecessary vanity and pulled her favorite navy blue sweater over a white T-shirt, stepped into her comfortably faded jeans and Nikes. She was contented knowing no one was ever going to call her a clotheshorse. She wolfed down a bowl of granola, a big glass of orange juice and grabbed a little box of raisins as she headed out the door. She whistled once and a small brown mutt followed her and jumped into the passenger's seat. He curled up and rested his head on his paws, his eyes trained on Lan. She was so deep in thought that she sped past the highway cutoff to the marina, something she hadn't done in years. She admonished herself severely as she made a U-turn and headed back.

"Wake up, Harding," she muttered. "You've got work to do."

She pulled into the first parking spot next to the front door. The marina looked forlorn this morning, as if it was wheezing and gasping under the strain of some terrible disease. Lan turned off the engine and sat quietly watching the crimson and gold leaves fluttering through the chilly autumn morning. The sky wasn't as full of them this year as it was in the past. The beautiful Oklahoma oak, birch, and maple leaves were noticeably absent. As much as she hated the annual raking chores, she missed the knee-deep piles that crowded around the marina, crunching under foot. The storm had taken away the autumn splendor. Dried leaves still held tight to the uprooted trees. She missed the trees. She missed the normality, the continuity of life before the storm. She had begun to find balance again. Balance of work and emotions and of spirit. Or was she merely hiding: Had she turned the monotony of her work into an emotional security blanket? Had she allowed the long hours of tedium to block out her loneliness?

She reached inside her shirt, pulled out the medicine bag, and held it between her fingers. She could feel the tiny stones and bits of bark and leaves Max had used to make her medicine. Her fingertips massaged the soft deerskin pouch. Tears welled up in her eyes and threatened to spill out. There would be none of that, she decided. No feeling fragile and vulnerable. She closed her eyes and opened her mind, flooding her thoughts with positive images, the image of Shared Winds, repaired and rebuilt, once again reigning over Grand Lake.

An energetic yelp from Koji, her trusted canine companion, brought her back to reality.

"Okay, okay. Let me unhook you before you strangle yourself."

She released the snap on his safety harness. The pup stood on her lap impatiently wagging his tail as she reached for the door handle. In one leap he was out the door and galloping toward the dock. She removed her jacket and tossed it into the backseat of the Jeep. Today was going to be better, somehow. She felt it.

But thirty minutes at her desk staring at the computer screen was enough. This morning was conspiring to test her patience. She turned off the computer monitor and stood up. She needed fresh air.

Once outside, she pushed up the sleeves of her sweater and began stacking the firewood she had cut from the downed trees. Each campsite and each cabin would have a fresh supply of firewood with plenty for the huge stone fireplace in the lobby of the marina. With the gas line for the furnace ripped out by uprooted trees, the fireplace was crucial. The cordwood was stacked in neat rows in no time. But that wasn't enough. She was on a mission. She eyed the pile still to be cut, checked her watch, and headed for the tool shed to gas the chainsaw. It was only a little after nine. Emma Bishop wasn't due until ten. More than enough time to cut a rick or two. Woods chips flew for more than an hour. The scream of the chainsaw seemed to go on without end. She hadn't noticed Emma drive into the parking lot and cross the slope to the campground. She hadn't noticed her sitting on a picnic table watching her work either.

"How long have you been there?" Lan asked with the startled look of a deer caught in the headlights. She turned off the chainsaw, set it down, and caught her breath.

"Not long," Emma replied. "That looks like hard work."

"They say firewood warms you twice. Once when you cut it, again when you burn it." Lan brushed the sawdust from her clothes and hair. "Messy job too."

"Is all that from the storm damage?" Emma pointed to the stacks of cut wood.

"Yep. So is that." Lan nodded toward the huge bulldozed pile of trees beyond the campground.

"Oh my," Emma gasped in astonishment. "That's a lot of wood."

"Those were beautiful trees. Cedar, oak, birch, walnut, couple wild cherry, and a few maple."

"And I bet the insurance doesn't cover that, does it?"

Lan raised her eyebrows and shook her head. "No. Some things you can't insure. Beauty in nature is one of them. You just have to take care of it. It's going to take a long time to get a mature stand of trees around the marina again. Some were pushed over roots and all." Lan pointed toward the crumbled pile of concrete. "The ones that lined the boat ramp were hundred-year-old walnut and cedars. The wind blew them over, pulling the roots right up through the concrete. Flipped it over like a pancake, then broke it into a million pieces."

"How big is that ramp?" Emma asked.

"Oh, about a hundred feet wide and maybe one hundred fifty feet long, with a flared apron at the top. We could launch anything but the *Queen Mary*," Lan said proudly.

"How far does it extend into the water?" Emma asked as she made notes in a folder.

Lan was impressed she knew to ask that. "With this lake level, about fifty feet. But there is a seam just below the waterline. Most of that part is still there. If you'll give me a minute, I'll show you around."

"Okay."

Emma continued to take notes while Lan returned the tools to the shed. By the time she walked back up the slope, Emma was busy calculating and sketching.

"I have to ask," Lan said after awkwardly clearing her throat. "What did you mean last night about helping each other?" She didn't know how else to broach the subject other than with her usual straightforward approach.

Emma finished her calculations and closed her notebook. "I have an offer for you, Ms. Harding." She folded her hands on top of the leather folder. "A proposition."

"Okay. Let's hear it. And you can call me Lan. Everybody else does."

"Well, Lan," Emma replied, trying out the name. "It's simple. I would like to be your contractor. I want to handle the repairs to Shared Winds. You have a lot of damage here but nothing too severe. As I see it, you have several small to medium jobs, and a few big ones. The roof over the boat dock and boathouse, the cabins in the campground, the concrete slab for the boat ramp, and of course the roof and window end of the marina building as well as the restaurant. I haven't looked at them in detail, but I don't see any insurmountable problems. There's the demolition work as well. We'd have to get this debris hauled away first. And set up a delivery schedule. Weather is a big factor."

Lan's eyes widened as she listened with growing interest. It was as if her prayers had finally been answered. This woman's words were almost too good to digest all at once.

"That's great. I'm glad Bishop's has reconsidered. I was getting worried there for a while. It's getting close to winter and we're losing precious time." Lan's enthusiasm was growing. The childish excitement of Christmas morning, the tooth fairy, and a new puppy all rolled into one couldn't equal her satisfaction at hearing Emma Bishop say they wanted the job of repairing Shared Winds. She didn't know why Quinn Bishop had changed his mind. It didn't matter. Whatever the reason, she was relieved.

"Is Quinn coming out later today to look things over?" Lan knew that sounded like she didn't trust Emma's judgment but she knew every big company had one boss who made the decisions and signed the orders.

"Not exactly," Emma replied.

"So you do the leg work, eh. Then he comes out later to look things over?" Lan said with an agreeable smile. "You take measurements and he makes bids, right?"

"My father isn't involved in this." Emma sat quietly while Lan absorbed this news.

"But I thought you said Bishop's was going to bid the repairs. I don't understand." Lan felt a terrible sinking in the pit of her stomach.

"I said *I* would like to be your contractor, not Bishop Construction." Emma spoke quietly but with confidence. "I think I need to explain."

"Yes," Lan agreed, crossing her arms. "Please do. I'm having a little trouble here."

"Yesterday I said we could help each other."

Lan nodded.

"You need a contractor. I know you've been trying to get other companies down here to bid this job. You'd be crazy not to. You need the work done now, not next summer or next fall. I'm a professional. I've been in the construction business for fifteen years and I have my own license. I can see this job through to completion. From planning and demolition to inspections and finishing. I will handle all the ordering, the hiring, the deliveries, all the subcontractors, all the headaches, and all the details. You decide what you want done and where. I'll make it happen. I can even handle the insurance company if you need me to."

"And what do you get out of it?" Lan asked warily.

"I get to keep my business." Emma stood up, tucked the leather folder under her arm, and headed for the dock. "I need a job to bid," she continued. "I've been working for my father for fifteen years and now it all comes down to this job." Emma looked to see if Lan had followed her. She had. "My father wants to retire. He wants time to do things, see things, while he and Mom are young enough to enjoy them. He can afford it. He invested well." Emma stood at the railing and watched the ripples rolling across the cove.

"Nothing wrong with retirement. But what does that have to do with me?" Lan asked.

"I've been saving up to buy him out. But this storm changed everything. He has decided he wants out now, not in a couple years. He doesn't think I'm capable of being the only Bishop in Bishop Construction." Emma turned to face Lan. "I'm his daughter, but he doesn't think I can handle it. He got a buy-out offer from a company in Kansas. He has six months to decide."

"Six months?" Lan asked. "When is that?"

"April first."

Lan took a deep breath. "Looks like we both are on a deadline here."

"This is what I know how to do," Emma declared. "And I'm good at it," she added with a wry smile. "I just have to convince you to hire me."

"I hire you so you can show your father you are capable of taking over the business. Is that it?"

"That's it."

"Have you ever been sole contractor on a job this size?" Lan asked.

"No," she answered quietly. "Shared Winds would be my first."

"And what happens if you can't handle it, if your father is right? Your business won't be the only one lost. I'll lose mine too." Lan wrinkled her brow then ran her hand through her hair. "I have to have Shared Winds ready for business as usual by the first weekend in March. All the marinas on the lake begin their season that weekend. It's tradition." Lan looked down through the missing boards on the dock. "And I have to put all this in the hands of a woman out to show her daddy she isn't all peaches and cream."

Emma stood motionless awaiting her verdict, as if anything more she could say would be superfluous. She had pleaded her case. It was now up to this woman to decide to trust her.

The trees across the cove swayed gently, dropping an occasional leaf as a reminder of the rapidly approaching winter. From high up in a nearly leafless cottonwood tree, a hawk left its nest and soared out over the water. It glided majestically then swooped down near the damaged boathouse. The powerful strokes of its wings sent it effortlessly back up above the treetops where it circled before returning to its nest.

At the same moment Lan felt her decision being taken out of her hands. She couldn't explain it, but she trusted it. Emma Bishop would be her contractor. There was no need to look any further. She had found the right person for the job. She knew it. She felt it. She trusted it. Lan extended her hand to Emma. "Miss Bishop, I'm putting Shared Winds in your hands. I trust you to do the right thing."

Emma took Lan's hand and shook it. They smiled cautiously at each other. Both took a preparatory breath at the same moment, as if realizing the enormity of the task they had set in motion with that one handshake.

"Thank you, Lan. I won't let you down."

"I hope you don't."

"I'll bring the contract out tomorrow morning for you to sign. How about showing me around now?" Emma asked, taking a deep breath. "I think we have some work to do."

Lan squinted into the morning sun and studied a sleek runabout as it rushed into the cove. The boat was zigzagging a path toward Shared Winds with speeds better suited for open water. She watched as the driver tossed what looked like a beer can overboard then leaned over and took another one from a cooler.

"He's going too fast," Lan announced harshly. The inboard engine coughed and sputtered as the boat roared toward the gas pumps mounted on the end of the dock. The driver put the can to his mouth and tilted it upright, holding it there until it was empty.

"Howdy," he yelled, gesturing wildly. He had the look of drunken foolishness. As the boat neared the dock, he seemed to realize he was going too fast to stop. "Oh shit," he muttered.

The woman in the seat next to him reached over and jerked the steering wheel, aiming the boat away from the dock. The boat circled out into the cove, its engine giving off an occasional sputter. With each circle, as it crossed its own wake, the boat roller-coastered wildly. The driver was thrown forward against the windshield then onto the floor. After stumbling over the seat, he grabbed at the steering wheel and pulled himself into the driver's seat. The boat continued to circle as both of its passengers swayed back and forth, clutching at first one railing then another. Neither one seemed capable of bringing the boat under control.

"Cut your engine," Lan yelled. She stood at the end of the dock, leaning as far out as she could. She cupped her hands to her mouth and yelled again. "Cut your engine."

"I don't think he hears you," Emma offered.

"At least he isn't hitting anything while he's circling tight like that," she reported. "But he looks drunk as a skunk. If he doesn't hold on, he's going to fall overboard."

Finally the engine sputtered for the last time, gave out a smoking belch, and fell mercifully quiet. After another half circle, the boat settled into the ring of waves it had created and rocked until the wake had dissipated.

"Thank goodness he turned it off," Emma said with a relieved sigh.

"He didn't," Lan replied. "The engine died. Probably out of gas. I heard it coughing when he rounded the point. I think he's been sucking fumes for five minutes."

"Then he's a lucky man," Emma said, shaking her head. "He could have been killed, or killed someone else."

"Hey! What happened?" the driver asked with a bewildered expression.

"I think we're out of gas, honey," the woman said as she studied the gas gauge.

"Now that was a kick," he said with a snort. "Grab me another can in the cooler, Judy." He held out his hand without looking at her.

She peered into the cooler and took out two cans. "Last ones, honey. We're going to have to get some more."

She handed him one. They both popped the tops and took a long draw. He belched then looked toward the dock.

"Hey you, toots," he yelled in a condescending voice. "Can you come on out here and tow us in? We're out of gas." He smiled a disgusting smile.

Lan perched her hands on her hips and stared without expression.

"Did you hear me, toots?" He leaned heavily against the side. "You could use one of those boats to come tow me over. You know how to drive a boat don't you, cutie?" He smirked while his eyes tried to focus on Lan.

Lan didn't answer. She watched and waited. It was a little late in the season for this kind of drunk. Usually they were the Fourth of July to Labor Day types. By October, the cool winds and colder water kept them home, drinking beer in front of the television.

"Hey toots," he said with a hiccup. The man hadn't noticed the boat had been riding the waves toward the dock.

"Toss me your bowline," Lan ordered in a calm voice.

"What?" The man looked at Lan as if she was speaking a foreign language.

"Toss me your bowline," she repeated slowly. "The rope, throw me that rope in the front." Lan pointed.

"This one?" Judy asked, leaning over the windshield.

"Yep," Lan answered with a nod. "That one."

The woman tossed the rope in Lan's direction with one hand while holding her beer can out of the way with the other. The rope hooked on the windshield and fell into the water.

"Oops," she declared with a giggle.

"Here, let me do that." The man grabbed the rope and managed a one-handed toss. This time the rope caught on the steering wheel and fell short. "Damn, Judy. Let go of the rope."

"I don't have it, honey," she said apologetically.

He gathered in the rope, perched on his knees, and made a bigger overhand toss. The end of the rope struck him in the back of the head, causing him to drop his beer can on the seat. In his scramble to grab it, he slipped and sat down in the spilled foam. The delayed shock of the coldness made him lurch out of the seat, whacking his elbow on the railing.

"Ouch!" he bellowed as the can slipped through his fingers into the lake, slowly filled with water, and sank out of sight. The man leaned over and watched as the last shimmering signs of the can disappeared. The woman rushed to his side of the boat to see what he was watching. The boat heaved to that side, dipping the man's face into the cold lake. "Goddammit, Judy." He wiped his face on his shirt and growled at the simpering woman.

Emma couldn't help herself. A large burst of laughter erupted. She quickly covered her mouth with her hand as muffled snickers tried to sneak out. Lan shook her head and blinked deliberately.

"One more time, champ," she said.

The man grumbled something at Lan and tossed the rope again.

It was a wild throw but Lan was able to catch it with her outstretched arm and pull the boat into the dock. The man climbed onto the dock, finding the hard surface difficult to walk on.

"Fill'er up, toots," he said, holding on to the railing. He began to dig in his pockets for his wallet. "Couple six-packs of Bud, too."

Lan looped the line around the dock cleat, and gave it another half hitch.

"I don't think so," she replied without looking up.

"What? You out of gas?" he asked, his speech becoming more slurred.

"Nope. Got plenty of gas." She flipped the lock on the gas pump and pocketed the key.

"I need gas, toots. What's the deal here?" He found his wallet and produced several twenty-dollar bills. "I'm a cash customer. Whatever it costs, I can afford it. Do you know who you're talking to, toots?"

"First of all, my name isn't toots. And second of all, I don't care who you are. You are drunk and I'm not selling gas to you. I'm not selling you any more beer either. You've had enough for one day." Lan returned his stare defiantly.

"What do you mean you aren't selling me any gas? This is a free country. I can, by God, buy gas if I want to." The man stepped closer to Lan, scowling at her as he swayed back and forth.

"Yes, sir. You certainly, by God, can buy gas if you want. You can go to any of the other marinas on the lake and buy all the gas you want." Lan pointed out to the open water past the entrance to the cove. "They might even sell you some beer. It just isn't going to be from me. If I sell you gas, you're just going to hurt yourself or somebody else. So I think it's safer to keep you off the water today."

"Look here, lady." He stepped closer, his beer-breath chokingly close to Lan's face. "If you don't want to pump it, I will. Get out of my way." He pushed Lan to the side and reached for the pump handle. He fumbled with the hose, losing his balance as he tried inserting it into the fill tube on the side of the boat. When he pulled the pump lever and nothing came out, he turned to Lan with a scowl. "Turn on the damn pump."

"Jerry, maybe we should go someplace else," Judy said from the back seat of the boat. He ignored her. She finished her beer and dropped the can overboard.

Lan heaved a deep sigh and looked down. She could feel her blood pressure rising, but she knew these people weren't worth the bother. It had taken her years to know what kind of customers she could live without. The motto about the customer always being right had nothing to do with these idiots.

"Jerry, why don't you let me call someone to take you home?" Lan suggested, reaching to take back the pump handle. "You really don't want any trouble here."

He turned to Emma and snarled, "You! Come over here and turn on the pump."

"No one is turning on the pump. So give me that and calm down." Lan stepped between Emma and his line of sight.

"Bitch," he snorted. "Sure, I'll give it to you." He dropped the pump handle and stepped forward, cocking his arm with a loaded fist. With a staggering lunge he extended his arm, aiming for Lan's face.

"Oh my God, Jerry," Judy shrieked.

"Lan," Emma gasped.

Before his fist could land, Lan leaned out of the way like an expert bullfighter. With his momentum to carry him, he stumbled to the edge of the dock and toppled into the lake with an awkward splash. He came to the surface, thrashing and choking.

"Oh my God, Jerry," Judy repeated. "Save him." She leaned over the side on the boat.

"Can't he swim?" Lan asked.

"I don't know. I've only known him three weeks," Judy replied.

"Oh swell," Lan muttered as she stepped out of her shoes.

"How deep is it here?" Emma asked as she watched Lan remove her sweater, revealing a white T-shirt with a small rainbow over the pocket.

"Deep enough. The lake level is up. Can you hold these for me?" Lan handed Emma her watch and the car keys from her pocket. She took several deep breaths to expand her lungs. An unexpected rescue like this made her thankful she had perfected her swimming skills in high school. As captain of the swim team, Lan's varsity achievements included a state championship in the hundred-meter freestyle her senior year. Even though she was rapidly approaching forty, she trusted the strength of her ability to save this man's life. She stepped to the edge and drove in, away from the splashing victim. She came to the surface behind him, then swam into position and secured her arm through his armpit and across his chest. She held him against her side, ready to pull him toward the dock, but fear had taken control of his senses. He grabbed and clawed at her, scrambling to pull himself out of the water. He may have been drunk, but he was still strong. With one hand pulling at her hair, and the other clawing at her shirt, he pushed her face under the water. She released her hold and grabbed for his hands, her face still submerged. His grasp was too strong for her to break. She grabbed his forearms and pulled him under with her. After several long agonizing seconds, they broke the surface together, he in the front, Lan behind, her arms locked around his chest. With powerful leg strokes, she headed for the ladder. The dunking had stunned the man long enough for her to get him to safety. Emma was waiting at the steps. She helped him up, then extended a hand to Lan.

"You okay?" Emma asked Lan with concern. "You must be freezing." She found herself surprisingly impressed with both Lan's athletic ability and her suddenly revealing wet clothing.

"Yep, I'm okay." Her lips had turned a nearly colorless blue. "How is he?"

"He's all right. He's too drunk to care." Emma watched as Jerry sat holding his head.

"Guess he can't read either." Lan nodded toward the sign suspended from the rafters.

"Shared Winds reserves the right to refuse service to anyone," Emma read and smiled. "Guess not."

Emma tried not to watch as Lan wrung out the hem of her T-shirt, the skin-clinging wetness fully revealing the outline of her bra and her small erect nipples. She pulled her sweater on over the wet shirt, her hands cramping from the cold water. Her legs began to tremble involuntarily. Lan wiped her face on her sweater sleeve and squeezed her hair through her fingers.

"You need any help, Lan?" yelled a voice from a lake patrol boat entering the cove.

"As a matter of fact, we could use you guys," Lan yelled back, pulling the man to his feet and patting him on the shoulder. He still hadn't recovered from the embarrassment and frustration of being dunked.

"We've been chasing this guy all over the lake today. Glad you cornered him."

"He kind of cornered himself."

"You two all right, Lan?" the uniformed patrolman asked, as he tied his bowline to the dock.

"We're fine. I'll lock his boat up for the night. He can claim it tomorrow."

"We saw what happened. You want to press charges?" the patrolman asked.

"No, not this time," Lan answered, her lower jaw shivering.

"You better get some dry clothes on. If this guy wasn't so drunk he'd be cold too." The patrolman helped the man into the boat and handed him a blanket. Judy climbed into the boat, took a seat as far away from the drunk as she could, and smirked disgustedly.

"That's the last time I go out with a guy from work," she sneered.

By the time the patrol boat had left the cove with the drunken boaters, Lan had locked the stranded boat and headed for the marina. Emma hurried along, following Lan's long strides.

"You need to take off those wet clothes," Emma said then realized that didn't come out the way she meant it.

Chapter 3

While Lan showered and found dry clothes in the locker room, Emma poked around the marina, measuring and taking notes on the damage, and admiring the view of the lake through the few windows still intact. The massive hand-hewn ceiling beams were the strength and backbone of the vaulted main lobby that housed the snack bar, ship's store, and rental counter. The wall of windows must have made a spectacular view of the lake, Emma decided as she calculated the square footage of broken glass by the number of sheets of plywood used to cover it. The undamaged tables and chairs in the snack bar had been stacked along the wall. The crushed ones had been piled together awaiting disposal. The snack bar counter had been crushed under what looked like a giant karate chop from a falling ceiling truss. The stainless steel sink and grill had been mangled beyond use. Two large refrigerators stood open, their doors torn off at the hinges. Three trash barrels were filled with broken dishes, glasses, and kitchenware. The ship's store was in no better shape. A rack of new fishing rods, all with their tops neatly snapped off, was still mounted to the wall. A display case was missing its glass panels and the fishing reel holders sat empty. Boxes of shredded maps and charts were pushed under the counter along with ripped life vests, broken sunglasses with the UV rating tags still attached, and a variety of broken marine light bulbs still on the cards. A barrel full of splintered water skis and foam kneeler boards blocked one aisle and a stack of boxes blocked another.

The marina was full of the vestments of business, each with some sort of war wound. Emma thought it was hauntingly like an emergency room, with the sick and injured parts of Shared Winds waiting quietly for help. She half expected to hear muffled sobs from these brave soldiers. The plastic five-gallon buckets of captured rainwater could easily have been the lifeblood of the marina. She remembered hearing how the time after an accident was called the golden hour, a time that was critical for a victim's survival. It was a time when all the skills and dedication had to work in harmony to save a life. With so much damage all around her and time ticking away, she knew this was Shared Winds' golden hour. Suddenly it became more than just a job. It somehow became a challenge, a duty for Emma. She felt a bond growing, a responsibility. As much as she wanted to tell herself this marina couldn't have a soul, something was reaching out to her. Something was touching her deep inside where she kept her courage and commitment, her skills and intuition.

"I'll do my best," Emma whispered. "I promise."

"I'm sure you will," Lan said.

Emma turned around with a gasp. She felt her face flush with embarrassment. Lan was rolling back the sleeves of a white shirt. She was wearing a pair of black jeans that looked new and stiff. Her hair was wet and combed back. A few locks had escaped and fell over her forehead like little feathers. She looked scrubbed and fresh with the faint scent of lavender floating around her.

"I just meant . . ." Emma stammered.

"Was she talking to you?" Lan asked with a devilish grin. She sat down on the stone hearth to tie her shoes.

"Was who talking to me?" Emma inquired timidly.

Lan looked up and let her eyes scan the room, as if to answer the question.

"She'll talk to you, if you stand real still and listen," she teased. Lan patted the stones on the hearth then stood up.

Emma wanted to admit the marina had communicated with her, but she knew it would sound ridiculous.

"Well, Emma Bishop, what do we do first?" Lan shoved her hands in her back pockets and gazed down into one of the buckets of rainwater.

"Prioritize the jobs," Emma said, opening her laptop.

"Oh geez." Lan rolled her eyes. "I hate that word. I hate the damn politically correct stuff."

"Okay then, we will make a nice list. How's that?" Emma inquired apologetically.

"Don't mind me. I'm just a little grumpy today. That happens when I have to jump in the lake before noon."

"Do you have to do a lot of that, lake jumping?"

"Fortunately, not too often."

The sound of little claws scampering across the tile floor became louder and louder, and soon the small brown dog with one perky ear and one droopy one, was circling Lan's legs and wagging its tail devotedly. Lan lowered her hand and pointed to the floor next to her left foot. The dog quickly stood on that exact spot and reluctantly lowered its rear to a nervous sitting position. With upturned face and panting tongue, the pup waited for Lan's approval. She smiled and leaned down to scratch behind one ear then the other.

"Good boy." Lan patted his back. "Koji Harding, I'd like you to meet our contractor, Emma Bishop."

"How do you do, Koji?" Emma said with an adoring smile. "He's so cute." Emma knelt down and held out her hand.

Lan snapped her fingers and pointed to where Emma was kneeling. Koji obediently trotted over to her, sniffed her hand, and then allowed her to pet him. Soon his tail was again wagging contentedly.

"Aw, he's so sweet. He must like strangers." Emma patted him and ruffled his curly fur with her fingernails. He was in heaven.

"Actually he was supposed to be a big mean guard dog. But no one told him that. Instead he is a little mutt who likes to ride in the boats and eat ice cream." Lan laughed. "He *will* bark if anyone comes snooping around at night. He also chases the gulls off the dock. They make a hell of a mess. He never catches them, but he likes to chase them."

Koji seemed to know Lan was talking about him. He returned to her side and sat by her leg, sweeping the floor with his tail. Emma went back to her computer, ready to put operation Shared Winds into motion.

"I have worked up a list of jobs, areas of the marina that need work. Demolition is first, naturally. I'll need different crews for different jobs, but basically we're looking at clean-up crews, carpenters, painters, and concrete work." She spoke and typed at the same time. "The dock has to have some understructure repair as well as roofing and walkways. Three of the cabins in the campground need to be completely rebuilt. The other two can be repaired. That gas supply line will have to be replaced by the Grove Municipal Services. It's on their side of the meter. All of our dump trucks and backhoes are at other job sites right now so as much as I hate to, rental is the only answer."

Emma searched her database for information as she itemized the tasks ahead of her. She had entered an all-consuming work mode oblivious to anything around her. She didn't look up until Lan dropped her insurance agent's business card on the table next to her.

"You might need this," Lan interrupted. "Gina Tucker has been my agent from the beginning. She's okay. She said when I found a contractor, she'd be glad to work directly with you. I'll let her know I found one."

Emma studied the card reminiscently. "I've worked with Gina

before." Slowly she ran her fingertip along the edge of the card. "She has a killer smile." Emma grinned to herself.

Lan watched as Emma seemed to tiptoe down memory lane. She wondered if it was just Gina Tucker or insurance agents in general that brought on this intense reflection.

"One other thing," Lan continued. "Recycling. Anything we can reuse would be great."

"Sure. I'm not big on wasting materials," Emma replied defensively.

"It's more than that. I like the idea of finding a use for things left behind. Maybe the storm left some of this debris for a reason. Like the wood I was cutting. All those trees, they still had a use. I just had to find it."

"I see what you mean," Emma murmured. She drummed her nails on the computer keys as she thought. "I did have something in mind along those lines. Those timbers up there." She gestured toward the beams supporting the vaulted ceiling. "The damaged ones will have to be replaced. No way around that. Especially the large center beam. But the ones you find at the lumberyards are all machine made. Those up there have a lot of aged patina. They weren't just rolled off the finisher. They're hand-hewn. It has to be done with a big drawknife and a broadax. They'll have to be matched to look right."

Lan squinted up at the beams, not sure what she was looking for. She hadn't given her ceiling much thought other than she knew they were some of the beautiful logs she had admired when she first saw the marina and knew she wanted to own it.

"You wouldn't want to put a Chevy fender on a Ford truck," Emma mused as she watched Lan's puzzled stare.

"Ah," Lan replied as the light went on. "I see what you mean."

"My guess is these are native timber. We might be able to use some of those huge trees you have piled up out there. Size wise, they look to be a pretty good match. And they look like either maple or hickory. There's a sawmill in Neosho that did some work for us like

30

that a couple years ago. I'll take a piece of a damaged log and see if they can do the millwork. All it will cost is the labor and cost of hauling the trees to the mill."

Lan smiled broadly. "Welcome aboard, Ms. Bishop."

"Call me Emma."

With so many worksites throughout the county using all of Bishop's crews, Emma was forced to hire new employees, a time-consuming job. She did find two foremen she had worked with before, one a grizzled older man who put up with no nonsense from his workers and the other a woman, considered by some the best finish carpenter in the state. Within a week, Emma was familiarizing the newly hired crews with the worksites. Three commercial-size dumpsters were delivered to the parking lot, ready to receive anything that was unusable and in the way. A glass company took measurements for the broken windows. Lumber, roofing, paint, tile, stain, docking, restaurant-grade appliances, tables and chairs, hardware, concrete, heavy equipment rentals, inspection certificates, and replacement fixtures all had a file on the laptop and a delivery date. Any marina employee that had been laid off because of storm damage was offered a job in the renovation. Most jumped at the chance to work even if it was nothing more than cleaning, shoveling, and fetch-and-carry. They needed the work and Emma needed some relatively unskilled workers.

The work was slow, but at least it had begun. For that, Lan was thankful. Through the pounding, sawing, and dust, she had marina business to conduct. There were still winter boat shows to attend, inventory to take, fishing tournaments to apply for, slip leases to renew, as well as keeping current on the changing fishing and lake regulations.

It was the same boring off-season stuff Lan had done before but doing it through a veil of plastic tarps, sawhorses, and earsplitting machinery were Excedrin headaches No. 23 through No. 94. She began carrying her cell phone in her shirt pocket so she could hear it ring. Koji had been excited with all the new people ready and willing to pet him, but he too soon grew tired of the noise and spent much of his time under Lan's desk in her office. It seemed to be the only spot not touched by the storm and therefore partially noiseless.

Max had a long list of boat repairs to keep him busy, but it was decided that he would attend the boat shows, manning a booth, singing the praises of the soon-to-be reopened marina, and selling boat slip rentals, the big-ticket part of any marina business. The contracts and monthly fees were what Lan could count on and budget for. Gas and store sales alone were not enough to keep the marina open. Max agreed, knowing Lan wanted to watch the construction progress and handle any problems that might arise. It would only take him away for five weekends through the winter months to Kansas City, Tulsa, Joplin, Oklahoma City, and Springfield. Lan promised the marina would pay for his wife to go along, too.

"Consider it five mini-vacations," Lan said. "Leona will love Kansas City in December. You can go see the Christmas lights at the Plaza."

"Okay, but I'm not wearing a suit," Max grumbled. "Clean jeans, but no suit."

"Agreed." Lan wasn't even sure Max owned a suit.

What he lacked in conversational skills he more than made up for in knowledge about boats and motors. Fixing boats was all he had ever done. Lan considered him a gift from above when she opened the marina and talked him into being her mechanic. Longtime friend of her grandfather, he had known her all her life. His youngest daughter, Nancy, had been her closest friend through elementary and high school. Max was the one who taught Lan to paddle a canoe when she was only six and too young for a powerboat. He had given her the first taste of power when he let her drive his 200-horsepower Evinrude across the lake at full throttle when she was twelve. And as she grew older, he was the one to first notice her indifference to dating boys. It was sometime during her junior year in high school when she began to balk at the "nice young men" her mother, determined to make a lady out of her tomboy, insisted she date. It was as if she was wearing her shoes on the wrong feet. They just didn't feel right. Max was more than a friend and employee. His family was her family. Leona mothered Lan with chicken soup and hot herb tea when she was sick and beamed grins at her accomplishments. Max quietly guided Lan while his wife chattered away and pinched her cheek when she saw her. They had earned the kind of love and trust usually reserved for parents.

By the time Lan graduated from high school, her own father, chronically unemployed, unskilled, and unkind, packed his spare pair of jeans along with his beer opener and went in search of greener pastures. Her mother was then free to pursue her image in the community, but it came at the expense of her daughter's needs for love and attention.

During Lan's freshman year at the University of Oklahoma, paid for by an athletic scholarship, she received a short letter from her mother. The only paragraph that had imprinted itself on her mind was the one that read: *I have met a wonderful man. His name is Robert and we are moving to Montana to try ranching. I'll let you know our address soon.*

She stopped looking for the letter with that address shortly after she graduated with honors and a master's degree. But somewhere in her deepest soul, the little girl still waits.

Chapter 4

"Is anyone here?" Emma asked tentatively as she tapped on the open office door.

"Right here," Lan's muffled voice announced.

"And where is right here?"

"Right here," Lan repeated as her head popped up from under the far side of the desk. "I'll be right there," she said as she grabbed a screwdriver from the desk and disappeared again.

"What are you building under there? A soundproof room?" Emma mused as she leaned down and looked in from the front of the desk.

"I'm trying . . . ouch, to fix this drawer so it won't keep falling on my feet when I close it," she grunted. The sound of a head whacking the underside of the desk was followed by a short string of expletives.

"Oh! Are you all right?" Emma grimaced sympathetically.

"Yes. But I can't come out now. Now this is war."

"Here, let me hold that," Emma said, crawling under to offer her help.

"Thanks. The drawer guide is loose and I can't hold it and the drawer and start the screws all at once."

"No problem."

It took some wiggling for both of them to fit but soon they each found a position to work in.

"Okay," Emma said. "I'm ready. Try that."

Through the grunting and groaning of trying to persuade the obstinate screws into the tiny hard-to-reach places, neither one of them heard the carpenter who had knocked on the opened door and was standing just inside the office. He could hear them, but he couldn't see them.

"Are you sure you are using the right tool?" Emma asked.

"It's the only one I brought with me," Lan replied with a groan.

"Maybe I should move over a little so you have enough room."

"You're fine. I need a better grip is all."

The carpenter's eyes widened at the conversation emanating from under the desk.

"I'll hold this while you rotate," Emma offered.

"I think I about have it. Yeah, hold it right there. Right there," Lan's voice groaned heavily. "One more second. Wait."

"You've got the spot. Go for it," Emma encouraged.

"Yeah, yeah, yeah," Lan said, expelling a gasp with each word.

The young man at the door had dropped his mouth and widened his eyes, embarrassed at what he thought he was interrupting but still curious about what was going on under the desk.

"Whew, there. Done."

"Yes, you got it," Emma agreed finally.

"I couldn't have done it by myself. Thanks."

"Anytime," Emma said.

"Um . . . Ms. Bishop?" the carpenter asked cautiously, ready to make a fast retreat if necessary.

"Yes?" she replied as they both popped their heads out from

under the desk. "Did you need something, Mike?" she continued as she crawled out, stood up, and straightened her clothes.

Mike blushed as if he had just heard something intimate, something that wasn't intended for his ears.

"I . . . um . . . did you . . ." he stammered. "That section of timber is in your truck," he finally managed to say. "You said to let you know when I had it cut and loaded," he continued defensively.

"Great, Mike. Thanks." Emma had no idea why he was acting so befuddled.

He nodded and hurried away, grateful for the chance to escape.

Lan tucked in her shirt and tried out the drawer.

"Works," she announced triumphantly.

"Mike sure acted strange," Emma pondered, looking out the door in the direction of his retreat.

"I didn't notice," Lan replied, replacing the dumped contents of the drawer.

"By the way, I wanted you to see this," Emma explained, laying a three-foot section of brown synthetic board across the desk. "You might want to consider using something like this on the dock."

"Is this that recycled plastic stuff?" Lan asked, examining the artificial wood. "I hear this stuff is better than when it first came out."

"Lifetime guarantee, one hundred percent recycled material, non-skid, waterproof, easier installation, and it is twenty percent more buoyant than wood."

"More buoyant? That would reduce freeboard," Lan muttered as she checked to see if she could bend the board.

"Freeboard?"

"It's the difference between the floating dock and the railing of the boat. Kind of like the amount you have to step up into a boat. Some of these big cruisers have quite a jump."

"I've never heard that term before, but it stands to reason," Emma acknowledged. "And, even though it doesn't biodegrade if you are worried about being environmentally kind, this material is completely recyclable. I thought you would like that."

"And how about cost?"

"It's a little higher than pressure-treated or cedar but with the guarantee and life expectancy, it more than pays for itself in just a few years. And you can pick from lots of different colors. Green, blue, white, redwood, dark brown."

"Gray?" Lan asked as if she already knew what she wanted.

"Yes, even gray."

"Okay, Ms. Bishop. Order up a dock's worth of gray."

"Just curious but can I ask why gray?"

"Matches the galvanized superstructure and isn't too hot to walk on barefoot. White gets dirty too fast."

"Good reasons," Emma replied with an agreeable nod.

"Here's my list, kid," Max said as he entered the office and floated a grease-smudged piece of paper onto the desk. "And here's the shaft bearing. Leave it with Charlie. He knows what I need. Hello, Ms. Bishop." He placed a newspaper-wrapped bundle on the desk.

"Hi Max," Emma replied with a smile. "Are you ever going to give in and call me Emma?"

"I'll give it some thought." Max grinned.

Lan heaved a sigh at the greasy bundle.

"Anything else?" she asked sarcastically.

"Yes," he said as he headed out the door.

"What?" she yelled after him.

"Gracie's," he yelled back.

"With or without?" Lan yelled even louder.

"With. Two quarts," he replied, almost out of earshot.

Lan smiled wryly.

"What is Gracie's? And what is 'with'?" Emma asked in amusement.

"Chili, with beans. Max thinks she makes the only chili worth eating. She has a little hole-in-the-wall place up by Seneca and been making it for twenty-five years."

"Is it any good? I love good chili," Emma asked enthusiastically.

"It's okay. But there's a better place in Joplin."

"Let me guess. Fred and Red's?"

Lan smiled broadly. "Yes, ma'am. Coneys from heaven. Have you been there?"

"You bet. But it's the Spaghetti Red that's sent from heaven," Emma argued.

"If I'm going to put a stool under my butt it's going to be for a Coney," Lan disagreed teasingly.

Emma shook her head as she tucked the piece of board under her arm and went to the doorway.

"I'll be back in a few hours. I'm going to the sawmill about milling those timbers," Emma said.

"I have errands to run, too," Lan replied looking at Max's list. "If you need me, I'll have my cell phone with me."

Emma instinctively felt her waistband for own cell phone. "Me, too."

Lan was loading the greasy bundle in the back of the Jeep as Emma pulled out of the parking lot and roared up the road. Two loud bangs and the sound of slinging gravel brought Lan's head out of the back seat. She watched with growing concern as Emma's pickup skidded along the shoulder before coming to rest on a precarious tilt into the ditch. Lan jumped into the driver's seat. With one fluid motion she started the engine and sped toward Emma's truck. The Jeep screeched to a stop next to the leaning pickup before Emma had a chance to regain her senses and open the door. Lan grabbed the door handle and swung it open, greeting Emma with an angry scowl.

"You okay?" she demanded loudly.

"Yes," Emma replied slowly. "I think so. I heard two bangs and the truck swerved toward the ditch."

Lan smirked then climbed down into the steep ditch and pushed back the tall weeds that blocked the tires.

"Two blowouts," she declared pushing her thumb into the front tire.

"Two?" Emma inquired sternly.

Emma squatted at the edge of the road and peered under at the flattened tires.

"I don't think this is a coincidence," Lan offered as she checked the back tire.

"Look at that," Emma said, pointing at the backside of the tire.

Lan stuck her head under the fender and felt the tiny silver buttons stuck to the treads.

"Nails," Lan grunted as she felt all the way around the inner sidewall. "Lots of them."

"Both tires?"

"All four of them," Lan replied, looking across at the two that were not yet flat. "Looks like galvanized roofing nails."

"Is there any way you could pry one out so I could look at it?"

Lan dug in her pocket and pulled out a small single bladed pocketknife. She pried one of the nails loose and handed it up to Emma.

"Galvanized decking nails," Emma said. Her eyes narrowed and her lips tightened. "Can you give me a ride back up there?" she asked with restrained anger. "I need to have a talk with some carpenters."

"Sure."

Emma took the keys from the ignition and slammed the door to the truck hard as if trying to release some of her rage. She kicked one of the outside tires that was now beginning to lose air. She climbed into the Jeep and clenched her jaw. Her eyes were riveted on the horizon.

"If you are interested, I could take you to the sawmill in Neosho. I will be in that area anyway," Lan offered, trying to appease Emma's anger.

Emma was fuming by the time she entered the marina. She positioned her hands on her hips, her eyes riveted on a group of carpenters working on the door framing. She didn't say anything until they noticed her standing there. One of the workers saw her smoldering stare and tapped the other two to get their attention.

"Is there a problem, Ms. Bishop?" one asked warily.

"Yes. There is a problem, Herb. A big problem, as a matter of fact."

Lan smiled to herself and went to wait in the office while Emma explained the virtues of picking up spilled boxes of nails and discussed their making arrangements for the tires to be repaired. Emma was demonstrating she could deal with problems with a cool head and administrative proficiency. She hadn't raised her voice or used profanity, but the workers knew she was unhappy and were ready to do whatever they could to rectify it. Lan was impressed. She had half expected Emma to become frustrated and resort to screaming and swearing at whoever dumped the nails off the back of the truck. She also expected an ugly scene in the parking lot with finger pointing and nasty remarks. There was none of that. Just explanations and apologies. Lan had also fought her urge to step in and deal with the problem for Emma. It was the kind of thing she had handled before with occasionally lazy and inept employees. Why she thought she had to do it for this woman was a complete mystery.

"Is the offer still open for a ride to the sawmill?" Emma asked, leaning on the office doorway, one hand on her hip.

"Sure. Ready?"

"I had Mike move that piece of timber to your Jeep, if that's okay?"

"I could have gotten it," Lan said.

"*He* needed to do it," Emma replied, with a raised eyebrow as if she was confessing his transgressions.

"Okay," Lan said, with an understanding nod.

After a stop at the sawmill where the replacement timbers were discussed, and a swing by Mid-West Marine for parts, Lan pointed the Wrangler north on old highway 71 toward Joplin.

"Time for lunch," Lan announced.

"Do you have a good place in mind?"

"Yep. The Undercliff. Great restaurant. Gives a whole new meaning to the expression 'hole-in-the-wall place.' Ever been there?"

"I don't think so."

"You'd remember it if you had," Lan advised. "It's kind of off the beaten path. That's one of the things I love about it."

It was after one before she crossed Shoal Creek and eased into a parking place in front of a wood-fronted café nestled in a rock cliff.

"Here we are," Lan announced as she stretched then combed her fingers through her hair.

Emma leaned forward and read the sign over the door.

"Undercliff," she said warily. "Are you sure about this place?"

"Yep," Lan insisted as she climbed out and tucked in the back of her shirt where it had crept out. "Best hamburgers you have ever tasted, next to the ones at Shared Winds, of course."

"I'm looking forward to trying those, too."

"Let's hope it's soon. When you're closed, it doesn't take long for people to forget about you."

"It won't be long," Emma said with a reassuring smile. "Bishops always finish under budget, and that goes for time as well as money."

"Always?" Lan asked as she reached for the door to the café and held it for Emma.

"Well, almost always."

"Uh-huh," Lan teased and followed her inside.

By the time their eyes had adjusted to the dimly lit interior, a cheerful man in his forties greeted them. He was wearing a blue T-shirt with the Undercliff logo on the back and a white towel draped over his shoulder.

"Howdy, ladies. Give me just a minute and I'll have a booth for you by the window." He hurried off to bus the only vacant table.

The high ceiling and walls were all covered with 1950s memorabilia and posters of classic cars. Several cozy tables were tucked under the slanted outcropping of granite striped with sandstone that was the back wall of the dining room. High wooden stools lined a counter where beer was served to hungry diners. Waitresses scurried back and forth from the kitchen with paper-lined plastic baskets of food and frosty mugs of drinks. Two pinball machines chinged and

41

flashed as a pair of teenagers gripped the sides, fingers pounding at the flippers and doing the pinball dance. A television set mounted in the corner over the counter silently showed whatever sporting event was being aired. Strands of twinkle lights draped from one rafter to the next. An old Wurlitzer jukebox played something country from the corner near the booth being cleared. By the time Emma had given the place a quick once-over, the man was back and gesturing them to the booth, where he spread out menus.

"What can I get you ladies to drink?"

"Just water for me. What would you like, Emma?"

"Iced tea please," she replied confidently. "Extra lemon."

"Gotcha," he said then returned to the kitchen.

"Great ambiance," Emma said, her head on a swivel to take it all in. "I've never been here before. You were right. I would have remembered. This is definitely a conversation piece in the world of cuisines and construction. And it is as off the beaten path as you can get. How did you find it?"

"Someone brought me here a few years ago. We sat right here in this booth and I did the same big-eyed stare you are doing."

"So, how's the food?" Emma asked as she looked over the menu.

"Nothing fancy. Just good old plain food. But then again you can't eat the décor." Lan pushed her unopened menu to the edge of the table. "The barbecue isn't bad, but I come here for the cheese-burger and fries in a basket. If you are one of those salad freaks, they have a big chef salad, too."

"Then I guess it is cheeseburgers and fries," Emma agreed with a smile and laid her menu on Lan's. "Would you order mine with let-tuce, tomato, and pickles?" Emma asked as she slid out of the booth.

"And grilled onions?" Lan suggested.

"Absolutely," Emma said, placing a hand on Lan's shoulder as she passed her. "What would a cheeseburger be without 'em?"

Lan stiffened under Emma's touch.

"I'll be right back," Emma said as she headed for the ladies' room.

Lan tried not to watch as Emma headed for the small corner door, but her eyes betrayed her, following like a beggar follows a rich tourist. After ordering the two burgers and fries, Lan's attention returned to the closed door. As she waited for Emma's return, the thought of her hand on her shoulder gave Lan a strange serenity. It was a warming she had almost forgotten and one she didn't have time to nurture. She remembered how Rachel used to squeeze her shoulders in a half-hearted attempt at massaging Lan's stiff neck muscles after a swim. She could see Rachel, dressed in her tiny black bikini and a towel wrapped around her long hair, sitting on the corner of Lan's desk with a dangerous come-hither smile aimed at stripping away any plans she had for work. She could hear Rachel's snicker as she teased Lan into leaving her piles of paperwork for a quick afternoon's sweaty tryst behind a locked office door then her devilish laugh as she pushed Lan away before reciprocating. Then there was Rachel's cute little tushy that filled out a pair of size three Levi's just right and her coquettish wiggle that got Lan's blood boiling even in subzero weather.

Emma was halfway back to the booth before Lan realized she had been watching her with a vacant stare. Lan quickly diverted her gaze to the jukebox, just a few feet away. She needed something to do. Anything. She didn't understand why she was so nervous or why she was so intrigued with Emma Bishop. Maybe it was the professionalism she brought to her work. Or maybe it was her tenacity. Whatever it was, this woman was different from anyone she had ever met.

As Emma slid into the booth across from her, Lan slid out and dug into her jeans pocket for some change.

"What kind of music do you like?" she asked, studying the selections.

"Lots of different kinds. What are the choices?" Emma asked, taking a long sip from her straw.

"Looks like a bit of everything. Country, rock, oldies, Barry," Lan announced with a chuckle.

"Oh boy, Barry Manilow. Can't we find something else?"

"Like what?" Lan hung a thumb on her front jean pocket while she read. "Boot scootin' boogie," she announced with an exaggerated Texas drawl.

Emma grimaced then slid out of the booth. "I see you are in need of guidance here."

"Just as long as it isn't heavy metal or rap," Lan declared.

"No kidding. I like to hear the melody," she agreed, joining Lan in reading the selections.

As simple as these music titles were, Lan found Emma's presence next to her clouding her ability to concentrate. No matter how hard she tried, her eyes were stuck in their peripheral position. For some strange reason, this wasn't at all like having Emma in charge of construction crews at the marina.

"Boy, there's about every kind of music you can think of on here. How about . . ." Emma drew her finger slowly down over the list.

Lan dropped two quarters in the slot. "There you go," she said then took half a step back.

Lan remained frozen, enjoying the view over Emma's shoulder. Her cheek was covered with soft peach fuzz. Her earlobe was small. Her neck was thin and graceful. The color of her hair was a mixture of honey and sunshine. It was obediently smooth, flowing over her shoulders in gentle curls.

"How about this one?" Emma asked as she turned and caught Lan's eyes watching her every move.

"Anything is fine. Surprise me," Lan replied, catching herself staring then quickly looking past Emma to the '57 Chevy poster on the wall. It wasn't polite to stare. Maybe it was because she had been a social recluse for the past three years since Rachel's death. But she couldn't help herself. She was powerless to stop. Lan felt a humiliating blush climb over her face as she heard the words, *Can't take my eyes off of you.*

Emma continued to read down the playlist, a wry grin on her face. Lan held her breath for a few long seconds as her gaze settled back on Emma. She estimated Emma was five feet seven, the same as

Rachel. But this was not Rachel. This woman was not sarcastic or sullen or moody. This woman had a twinkle in her eye, an interest in everything and everyone, a sense of humor. Lan's senses told her she was sensitive and compassionate. She was also too nice not to be already involved with a similarly caring and intelligent person, and Lan's senses told her it had to be with a woman.

Emma pressed another selection then smiled at the jukebox.

"Here's a good oldie," she announced, grinning devilishly then patting the top of the jukebox and sliding into the booth. "Frankie Valli," she said with a satisfied smugness.

"Umm," Lan stammered, tugging at her earlobe. "I, ah . . ."

She tried to smile apologetically if she had made Emma feel uncomfortable but now she was convinced she was only making it worse. She hadn't meant to be obvious and now she was embarrassed, something she didn't handle well. Lan began making elaborate promises to the Great Spirits of her forefathers if only the cheeseburgers would appear within the next four seconds.

"Here you are, ladies," announced the man as he placed the plastic baskets on the table and took a bottle of catsup from his apron pocket. "Let me know if you need anything else."

The cheeseburgers lived up to Lan's rave reviews.

"I'll have to remember this place," Emma declared. "You were right. Great burgers."

"Glad you like it," Lan said, dragging a french fry through the catsup.

"When you aren't running Shared Winds or eating hamburgers, what do you do?" Emma asked over her iced tea. "For fun?"

"For fun? Shared Winds is my fun. It's my work and my play," Lan replied instinctively.

"Don't you have any hobbies? You know, golf, fishing, hang gliding," Emma teased.

Lan smiled and wiped her napkin across her mouth.

"Camel herding, goat roping, flagpole sitting?" Emma continued as Lan's smile grew.

"Well, I do have a nineteen forty-eight Chris-Craft runabout I am restoring," Lan offered.

"One of those wooden inboards?"

"Yes, mahogany," Lan replied proudly, pleased that Emma seemed to know what a Chris-Craft was.

"Those are great-looking boats. Real classics. How long have you been working on it?" Emma asked, leaning forward slightly.

"About four years."

"Four years? Wow! It must have needed quite a bit of restoration."

"Almost everything," Lan said resolutely.

"Is it ready for a test drive yet?" Emma asked with enthusiasm that surprised even her.

"Not quite. It needs a transmission seal and a new intake manifold, and a camshaft. There was lots of dry rot after fifty years so most of the hoses and belts were shot, too."

"Uh-huh," Emma agreed with interest even though she had no idea what those parts were.

"But she looks all shipshape. I've replaced the rotted wood, replated the brass railings and fittings, and reupholstered the seats." Lan's face lit up as she relayed her progress on the boat. "It spent twenty-five years in a leaky barn without a cover and no maintenance, so the engine looked like a rusty anchor."

"Where is this wonderful creature? Down at the marina?" Emma asked.

"In my garage at home. She's almost ready to come to the marina. I don't want her maiden voyage to be her last so I have a few things left to do. But I haven't had much time to work on her lately."

"Those old wooden boats have such class. They sort of glide over the water like a mahogany swan," Emma said as her hand gestured gracefully.

"Mahogany swan. I like that," Lan replied with a nod.

"I'd love to see it sometime."

46

"Sure."

"I bet it's a lot of work to rebuild a boat," Emma offered.

"Not as much as rebuilding a marina," Lan said, leaning back and resting one arm over the back of the booth.

"By the way," Emma said, looking at her watch, "I think we should be getting back. The crew will think I got lost."

"Yeah, I think we better," Lan agreed as she dropped the tip on the table and grabbed the check before Emma could reach it. "At least we had a couple hours without phone calls and nagging details."

Lan turned onto the highway and shifted through the gears.

"And what do you do for fun?" Lan asked. "Done any camel herding lately?"

"Sometimes keeping the crews on schedule is a lot like camel herding."

They both laughed.

"There has to be something you like to do when you aren't cracking the whip."

Emma looked out her side window for a long moment thinking. What she wanted to say would sound silly. The desire to sit quietly and watch a sunset or sip hot tea by a fireplace didn't seem like much of an ambition. A longing to go camping where telephones couldn't reach her or demanding clients couldn't hound her seemed childish and simple-minded. Not much of a hobby.

"I haven't given it much thought lately," Emma replied as she began flipping through her day planner. "I haven't had much time for hobbies either."

"It isn't good to be consumed with work twenty-four-seven," Lan announced. "At least that's what I hear."

"Sounds like you have that twenty-four-seven affliction yourself."

"True. My life is definitely twenty-four-seven." Lan smiled at the thought. "But I wouldn't have it any other way."

"I know what you mean. Gives you a sense of direction and purpose," Emma said with satisfaction.

"Balance," Lan added.

"Balance? Wouldn't that be equal parts of work and relaxation?" Emma asked.

"Equal parts work and pleasure. If you enjoy what you're doing, then you are at peace, balanced in your existence," Lan said confidently.

"But there has to be time in everyone's life for something other than work, if you can squeeze it in. Like relationships, or vacations, or hobbies. I love my job, but I still look forward to those times when I don't have to answer the phone, read blueprints, listen to OSHA regulations, or argue with suppliers about delivery dates. There has to be a time to recharge our inner batteries, to sleep late, to wear sweats all day, to take two hours to sip tea and read the paper, to put an extra log in the fireplace and take the time to enjoy it burn down," Emma explained. She spoke as if offering up a prayer for the future.

Lan didn't reply. She too was deep in thought. Emma had just described the perfect getaway and Lan wanted to enjoy the image while it lasted. Suddenly she wanted to know who Emma envisioned stoking the fire and sharing the warmth of the fireplace with her. She knew it was none of her business, but it seemed important somehow.

Chapter 5

"Hey, Lan," yelled a woman standing by the railing of the deck.

"Hi, J.T.," Lan replied as she crossed the deck to where she and another woman were waiting. "Hi, Annie."

The two women were dressed in jeans and sweatshirts. They stood at the railing, holding hands and seemingly lost in quiet conversation. J.T. was slightly taller than Annie, somewhere about five feet eight. Her thick shiny black hair, cut just below her ears, was full of restless curls. Her shoulders were muscular and square through her sweatshirt, which was appliquéd with an emblem of the Cherokee tribe. Her jeans hugged her hips and tush like faded blue paint. There was an unmistakable mark of a wallet in her back pocket and a small ring of keys dangled from her belt loop.

Annie's sweatshirt was embroidered with a small rainbow over one of her well-endowed breasts. Her hips were full and round as well. Her reddish brown hair flowed over her shoulders in bouncy waves, which J.T. occasionally stroked with two fingers. A day planner was tucked under her arm with yellow sticky notes protruding from several pages. Annie watched J.T. with an adoring attention reserved only for those deeply in love.

"*'O si' yo, To hi tsu?*" J.T. said, then gave Lan a firm handshake. J.T. spoke the Cherokee language with confidence and ease.

"*O si Tsu*," Lan replied softly.

"Oh for Pete's sake, you two," Annie declared sarcastically as she gave Lan a hug. "Will you make her speak English, Lan?"

"That's your job," Lan teased. "She's just my friend. You're the one who's going to marry her."

"I just said hello and how are you, babe," J.T. informed Annie. "I'm going to have to start teaching you some Cherokee words."

"I can speak Cherokee. I can count to three," Annie said proudly then took a deep breath. "*Saquu, tali, tsoi.*" She grinned like a child winning a spelling bee.

"That's great," Lan said as J.T. kissed her on the cheek for her accomplishment.

"Hiya Emma," J.T. called out as Emma climbed the stairs to the deck. "What are you doing here?" J.T. grinned broadly and winked at Lan.

"Working," Emma replied. "How are you two love birds doing?"

"We're fine. In fact I tried to call you this morning. They said you were out on a job site somewhere."

"That's right." Emma continued as she hugged Annie and J.T. "And why aren't you two working today?"

"It's called a perk for being self-employed," J.T. said proudly.

"And my computer work will wait for me, it always does," Annie whispered secretively. "Besides, we have a lot to do this week, what with the change of wedding plans and all." She smiled shyly at J.T. and winked.

"Change?" Emma asked. "I thought the ceremony was next month."

"Yeah, next month," Lan said with a scowl.

"It was," Annie said, throwing an accusatory eye on J.T. "But someone, who will remain nameless, changed it. Something to do with fuzzy worms and squirrels' tails and hawk feathers. I thought those silly old wives tales were just that, silly. Now she tells me those are actual signs that winter is going to be severe."

"Huh?" Emma said, joining Annie and Lan in staring at J.T.

"Emma, she thinks just because caterpillars' fuzz is darker and thicker we are in for an early winter. And just because the squirrels have bushier tails and the hawks aren't losing their long tail feathers we are going to have lots of snow." Annie sounded like a tattletale.

"Hey, you wouldn't want to be standing out on an island in the middle of Grand Lake in a blizzard, would you?" J.T. explained.

Lan began to laugh then patted J.T. on the back.

"What's so funny? It's only common sense. You have to respect the forces of nature, to accept the seasons as they are presented to us," J.T. pleaded. "The signs are there, plain as day."

Lan continued to laugh, shaking her head and leading the group inside the marina.

"See, J.T.," Annie chided. "Lan thinks you're crazy, too."

"I'm not crazy," J.T. explained. "I'm only listening to the spirits and the messages they have given us."

"I know you think you are, sweetie, but I had all the plans made. Now I have to change everything," Annie argued. "Everything."

Annie opened her day planner and leafed through the pages, stopping at various dates and lists.

Lan laughed so hard, tears began running down her cheeks.

"I don't understand," Emma said quietly. "What are you all talking about?"

"Let me guess," Lan said, trying to stifle her laughter. "You have been talking to Max?"

"Well," J.T. started.

"You heard him say how to tell if there was going to be a severe winter by the signs in the forest, right?" she continued.

"Can't you do something, Lan? Tell her Max was only teasing. Tell her it's all made up. Please," Annie pleaded.

J.T. took Annie's hand and kissed the back of it then held it against her chest.

"Sweetie, you'll just have to trust me on this," J.T. said calmly.

"I have *no* idea what you all are talking about," Emma said, shaking her head. She sat down at a table and opened her laptop computer.

"Oh, Emma, it's all hogwash," Annie insisted. "Pay absolutely no attention to them. It seems there are some sort of signs they use to tell if there is going to be a harsh winter. Max said the caterpillars have a darker and thicker fur this year. And the tails on the red squirrels are thicker. And something about the hawks not losing their feathers as much."

"There are other signs, too," J.T. insisted. "But it is true. You watch. This is going to be an early winter. The Trading Moon will be short."

"The Trading Moon?" Emma asked.

"November," Lan replied. "The Cherokee called November the Trading Moon."

"How do you think our forefathers predicted the seasons? They didn't have Doppler radar, you know. They listened to the messages from the spirits, the signs," J.T related. "I'm not fanatical about much, but I do believe this. I have seen it for myself. If you watch the squirrels you'll see they're making deeper nests and spending more time than usual gathering food. The migratory birds have all left. The eagles have come to their roosts early this year and have built nests in lower branches. We've been lucky. We've had several mild winters, but this one is going to be a doozey."

"Geez, I hope she's wrong," Emma whispered in Lan's direction. "We don't have time for bad weather."

Lan released a sigh and shoved her hands in her back pockets.

"We had the same signs last year, J.T. And the only snow we had was that one skiff in January. There was never any ice on the cove and I had boats coming to the dock practically all winter."

J.T. held up her hand as if halting the discussion dead in its tracks.

"Even if I am wrong, what will it hurt to change the date?" she asked, smiling a wonderfully charismatic smile at Annie.

Annie looked into her eyes and seemed to melt like summer butter.

"Awwww," Annie cooed. "Okay, honey bunch. If you feel that strongly about it, it's fine with me."

"Are you sure it's all right with you, my little jelly bean?" J.T. cooed back, seemingly lost in Annie big dark eyes.

"Whatever you want, baby cakes."

"Oh my God," Lan declared. "Will you two just kiss and get it over with. I'm getting a toothache here."

"Yes, please," Emma pleaded from behind her computer screen.

Lan turned and strode toward the table where Emma was working, allowing J.T. and Annie a small amount of privacy to finalize their kiss.

"Tell me when they're finished," she said with a smirk as she leaned on the table.

"Okay," Emma said quietly with a small giggle. "By the way, I sure hope she's wrong. There's a lot of work that can't be done if it's too cold. The boat ramp is one of them. It can't be poured until the gas company replaces the damaged line that ran under it up to the marina, unless you don't mind not having heat up here. They can't even spread the gravel and lay the rebar until it's repaired. And the concrete has to have temperatures above freezing to cure or it will turn to mush."

"I know," Lan agreed quietly. "The thing is, I've seen the signs, too. This winter might just be as bad as she said. Let's hope not. I need to keep the gas pumps running out there to remind folks I'm still in business. The last time the cove froze over . . . let's just say, I got pretty tired of eating beans and bologna."

"I think we need to rearrange our priorities a bit." Emma flicked her tongue back and forth across her upper teeth. "One way or another, I'll get the gas company out here this week. I hate to be sneaky but you know, I think I heard someone say they thought they smelled a gas leak out there," she said, beaming mischievously. "They'll have to come out and get busy on that line. Then the concrete crew can start work. It'll take a couple weeks to get it cleaned out and readied for the pour," Emma said as she looked over her schedule.

"Good. I need that ramp as soon as possible," Lan declared, then tapped her knuckles on the table. "The sooner, the better."

"Even in this weather it will take two, maybe three weeks to cure enough to be usable."

"That long, eh?" Lan stood up straight, her forehead wrinkled with concern.

"It's called patience," Emma said, patting Lan's hand then smiling up at her. "We'll get it done."

"Yeah, I know."

"So, are you both available next Saturday?" J.T. announced as Annie clung to her side adoringly.

Emma and Lan turned to them in unison.

"We have decided to move the ceremony up to next Saturday, on Two Tree Island, at noon," Annie said, beaming. "So we hope you two can be there."

Lan and Emma looked at each other as if someone had just told a secret no one else was supposed to know.

"You two didn't know the other one was invited, did you?" J.T. said with a proud laugh.

"Nope," Lan said, looking at Emma.

"No, I didn't," Emma agreed.

"I bet you two didn't even know you knew the same people, now did you?" Annie said with a coquettish giggle.

"Learn something new every day," Lan declared. Her intuition may have been right. If Emma knew J.T. and Annie, could it mean she too was a lesbian? She hadn't used it in a long time but Lan was glad to know her rusty old gay-dar still worked.

"Indeed you do," Emma added with an inner twinkle.

"So," J.T. mused. "Are you two still going to be there?"

"Remember, you promised to sing, Emma," Annie reminded her. "We can't imagine having a ceremony without your beautiful voice."

"You sing?" Lan asked.

"Well, sort of," Emma replied modestly.

"Sort of? Sort of?" J.T. gasped. "Damn, woman."

"She should have been a professional singer," Annie offered confidently.

"Oh, stop it, you two," Emma interrupted in full blush.

"No kidding?" Lan said with genuine curiosity. "A singing contractor. What are you going to sing at the wedding?"

"Actually, I have no idea. No one has told me what I'm supposed to do," Emma said, raising her eyebrows at the couple.

"Didn't you tell her what you wanted, sweetie?" J.T. inquired.

"No. I thought you did, baby." Annie's eyes got big at the thought.

"I need a little bit of time to learn the song," Emma said matter-of-factly.

J.T. and Annie gave each other a blank stare then began to snicker.

"Can we let you know tomorrow, Emma," Annie said apologetically. "I'm so sorry, but it looks like this detail got overlooked. We know we want you to sing, but we just aren't sure what."

"Yeah, Em," J.T. offered as she nodded her head. "We'll let you know in the morning. We'll come up with something."

Emma smiled broadly and went to hug both women.

"Tell you what," she announced. "Why don't you let me pick something? I'm sure I can find something just right that you will both like."

"Oh, that sounds terrific," Annie replied, sounding genuinely pleased. "Would you?"

"Whatever you pick will be fine, Em," J.T. added.

"No problem." Emma stood between them and draped an arm around each one. "You worry about the rest of it. I'll take care of this." She kissed each on the cheek then went back to the table and her laptop.

The couple seemed relieved that Emma had removed one of the details on their long list of to-do's before next Saturday. The overwhelming chaos of changing the ceremony had put a dazed look on both their faces.

Lan wanted to tease them about their nerves and giddiness but thought better of it. J.T. and Annie were deeply in love and they had stepped onto a path many didn't have the wisdom or the courage to attempt. She was very proud of them. She wanted to tell them how pleased she was with their diligence and determination, but the words stuck in her throat, causing a small tear to well up in her right eye. Strange. Lan blinked it away and broadcast a satisfied smile instead.

By the time Lan had walked J.T. and Annie to the front door and returned, Emma had called the gas company and was now on the phone with someone about scheduling a dump truck and front-end loader.

"So you sing?" Lan inquired as she leafed through the mail.

"A little," Emma replied as she pushed the buttons on her cell phone with the end of her pen, then frowned at the busy signal.

"What are you going to sing at the ceremony?"

"Good question. But J.T. and Annie didn't seem to know either."

"Takes a lot of guts to do what they are doing." Lan continued to open mail.

Emma nodded in agreement. Lan headed to her office, Koji trailing along with an energetic tail wag.

"By the way," Emma called to Lan. "Since it looks like we both are going to the ceremony, any chance I might catch a ride out to the island with you? I hadn't quite decided how I was going to get there."

"Sure," Lan answered. A flutter of excitement stirred deep inside her at the thought of taking Emma to the ceremony. "We'll leave about eleven."

"I'll be ready," Emma replied before heading outside to take some measurements.

"Me, too," Lan whispered as she watched Emma energetically bounce down the steps. She had no idea where that remark came from but something was tugging at her, something she was desperately trying to ignore. This was not a date, she told herself emphatically. She shook her head then buried herself in work.

Chapter 6

That week leading up to the wedding was marked by twelve- and fourteen-hour days and two days of rain that slowed the work on the dock. Emma's first big headache was an overdue shipment of galvanized pipe and a load of latex stain instead of the oil-based stain that was ordered.

"Aren't you going home?" Lan asked, stoking the fireplace. "It's getting late."

Emma dramatically punched the button to shut down her laptop then stretched.

"I would love to. It's been a long day and I'm pooped." She covered her mouth to hide a yawn. "But I can't. I have to wait for a delivery truck. It got delayed somewhere in Texas with mechanical trouble. It should be here soon."

"I'd volunteer to wait for it, but I have to run in to the Fed Ex office. These fishing tournament applications have to go out today."

Lan picked up a stack of brown envelopes and checked the addresses. "I'll be back later to lock up. You can flip the lock on your way out if you leave before I get back."

Lan snapped her fingers and Koji followed her out the door. It was well past seven when she finished at the Fed Ex office, stopped for gas and groceries, then returned to the marina. She was pleasantly surprised to see Emma's truck still in the parking lot.

"You still here? What happened to your delivery?" Lan asked, setting the grocery sacks on the counter.

"The driver called from Joplin. Can you believe it, he got lost. Took the wrong exit." Emma was sitting on the hearth, her eyes heavy from the long hours.

"I'm sorry. I should have stayed with you."

"No. You need to go home. You've had a long day, too." Emma leaned back against the warm stones and slipped off her shoes. "He'll be here soon."

"Okay, then I'm waiting with you. And I'm providing you with dinner."

"You don't have to do that, but thank you. That's very sweet and I'm famished."

Lan opened the grocery sacks and pulled out a loaf of bread, a jar of peanut butter, two apples, and a quart of milk. She found some napkins, foam cups, and a clean plastic knife in the snack bar.

Emma watched with amusement as Lan busied herself with picnic making.

"Sorry I didn't buy any jelly today," Lan apologized as she spread their sandwiches.

"No problem. Can I help?" Emma offered, watching Lan diligently work the peanut butter into a smooth layer.

"Nope. I'm preparing the whole meal." Lan grinned broadly then handed Emma a napkin and a sandwich. "And here's the second course," she added, giving Emma a freshly washed apple.

"Thank you very much," she replied, bowing to Lan's achievement. "And on your best china, too."

"Nothing's too good for my dinner guest." Lan touched her sandwich to Emma's as if clinking glasses.

They ate peanut butter sandwiches and apples in front of the crackling fire. Lan poured them each a large cup of milk. They teased each other about how big their milk moustaches were then took turns wiping the milk off each other's upper lip.

"You're quite the cook, Ms. Harding," Emma teased, tossing her napkin into the waning fire. "I can't remember when I've had so much fun eating a sandwich." She looked at Lan tenderly. "Thank you, really. I loved it."

"You're very welcome." Lan found herself lost in Emma's warm and caring eyes. "Maybe we can do it again sometime," she said softly, a warm shiver shooting up her spine.

"I'd like that," Emma replied, barely audible.

For a long moment, a silence hung over them as they sat staring into each other's eyes. Neither could find words to speak. Suddenly the air was split by the blast of a truck horn in the parking lot. Emma flinched, then stood up.

"Guess I better go see about the truck."

"Okay," Lan replied. She watched as Emma walked to the door then turned back for a last look before going outside into the darkness.

Lan blew a soft whistle acknowledging something new and unexpected had just happened during that tender moment. She collected her groceries, waited for the truck to be unloaded, then locked up the marina. After Emma pulled out of the parking lot and disappeared into the night, she too headed home.

By Saturday morning both Lan and Emma were ready for a break and time away from the marina. Attending J.T. and Annie's wedding had become a goal, a target for both of them. Lan stood on the dock and rested one foot on the gunwale of the boat to steady it. She offered Emma a hand and once she was settled into the passenger's seat, Lan released the bowline and tossed it onboard. She then released the stern line and gave the boat a shove. As it began to slide out of the slip, she stepped onboard and eased into the driver's seat next to Emma.

"Even with the windshield, it's going to be a little chilly once we get out into the open water," Lan said as she turned the key and started the big engine rumbling.

Emma slid down in her seat and buttoned the top button of her coat.

"I'm ready. How long a ride is it?" she asked, almost afraid of the answer.

"Either fifteen minutes of cool, or five minutes of cold," Lan teased as she steered clear of the dock and slowly chugged out of the cove.

"You mean we can take our time and only get slightly chilled or go really fast and have the wind freeze our eyeballs?"

"You got it," Lan chuckled as she buttoned her jacket and wiggled her long fingers into the well-worn pair of leather gloves. "What's it going to be?" she asked, tapping the RPM gauge with her knuckle.

Lan usually roared across the lake with the throttle wide open, her hair blender-combed, the hull bouncing and skittering just this side of reckless.

"We'll try slower," she advised, nudging the throttle enough to pull the bow up.

Emma quickly realized her fate as the late fall temperatures tweaked her cheeks. Even slow was going to be agony. She pressed her collar up to cover her ears, squinting at the sharp wind. She took in gasping breaths, trying to avoid deep intakes of cold. Her legs began twitching involuntarily. The tip of her nose tingled like being pierced with a thousand pins. She tucked her chin down inside her coat, allowing only her eyes to peer out. The more the biting wind beat against her face, the farther down she slid in her seat. She closed her eyes, waiting for her blood to turn to slush.

"You okay?" Lan asked as the boat slowed to a gentle roll.

"Uh-huh," Emma grunted from inside her coat. "Are we there?"

"Not even half way yet." Lan scowled at Emma with deep concern. "You're white as a ghost."

"That's 'cause my blood has turned to ice and is clogged up in my veins." She gave a deep shiver as her frozen breath escaped up through her collar.

"Come here," Lan ordered as she unbuttoned her coat and held it open, ready to close around Emma's shaking body. "You should've said something."

Emma eased over in the seat, where Lan's warm coat looked so inviting. Whether it was Lan's body or the thick coat, Emma found warmth worthy of a good snuggle. She turned her face into Lan's chest, pressing her cheek into the delightfully warm sweater.

Lan rubbed vigorously at Emma's back, trying to stimulate circulation for warmth as well as find something to occupy herself as Emma snuggled closer. She expected to give up some warmth with her gallant gesture, but something else was happening. Something she hadn't expected. A chill had incited her left nipple to a full erection, eager to press back at the cheek that nuzzled relentlessly against it.

"This is a wonderful sweater," Emma cooed with relief. "Thank you. Aren't you cold though?" She pulled the open side of Lan's coat around her shoulder.

"No," Lan gasped as Emma's hip pressed firmly against her own. She suddenly had to remind herself to breathe. For a brief moment, she closed her eyes and bathed in the intoxicating scent of Emma's fresh wind-blown hair. As Emma snuggled into the cozy cocoon, the warmth of her breath rose against Lan's neck sending a shiver coursing to places long denied. "I'm fine. We better get going." She forced her attention to the task at hand, namely getting them to the island ASAP.

Lan kept her left arm around Emma, operating the throttle and steering wheel with her right. She urged the throttle up slowly but steadily until the boat had planed out and raced across the top of the water.

"Hold on. I'll have us there in just a minute," Lan announced as she shielded Emma's face with her gloved hand. A cutting spray of mist stung at Lan's face. She pulled the coat collar up over Emma's head and held it there. It could have been fifty below zero, but Lan couldn't feel it, not with this radiant woman squeezed up against her. She was producing her own throbbing source of heat.

By the time the boat eased up to the narrow dock at Two Tree Island, Emma had stopped shivering. She peeked out from inside the coat as the hull tapped against the old wooden walkway. A wave followed the boat, heaving it up and over a deep swell, throwing Emma's body tightly against Lan.

"We're here." Lan sat motionless, looking down as Emma's head extended from deep inside her protection like a brave little turtle.

Several boats were already tethered to the narrow strip of sidewalk that ran out into the lake supported precariously on a few recycled telephone poles. A small armada of fiberglass runabouts, aluminum pontoon barges, and two larger day cruisers had brought Annie's and J.T.'s friends and relatives to the island. Through years of use by the locals, the island had been cleared of brush and was dotted with picnic areas. Downed trees had been stripped of their branches and converted into benches. An open-sided shelter stood on the high ground, providing the only protection from the sweltering Oklahoma sun and torrential downpours. Surprisingly it had weathered the storm that claimed Shared Winds and so many other lake properties. In fact the wind had been a blessing, sweeping away the litter, leaving a pristine area of natural beauty.

"Please don't remind me about the trip back until later, okay?" Emma requested as she gathered her wits and combed her fingers through her tangled hair.

"Are you going to be all right? I mean will you be able to sing?" Lan asked then shut off the engine.

"I think so. I'm not sure what octave I will be singing in, though," Emma replied. "And just why is it J.T. and Annie are doing this out here this time of year?" she asked sarcastically.

"You got me," Lan mused. "It must be true love."

"Oh Lord, I hope so," Emma said as she stepped onto the dock. "By the way, thanks for sharing your coat. I hope it wasn't too uncomfortable for you."

"No problem. I guess I'm more used to the cold," Lan replied as she secured the lines to the dock.

"I've worked outside in the winter before. Cold is one thing, but cold wind is another. How can you get used to bone chilling frigid?" She gave a deliberate shiver.

Lan stepped onto the dock with the cardboard box that had been stowed in the storage compartment. She gave an embarrassed chuckle and tipped the box so Emma could see. "I forgot all about these. They are the blankets for the ceremony. You could have used one of them to keep you warm."

Emma shot back a suspicious stare.

Lan caught sight of J.T. heading for the dock. She had an expression similar to someone whose puppy was about to take a header down a well.

"Oh my God," J.T. whispered through her teeth as she grabbed Lan's arm, squeezing it until she winced. "I lost it."

"Lost what?" Lan scowled, peeling J.T.'s fingers off her arm.

"Shh," she insisted, looking around to see if any one was listening.

"What's the matter?" Emma inquired.

J.T. pulled Emma into her huddle with Lan.

"The tobacco. I had it yesterday. I laid it out. It was right there with my clothes, but now I can't find it. What am I going to do? We have to have the tobacco for the blessing." J.T. began digging through her pockets.

"Well, that's it," Lan said with a straight face. She winked at Emma so J.T. couldn't see. "You are just going to have to call it off. You can't have this ceremony without the tobacco offering. But no big deal. Just get some more tobacco, and we can come back and do this next weekend."

J.T. stared up at Lan with a terrified expression.

64

"Oh shit," she said then began scanning the crowd. "How am I going to explain this to Annie? You thought there was hell to pay for changing the plans last time, I don't even want to think what she is going to say about this." She nervously rubbed her hands up and down on her thighs. "I am dead meat, Lan. And I mean DEAD! We wanted to do this right. This was the way my Cherokee ancestors did it. I wanted it to be perfect for Annie."

"Gee, that's a shame, hon," Emma cajoled, scratching the corner of her mouth to hide a snicker.

"Yeah. Too bad, kiddo," Lan smirked with a tilt of her head. "You want me to tell Annie for you?"

"No," J.T. said reluctantly. "It's my mistake. I'll do it. I can't believe I lost it."

She wiped her fingers over her lips then hesitated a long moment before heading off to break the bad news. Lan looked at Emma and shook her head then reached out and grabbed J.T. by the arm. Lan's familiar impish grin greeted her.

"Get back here. You are so easy," Lan declared as she patted her on the shoulder. "Relax, will you. I have never seen anyone so uptight."

"What?" J.T. still had a vacant stare.

"We'll get you some tobacco. Don't worry about it."

"I'm sure some of these people smoke," Emma agreed, smiling encouragement.

"I don't know. Annie spent an hour picking out some special blend just for this occasion," J.T. argued.

"It doesn't matter what kind of tobacco it is. Look at this as a good sign."

"A good sign? How?" J.T. was a hard sell.

"Think of it as your friends all contributing to the start of your new life together," Lan explained as she straightened J.T.'s collar.

"It will be fine. Don't let a little thing like this ruin your day." Emma rubbed J.T.'s arm as if this future lesband needed blood to flow north to keep her brain from atrophying.

"Okay," J.T. replied reluctantly. She headed off into the crowd, still dazed and befuddled.

"Do you think she will make it through this?" Emma asked.

"Oh sure. But we'll have to tell her about it next week 'cause she isn't going to remember any of this." Lan carried the box up the hill to what looked like the staging area.

J.T.'s younger sister and Annie's niece were arranging sprigs of lavender, sage, and dried rosebuds around a twenty-foot circle. The crowd, mostly women, was dressed in everything from jeans and turtlenecks to suits and long cotton dresses with colorful shawls. They visited in little groups, laughing, hugging, and renewing old friendships. One couple, women in their fifties, was dressed in matching tuxedos and short blonde haircuts. They held hands as they moved from one group to another, laughing and telling stories of their own ceremony twenty years ago.

Annie arrived with her relatives and was immediately hustled off to be hidden until the moment she was to enter the circle with J.T. If they had any reservations about their daughter's gender bias or her public ceremony to express it, they not only didn't show it, but appeared even more jubilant and supportive than most parents.

J.T. had been brought to the island by her sister and a few close friends in a boat fast enough to outrun the Miami Vice Squad. She too had been encircled by well-wishing giggling women, bent on ensuring she didn't see Annie until the absolute moment the ceremony began. Not only did they want this wedding tradition observed, but the night before a posse had connived to secretly pirate Annie off to a friend's house, insisting the couple could not sleep together. It didn't seem to matter they had begun sharing their new apartment four months ago.

Lan found a small hollowed-out piece of driftwood and went about collecting tobacco from anyone who had a pack of cigarettes or box of chew. The story quickly circulated of how important the lost tobacco was. Those who didn't smoke wished they had so they could contribute to the offering, even if they didn't understand the

Native American custom of blessing the four directions with bits of tobacco. Soon Lan had more than enough. She took the tiny leather bag that hung around her neck and dug out a few bits of tobacco to add to the pile. Earlier that morning she had considered not wearing her medicine bag. She was glad she had ignored that thought.

Even though she was not a steadfast follower of her Cherokee heritage, some parts seemed easy to reconcile. The traditions and teachings that put her inner soul at peace were the ones she acknowledged. Like her homosexuality, it was a private matter, not for public display or discussion. Most of her friends had known she was a lesbian from her confused days in high school. But she had moved through her world without screaming it from the rooftops. That was just her way. It had nothing to do with being or not being gay. It had to do with being a private person. It was like a suit of armor, a shield from being hurt, in relationships as well as life. She was happy for J.T. and Annie nonetheless. They were some of the brave ones, the few who spoke up for all those that wouldn't or couldn't. This was their day, their day to be married. She was both proud and humble to have been asked to assist with the ceremony. She set the tobacco-filled piece of wood on the stump where a vanilla-scented candle was burning, and a book of poetry had been opened to some obscure ode to flowers and nature.

Annie stepped out of the picnic shelter, beaming with expectation, dressed in a white Cherokee tear dress. This was a gift from Max's wife, Leona. An accomplished seamstress, she made many authentic Native American garments for those who sought the heritage and tradition of their ancestors. The dress had been copied from one found in Leona's great-great-grandmother's trunk believed to have been worn during the Trail of Tears era in the late 1830s. During the Cherokees' removal from their homelands in the Carolinas, the most basic household belongings were confiscated so most women did not own scissors. The material had to be torn from larger pieces of calico print. True to her heritage, Leona appliquéd a sacred seven-sided star of the Cherokee on the flounce. The white-on-white dress with full skirt flowed down over Annie's knees. She wore a pair of deerskin boots, a gift from J.T. to her partner. A single yellow rosebud decorated her hair on one side. J.T. was enchanted with Annie as she met her with a kiss and led her to the circle of gathered friends. J.T. wore black pants and a rainbow ribbon shirt, also a Cherokee traditional wedding garment made by Leona's nimble fingers.

Together they placed bits of the tobacco at each of the four directions, North, South, East, and West, representing the four sacred parts of their world—fire, wind, earth, and water. They asked the gods for guidance and protection. An older woman, leaning heavily on her cane, burned a sprig of sage, allowing the smoke to cleanse and purify the circle.

Some of the guests stood alone, smiling encouragement and approval. Some stood with their partners, holding hands, hugging and leaning together as they watched the ceremony begin. Two women with raven black hair and dark eyes strummed a Cherokee folk song on acoustical guitars.

When J.T. and Annie were finished with the tobacco offering, they stood together just outside the circle where Lan was waiting for them.

Lan took two blue blankets from the box. She placed one around Annie's shoulders, the other around J.T.'s shoulders. She then took a white blanket from the box, draped it over her arm, and found her place in the circle of friends.

J.T. and Annie gazed at one another as if seeing an old friend with whom they shared many memories. There was comfort in their gaze and warmth each could feel even without touching. They stepped into the circle, wrapped in the blue blankets, symbolizing their separate and independent lives, and representing their old ways of weakness and sorrow. J.T. handed Annie a small bundle, wrapped in deerskin, containing some meat she had dried into jerky. This symbolized her intent to provide and protect her from this day forward. Annie handed J.T. an ear of corn and a small loaf of bread she had baked fresh that morning representing her promise to nurture and support J.T. for the rest of her life.

Lan waited for them to complete the exchange of ceremonial gifts, just as Cherokee couples had been doing for generations. This was her cue. She spoke with her usual clear confidence, her eyes fixed squarely on the large oak tree across the way. If she were to get through this without letting her voice crack, it would be nothing short of a miracle. She hated the thought of losing control.

"We are all friends here, and have come to stand in a circle with you, to witness the celebration of your love. And like the circle, you are at both the beginning and the end of your journey. The end of your life of loneliness, and the beginning of your life together. This is your covenant. You shall now be as one, protecting each other. Like a tree in the wind, you will bend and sway with the changes of your lives, but you will stand tall together. Benjamin Franklin said, those who love, never grow old. May you be young forever." Lan looked at Annie and then at J.T. "This is your beginning, your time to celebrate. Like a weary hunter, J.T. and Annie, you don't have to search any longer. At the end of each day, regardless of the hardships and pain, you can rest in each other's arms. This is your prize. This is the trophy you have been awarded for the courage and dedication of your love. You have each other. You have a marriage of souls."

J.T. took Annie's hand, seemingly grateful for something to hold on to. She spoke slowly and deliberately, hoping she could remember the vows she had researched and practiced for weeks.

"Annie, this is my promise to you. I will walk where you walk. I will laugh when you laugh and cry when you cry. Wherever you sleep, I will sleep. If you are happy, then I will be happy, too. If you are sad, I will comfort you. I promise to share my life with you and only you. I will love you and only you. You are the one that fills my heart and satisfies my soul. And I will forever find heaven in your presence."

J.T then placed a simple gold band on Annie's finger. Annie smiled and swallowed back the lump in her throat. She tightened the grip on her lover's hands, unwilling to give it up for even a second.

"J.T., my love, I have waited my whole life for this moment. Sometimes I thought it might never happen for me. But here we are, ready to start our lives together."

Annie stopped and discreetly wiped away her tears of happiness then continued. Sighs flowed around the circle, as if each of the guests knew the depth of this emotional moment.

Emma sniffled quietly, embarrassed at herself for letting the words touch her so deeply. She wondered if Lan was at all affected by the tender words, however sappy they might be. She wanted to look up at Lan, standing next to her, to see if even the smallest drop of moisture crowded the corner of her eye. Surely not. Annie continued.

"Whatever is over the next horizon, I want you to go there with me. But I know we are not the same. Some of our interests are different. So I promise to encourage your dreams and celebrate your accomplishments." She took J.T.'s hand in both of hers. "In honor of this day, our day, I wanted to bring you a gift, something to let you know how much you mean to me. But unfortunately, I can't offer you my heart, since it's already yours. Nor can I offer you my hand since it will be forever holding yours. Nor can I offer you any great worldly possession since no amount of money can be enough to equal what you mean to me. So you will have to settle for my love. This I give you completely and forever."

Annie then slipped a matching gold band on J.T.'s trembling finger. Another round of sighs raced around the circle. Following the Cherokee tradition, Lan walked to the center and removed the blue blankets. She encircled the couple with the white blanket signifying their moment of unity. She handed them a small leather pouch, like the one she wore around her neck. This was a medicine bag she had prepared for them, to protect them and guide them, to enrich their spirits and soothe the storms of their lives.

"May you always find rainbows," she said softly so only they could hear.

"Thank you," they replied in unison. Through the smiles of joy, tears welled in both their eyes.

Emma moved to stand next to the guitarists who strummed a chord for her to find her key. As J.T. pulled Annie in to her for their kiss, Emma's rich voice filled the air. There was no trace of the cold boat ride as she reached every note clearly and completely.

"Could I Have This Dance for the Rest of My Life?" she began.

The guests all recognized the words as she sang but no one wanted to join in. It seemed somehow sacrilegious to interfere with such a beautiful sound.

J.T. and Annie leaned their foreheads together and began to sway to the music. The song was perfect. Lan took a deep breath as she watched Emma sing. The fullness of her voice took Lan completely by surprise. The breeze stirred Emma's hair gently around her face. Once again Lan knew she was staring, but this time so was everyone else. There was no reason not to. She had every right to study the perfect shape of her mouth, the delicately arched eyebrows, the pale freshness of her skin. She hoped it was a long song. They were right. This woman could most definitely sing. She was also stunningly beautiful.

As the song came to an end, the crowd applauded and whistled wildly. J.T. and Annie cheered the loudest. J.T. whistled sharply. Emma blushed, her eyes lowered in genuine humility.

"That was wonderful, Em. Perfect. We love that song," Annie announced over the applause. "Do another one? Please?"

"Thank you. But I didn't prepare anything else," Emma replied.

"Anything," Annie pleaded.

The guests began yelling out song titles, hoping to suggest something acceptable.

Emma's eyes discreetly searched the crowd for Lan's approval. When she saw her proud grin and thumbs up, she returned the smile and shrugged her shoulders. Lan nodded and crossed her arms, ready to enjoy anything Emma wanted to sing.

Emma thought a minute then huddled with the guitarists, who agreed with whatever she had said.

"Okay. I'll sing one more. But you all have to dance or help me sing it. Okay?" she asked as the crowd cheered encouragement. "This is an oldie. One of Elvis's," she announced then cued the guitarists.

Several couples joined J.T. and Annie dancing to Emma's song. As the dancers moved back and forth in the circle, Emma could occasionally see through to where Lan stood on the other side. Lan's eyes never looked away, as if waiting for each fleeting glimpse through the crowd.

When the song was over, Emma was surrounded with congratulations and well-wishers. Like any party, once the ceremony was over, the food came pouring out. Sandwiches and dips, exotic hors d'oeuvres and desserts, salads and relish trays, and every conceivable drink from juice to champagne. Someone had brought a large battery-operated boom box. What had started out as a celebration of love soon became a wonderful excuse to dance, everybody with anybody. Lan spent her time visiting and keeping up with the trash bags. She watched and laughed at the fun but was careful to stay clear of wandering single women who looked like they wanted to dance.

Emma, on the other hand, had a full dance card. She had been invited to dance nearly every song by one woman or another. She moved gracefully, following even the clumsiest dancer. It was nearly sunset when the call went out for the last dance, a slow dance. Lan had begun gathering and packing when she felt a tap on her shoulder. She turned around to see Emma's beaming face.

"How about the last dance with me, Ms. Harding?" she said, holding out her hand.

Lan looked around, hoping someone needed her immediately for something, anything. She had just been asked to do the one thing that struck terror all the way down to her toes. To dance. She didn't dance. She never learned how, never needed to know how, and was now too old to learn. Rachel had never suggested she learn to dance.

She didn't need her to. Whether they were out together or she was out alone, finding a partner was never difficult for Rachel.

Now if Emma had asked her to balance receipts or check the oxygen saturation level in the lake or change the oil on a 150-horsepower inboard she would be happy to oblige. But dance? No way. No damn way. She'd rather eat fish guts on toast.

With as much dignity and tact as Lan could muster, she declined the invitation to dance. Using an armload of full trash bags as her excuse to get out of the humiliation of not knowing how to dance, Lan smiled politely, excused herself, and hurried to put the trash in the boat for the trip back to the marina. Emma watched her retreat with narrowed curious eyes, but did not want to push the matter.

Chapter 7

Koji spent several minutes choosing his observation post for the big concrete pour—spindles on the deck, behind the bottom step, hanging out the opened tailgate of Emma's pickup, or pacing back and forth in the grass. The pup finally settled on the deck, front paws hanging over the top step, back haunches down but ready to spring into action if a concrete truck got out of hand.

"You keep an eye on them, Koji," Max admonished as he stepped over the pup on his way down the stairs.

Lan's curiosity brought her out onto the deck to watch the first big truck back into position and begin expelling its gray lumpy ooze. A platoon of concrete finishers watched as a long chute was guided from one side to the other, filling the first section. Two men with their cuffs tucked inside rubber boots, waded in and began muscling shovelfuls into corners and low spots.

"It's like watching a Zamboni on an ice rink," Emma said as she climbed the stairs to Lan's vantage point.

"I beg your pardon," Lan said, half in a fog.

"Pouring concrete, everyone likes to watch it being spread."

"It is kind of mesmerizing. How many trucks will it take?" Lan asked.

"Just one. We're going to spread it real thin. Saves money that way," Emma replied seriously.

"Good idea. That way the grass can grow right up through it and give it some color," Lan added, realizing she was being teased.

"Two hundred sixty cubic yards of gray gold, thirty truckloads, and an option on two more." Emma checked her watch. "The first truck is here right on time, too. By dark, you'll be the proud owner of one bright shiny new boat ramp." She smiled broadly and took a deep breath. "And I hope the weatherman is right about the temperatures tonight. He said it would stay above fifty through the weekend."

"Oklahoma autumns are great. I love the cool evenings and crisp mornings," Lan replied, breathing in the first hint of the changing seasons.

"Don't even joke about it. Just concentrate on temperatures above fifty degrees. Too cold or too hot and we won't have proper hydration." Emma didn't notice Lan's look of complete ignorance. She might as well have been speaking Portuguese.

"You want to check the slump, Ms. Bishop?" called a man taking a metal cone-shaped container from the back of her pickup. He placed it on the ground by the concrete truck near the chute.

"I'm coming, Jason. Fill it up." Emma and Lan joined him, keeping clear of the crew and the swinging chute delivering the slurry into place.

Jason shoveled the concrete mix into the cone until it was half full, tamped it down with a piece of rebar, then filled it to the top and smoothed it off level. He released the lever and removed the cone shell from the platform. Jason and Emma watched as the wet concrete began a painfully slow melt like a snow cone in a paper cup. Within a few seconds, Jason measured the height of the pile and nodded, satisfied with what he saw.

"Is this something important or just for the fun of watching cement droop?" Lan asked, watching every detail.

"We test the amount the concrete sinks down or slumps. It's a loose measure of the consistency and flow. We have a six-inch slump here and for these conditions and this job, that is just what we want." Emma nodded to Jason and gave him the thumbs up. "It's all yours, Jason. Make me a boat ramp."

"Do you want me to test every truck?" he asked, dumping the slump pile into the form.

"Yes. Let me know if there is any variance," she added.

"Will do."

One by one, the trucks arrived, dumped their load, and left. It was a slow, methodical process of filling the frames, shoveling it out, then smoothing it off and adding a raked finish. For the middle sections the chute couldn't reach, a pump truck was used, its hose and crane-like frame arched over into the center sections, plopping out concrete in a never-ending trail. The crews took shifts through the lunch hour to keep the pour moving on schedule. Little by little the ramp was taking shape. The clumsy ballet of trucks, drivers, finishers, tools, and the precious recipe of gray slop all moved from one side of the ramp to the other, transforming the wood-framed slope into a wide smooth boulevard into the lake.

Lan wandered in and out, trying to keep her mind on her own work, but the curiously magnetic concrete show kept her returning for periodic updates.

"How are you going to do the part that goes into the water?" she asked as the crews moved down closer and closer to the waterline.

"The concrete is heavy and sinks so they just smooth it out under water. They have special tools to do that," Emma replied, looking up from her laptop.

"But how about the lake water, doesn't that make it too wet?"

"No. It doesn't affect it. The water that's used to mix the Portland cement with the aggregate is what is causing the reaction, not the outside water."

"Oh," Lan replied, giving another look out the window before returning to her office, trying to look like she understood. She couldn't help wonder if dumping load after load of concrete into the lake would pollute the water or just make a big mess at the bottom of the cove.

After fifteen minutes, she couldn't sit at her desk any longer. She decided Max needed supervision. She headed down to the dock where he was replacing a manifold on a big inboard.

Koji had grown tired of the concrete ballet and relocated. He was sitting on the end of the dock studying a small fish circling beneath him. He had outgrown the temptation to stick his paw in the chilly lake water in a feeble attempt at catching the fish. He settled on watching, his head hung as far down as he could reach, his nose just above waterline.

"You want to replace the trigger guard on the gas pump handle? It's in the bucket over there," Max said, looking up from the engine compartment as Lan ambled within view.

"Sure," she replied, digging in the bucket of tools for the part and a screwdriver. "Watching and waiting for them to finish that ramp is driving me crazy." She sat down on the dock cross-legged and went to work on the handle.

"It's called patience," Max replied, straightening up from his back-wrenching position.

"I'm patient. I can wait," Lan replied, looking up the hill at the workers, mentally counting how many were shovel-leaning and how many were shovel-pushing.

"That Miss Bishop seems to have everything running smoothly. She's a real stickler for details," Max said, giving a loud groan as he once again crouched over the engine compartment.

"She seems to, doesn't she?" Lan smiled to herself.

"Ain't bad to look at either," Max added without looking up.

Lan raised her eyebrows in silent agreement.

"How's your boat repairs coming, kid?" Max asked. "Did you ever get the motor put back together?"

"Can't find a camshaft for it. The one I bought from that idiot on eBay was the wrong one. It was for the thirty-eight model, not a forty-eight. He didn't know what he was talking about. It was two inches too long and the bolt pattern was different."

"Damn. Did you send it back and get a refund?"

"Heck no. I listed it on eBay for what it really was and got twice as much for it. The guy who bought it said he had been searching for one for ten years." She laughed victoriously. "But I'm still without a camshaft. I have the upholstery finished and the varnishing about done. A few of the brass pieces need a little work still. But you know what they say?" She looked over where Max was working.

"What?" he asked, his head still buried in the engine compartment.

"I have no idea, but I'm sure there is some Cherokee saying about boats without a motor."

"No-go-em-fast," he muttered.

Lan smirked and re-hung the finished handle on the pump.

"I'm finished here. You need any help?" she inquired as she wiped her hands on a rag and dropped the screwdriver back in the bucket.

"No thanks. I want to finish today," Max said, giving Lan his customary tease. It was his way of telling her he was proud of her for finding a contractor, getting the marina repairs underway, and being a good boss. But giving her a hug and direct words of encouragement weren't in his nature to say any more than they were in Lan's nature to hear. Like the way he joked with his children and grandchildren, he and Lan settled on teasing, good-natured ribbing, and an occasional poke in the arm.

"Hand me a left-handed crescent wrench, will you?" he asked, holding out a greasy hand. "Should be one in the bucket."

Lan looked in the bucket without leaning down, giving a quick scan of the tools. "You only have right-handed ones. Maybe I should run into town and buy you one."

Max stood up and wiped his hands on a well-saturated rag.

"Get me some lightbulb grease while you're there," he mocked, enjoying the joke.

Lan handed him a wrench and tossed him another rag.

"Do you really think she can handle it?" Lan inquired, wondering why she felt the need to ask. "I mean, don't you think she seems like a real professional?"

Max looked over at Lan before answering. He studied her face, as if measuring what kind of response she expected.

"She's good, kid. Very good." He nodded matter-of-factly. "Have you ever met her father?" he asked, narrowing his eyes. He looked at the group of workers in the parking lot crowding around a shiny new GMC dually with a Bishop Construction logo on the door.

"No," she replied.

"Well, I think you are about to." He tilted his head toward the parking lot.

The workers crowded around the man as he stepped out of the truck, shaking hands and distributing slaps on the back. He was a tall large-framed man in his fifties with gray hair and a well-trimmed beard and mustache. Whatever he was saying to the crew had them laughing and nodding in agreement. He was dressed in a brown leather jacket and corduroy slacks. Lan watched as he headed for the marina door, perusing the job site and seemingly passing judgment on the progress.

"Are you sure that's him?" Lan asked curiously as she studied the man.

"Yep, I'm sure," Max replied then returned to his work.

So Quinn Bishop had come to see how Peaches and Cream was doing.

"Aren't you going up to meet him?" Max asked.

"I don't think he has come out here to meet me." Lan leaned back against a post and hooked a thumb in her pocket.

Lan couldn't keep the image of Emma and her father out of her mind. Was he there to give her support or was he there to create a problem for her and the completion of the repairs? Lan took a deep breath and focused on the medicine bag around her neck. She wanted to grab it and let its strength flow through her and up the hill, surrounding Emma and protecting her.

"You want me to go ahead of you and scout out the situation? I can tell the white man to be nice to the tall Indian woman." He mused, "I could offer peace pipe."

"Oh, shut up," Lan replied jokingly as she headed down the boardwalk.

"I have some beads in my truck for trading," he called after her. "Make good wampum."

She ignored him although the thought of meeting Quinn did hold a certain amount of curiosity.

"Dad, this is Lan Harding. Lan, this is my father, Quinn Bishop," Emma announced as Lan entered the marina.

"Nice to meet you, Lan," Quinn stated, his big hand extended to Lan as she crossed the room to where they were standing at Emma's work table. His voice was quiet but commanding. His eyes were bluer than the sky.

"Nice to meet you, Mr. Bishop." Lan took his hand and shook it firmly.

"Mr. Bishop?" he laughed. "I'm not Mr. Bishop, unless you are my doctor or the guy who repairs my trucks. Call me Quinn."

"Quinn," she replied.

"Dad came out to see how things are going."

"We're doing fine. Emma has repairs right on schedule. No problems here." Lan nodded and smiled contentedly.

"Oh really?" Quinn replied as he studied the damaged ceiling and window wall. He then turned his attention to the restaurant area still disheveled.

"Yes. Your daughter is doing a great job. I'm very pleased with the progress." Lan fixed Quinn with a determined stare, letting him know she had no doubts about her confidence in Emma's ability.

Quinn saw her stare and matched it with one of his own.

"Dad is working on a project over by Grove so he was in the area," Emma included with the eyes of a mediator.

"Shared Winds is the talk of the construction business," Quinn announced, looking first at his daughter then back at Lan. "Yes sirree. Bets are flying about it." Quinn sank his hands deeply into his pants pockets.

"Bets?" Lan asked warily.

"It's nothing," Emma interjected. "Pay no attention to him, Lan." Emma glowered at her father.

"Bets are on whether you will still be open on Welcome Back Weekend in March," he continued, ignoring Emma's roadblock. He narrowed his eyes and watched Lan for a response.

Lan swallowed then forced a half smile. The thought of failure never crossed her mind.

"We'll be open. Come on by. I'll treat you to a free hot dog and pop. I'm planning a big grand reopening that day." Lan surprisingly felt the need to impress. She hadn't thought of any such grand reopening until her mouth just obligated her to do so.

"I didn't know you planned on a grand reopening. That will be great. Show Shared Winds off to the customers. I like the idea, Lan," Emma said, giving the notion some thought. "Yes, I really like that idea. Hot dogs, pop, maybe balloons for the kids."

"Sure. Balloons, too," Lan agreed, keeping her eyes on Quinn. She wasn't sure why this man made her nervous, but he did. Maybe it was because he held Emma's future in his hands. Or maybe it was his condescending look. Whatever it was, Lan wanted him to know his lack of confidence was misplaced.

"Put mustard and onions on mine and you have a deal." Quinn kissed Emma on the cheek then offered Lan his hand again. "I have to get back to work."

"Nice to meet you, Quinn." Lan shook his hand as hard as she could. She felt his hand shift into high and respond to hers with even stronger power.

"Same here, Lan."

"I'll talk with you tonight, Dad," Emma replied, watching the dueling handshake. "Tell mother I'm bringing over that rice dish she likes," she added, placing her hand on theirs and stopping the battle. "Come on. I'll walk you out. You can tell me all about the jobs you are working on."

Chapter 8

Koji scratched at the door inquisitively. Something wasn't to his liking outside. When the door didn't open of its own accord, he trotted into Lan's office and circled her desk. This usually got him attention. But the person in jeans was just sitting there at the desk. He sat next to her leg and waited. One minute was long enough. He pawed at her shoe and included a small insistent yip.

The sound of snoring quickly stopped and Lan dropped her hand down to scratch his head.

"Is it time to go, Koj?" she said through a yawn.

Koji barked and went to the door to wait. Before Lan could get her jacket on and turn out the lights, he was barking persistently.

"What is it, boy? What's out there?" Lan opened the door and looked out. Koji shot out like he had been launched. He soon disappeared into the darkness, the sound of his barking echoing through the still cold air. "It got cold out here, damn," she said, zipping her jacket. Her cold breath curled up around her head. "Koji, get back here." The sound of a small gasoline engine being started floated up from the direction of the water. Then another started up, humming in unison. Koji yipped then stopped barking.

"What the . . ." Lan squinted into the blackness.

Another engine started, died, then started again. Lan followed the sounds, straining to see through the darkness. By the time she had groped her way down through the trees to the clearing near the boat ramp, several more engines had been whip-started into action. The lights of a pickup truck were pointed at the freshly poured cement. The tailgate was down and Koji was hanging over the side, his tail wagging exuberantly. A long flatbed trailer carrying more than a dozen torpedo-shaped heaters was hitched to the pickup. Someone in a bulky coat and stocking cap was struggling to align a row of the heaters along the side of the ramp, spacing them all the way down to the waterline. The shadowy figure dragged another heater into position and pulled the starter cord. It took several attempts and a kick in the side before it joined in the noisy chorus. Lan stood next to the open pickup door, holding her finger up to her mouth to hush Koji from yipping his excitement.

"Ouch!" A woman's voice screeched as one of the engines couldn't be convinced to start even after repeated tugs on the cord. "Dammit," she cursed, examining an injured finger.

Lan smiled broadly. "I know that voice, Koj," Lan whispered into the dog's ear. "Do you think we should help? We wouldn't want her to break all her nails."

Lan walked over and reached down to give the cord a try. Emma looked up in surprise and jumped back, grabbing her throat.

"Oh my God," Emma gasped. "I didn't know you were here."

"Need some help?" Lan asked as she adjusted the choke then tried the cord again. The engine finally coughed and sputtered, then chugged into action.

"How long have you been here?" Emma asked, still breathless from the surprise.

"Long enough to know you should have brought some help with you."

"There wasn't time." Emma lined up the newly started engine then went back to the trailer for another one. "I was watching the late news and the weatherman said we are in for an unexpectedly cold night." She rolled the three-foot-long red metal machine down the back of the trailer and across the gravel. "Temperatures are going to drop into the twenties. Some front decided to drift down from Canada and it caught everybody, including me, off guard. That fifty degrees we were supposed to have is now just a pipe dream."

Lan grabbed the handle and helped pull it into place.

"Are you saying the temperature has something to do with my new boat ramp?" she asked, holding the starter cord, poised to pull it.

"I checked the forecast before I ordered the concrete. I sure wouldn't have poured fifteen thousand square feet of marine grade cement if I knew it was going to get down in the twenties." Emma shook her head as if she was chastising herself. "If the water in this ramp freezes, we will have to bulldoze it all out and do it all again. It will be a worthless crumbly mess." She heaved a disgusted sigh and pulled the heater closer to the edge of the ramp.

Lan pulled the cord and sent the engine churning.

"These heaters should keep the ambient temperature above freezing long enough for the cement to start to cure."

Emma filled the remaining heaters with kerosene while Lan dragged them into line and started them going.

"Do we need all these?" Lan asked as she positioned the last one to spray its precious warm air over the surface of the ramp.

"Yes. And if I could have found more in our warehouse, I would have brought them, too." Emma walked the line of heaters, checking each one for position. If one dared to be out of line, she gave it a tyrannical shove.

"I thought that was why they spread the straw and tarps," Lan muttered as she fine-tuned the engine speeds on each unit.

"Normally, it would have been enough. But twenty-six degrees," Emma said, her voice trailing off at the thought.

Lan heard the emotion growing behind Emma's normally proficient exterior. She tried not to stare, realizing this was far more than just a worrisome development. But Lan knew how careful Emma had been in her attention to detail. If the weatherman had even hinted at such a drastic drop in temperatures, pouring the concrete would have been postponed.

"This wasn't your fault, you know. It was just one of those things that happen." Lan spoke with as much reassurance as she could find.

Emma finished aligning the heaters, saying nothing. She couldn't escape the guilt that scratched at the pit of her stomach like fingernails on a chalkboard.

Lan reached in the cab of the pickup and switched on the radio. A loud country western tune blared out, echoing across the water. It was obnoxiously loud but she left it, hoping to get Emma's attention away from her anxiety. It worked.

"All right, already," Emma groaned. "I hear you."

Lan lowered the volume and pushed the search button to find something better.

"How long do we have to stay and supervise these things?" Lan asked as she perched half in and half out of the truck cab.

"I want to stick around awhile, just to make sure they don't conk out. Some of these things haven't been used in several years." Emma wandered up to the truck and stood leaning against the side, giving Koji a brisk scratch behind the ears. "Thanks for your help."

"No problem. After all, I have a stake in this, too," Lan added.

Emma forced a smile, realizing she wasn't the only one worried. "But I think it will be okay."

"So we just have to keep the water in the cement from freezing so it can dry correctly?" Lan asked, giving up on finding anything reasonable to listen to on the radio.

"The water doesn't dry when concrete cures. It is a chemical reaction, not an evaporative one. We have to give the cement in the concrete a chance to cure slowly. If the water freezes, the reaction is halted and the rigidity will be compromised." Emma related the technical information as if it was second nature to her.

"Oh." Lan tried not to look ignorant. "So we are keeping the air above the concrete warm enough for the chemical reaction to take place, right?"

"Yes, exactly."

"I'm learning every day."

"Speaking of learning," Emma said, folding her arms and digging her toe in the gravel. "How come you wouldn't dance with me at the wedding? I think those trash bags could have waited a few minutes. Is it because you don't know how?" Emma looked up at Lan with a sideways glance. "Or is it because you just didn't want to dance with me?"

Lan cleared her throat and looked down, feeling a blush shoot up over her face. "I was hoping you had forgotten that."

"Nope."

Lan scrunched her mouth one way then the other. She knew Emma was going to stand there and wait for some kind of explanation. There was no way around it.

"I guess I never got around to learning how to dance."

"Everybody has to dance sometime or other, whether they know how to or not."

"I never have. I've always been the one who operated the jukebox or the stereo. I just never thought it was that important." Lan knew she sounded like a scared rabbit but she couldn't help it. On the subject of dancing, being scared came naturally.

Emma reached in over Lan and found a radio station with slow music.

"Let me teach you. It's really very simple." Emma extended her hand and waited for Lan's decision.

Lan hesitated, her apprehension visible in her eyes.

"I don't think . . ." Lan started to say.

"Come on," Emma coaxed reassuringly. "I promise it won't hurt." Her eyes relayed her calm assurance.

Lan wanted to say no. She didn't want to be made to feel clumsy and awkward. She didn't want to be cornered like this. But she felt her defenses collapsing. She knew she was going to end up doing this. A vision of Fred Astaire and Ginger Rogers flashed across her mind. She wondered if they started out this way. She was, in spite of her determination not to, about to learn to dance. As if her life was passing before her, if she ever knew anything about being graceful, she wished it would return to her immediately.

"I ought to tell you, when I was a freshman in high school, I went out for the varsity basketball team. I was all cocky and sure of myself. I practiced my foul shooting and had a good set shot. The coach tried to tell me I should try out for the junior varsity team first, to get some experience. But not me. I wanted to be on the varsity team. So she sent me in, first home game. I took three steps and fell on my face." Lan chuckled defensively. "My shoelace was untied."

Emma looked down at her shoes. "They're both tied. You're all right."

"It took me months to get over that," Lan replied quietly. "Um, I didn't get in line when they were handing out grace, ya know."

"Oh, I think you did. You just don't know it."

Lan raised her hand slowly and placed it across Emma's outstretched fingers. Emma closed her hand around Lan's and pulled her to her feet.

"First you put your right arm around my waist, like this." Emma showed her. "Then you put your left hand in mine, like this." Emma took Lan's hand in hers and extended it.

"Who's leading?" Lan asked, looking down at her feet.

"You are," Emma replied. "And don't look down. It's confusing. Look at me."

Lan raised her eyes. She had wanted to look at Emma but thought it would be too forward. Now she was told to do it. It was like an early Christmas present. Concentrate. She had to concentrate. Breathe, in and out. What was that wonderful smell? It was a delightful mixture of roses and lavender. Emma's hair brushed against her cheek. It felt soft, like the satin binding on her blanket. Between the soft curls of her hair, she could see Emma's ears, small and delicate. The lobes were dotted with tiny amethyst stones. February, she thought. Her birthday must be in February. Lan's senses were flooded. Emma's skin against hers, the feel of her body beneath her arm, her legs against hers.

"Now start with your right foot. Step back."

Lan moved her left foot.

"Ouch!" Emma whispered with a grimace.

"I'm sorry." Lan stepped back and released her hold on Emma. "I told you I couldn't do this."

"Oh yes you can." Emma grabbed her and pulled her back into position. "We'll just start with your left foot. Like this. One, two, three. One, two, three." Emma held Lan tightly and maneuvered her in little steps. They weren't in time with the music but at least they weren't stepping on each other's toes.

Lan moved stiffly. Her long and normally agile legs seemed uncooperative. She didn't like being put in a position of possible failure. She had always taken the time to research a project, to learn all the ins and outs, to be proficient at whatever she tackled. She didn't like doing things she had no knowledge of and this was definitely high on that list. She desperately wished a boat would pull into the cove with engine trouble. Lan held her head erect but her eyes strained downward to see what her feet were doing.

"You're going to get a cramp if you don't relax. This is supposed to be fun," Emma said with a grin.

"Uh-huh," Lan replied dryly, then stopped moving. "I lost count."

"One, two, three. One, two, three," Emma said as she nudged Lan into motion again. "Very good."

Soon Lan was able to move her feet and talk at the same time.

"Are we in time with the music?" she asked.

"Pretty close," Emma answered. She hesitated a moment then launched them again. "Now we are." Emma cocked an eyebrow at

Lan's overly serious expression. "Come on. Loosen up." Emma grabbed Lan tightly around the waist and spun her around. Lan surprisingly stayed with her through the dizzying spin.

The song on the radio changed, leaving a few seconds of dead air. Emma continued to dance, refusing to let go of Lan, fearing she would run for the hills. A new song began at a slower pace.

"Oh, great song," Emma said, throwing her head back. "I love Jane Olivor." Emma hummed softly as they moved to the soothing strains of the woman's voice. Emma closed her eyes and sang along quietly.

Lan watched Emma's face express every word of the song, her voice matching the one on the radio perfectly.

"Stay the night, need you to love me, stay and love me, stay the night." Emma continued as if she was singing alone in the shower.

"You have a beautiful voice."

"Thank you. I forget myself sometimes and get a little carried away." Emma blushed.

"When you have a voice like that, you should sing."

"Sing with me," Emma insisted. "I'll teach you the words."

"No way," Lan said emphatically. "I do *not* sing. Period." Lan shook her head, leaving no doubt that she was not going to be talked into a song and dance routine.

Emma could recognize a boundary when she saw one. "Okay," she said with a chuckle.

Lan adjusted her hands as she became more comfortable with her dance.

"You really are doing great. I'm impressed how fast you've picked it up."

"You sound like you have done this before."

"Once before," Emma replied reminiscently. "Long time ago."

Lan was moving with more confidence. The steps were becoming more automatic. She began to guide Emma in graceful circles and arcs. Emma surrendered to her lead, even when it occasionally faltered.

Lan lightened her grip on Emma's hand, satisfied to support and guide, rather than grab and turn.

"How did that dance lesson turn out?" Lan asked with guarded curiosity.

"What dance lesson?" Emma asked, still lost in the song.

Lan watched Emma linger in the world of Jane Olivor's words. She wondered who was swimming with Emma in her sea of illusion, whose face she was smiling at.

"I just wondered if that person you taught to dance was as awkward as I am," she asked with a defensive smile.

"No," she replied softly. "She was worse." She lowered her eyes and leaned into Lan's shoulder.

A small relieved smile crossed Lan's mouth. She turned her head to get her bearings and when she turned back Emma's forehead brushed against her lips and stayed there. It was soft and warm. The soft sweet smell of her hair invaded Lan's nose. She closed her eyes and drew in a slow quenching breath. The taste of her skin against her lips was sweet. Lan's heart pounded so hard beneath her coat she was sure Emma could feel it.

"It's getting colder out here," she said in barely a whisper. "Are you warm enough?"

"I'm fine." Emma pulled Lan's extended hand between them and snuggled against it. "Just fine. How about you? You okay?"

Lan's mind had begun a downward survey over the feel of Emma's body. Firm breasts pressed against her ribs, hips sliding back and forth, Emma's thighs responding to each step Lan took. One of Emma's legs had slid slightly off center and was nestled between Lan's legs.

"Yes. I'm fine."

She pressed her lips into Emma's forehead. Without the sounds of a kiss, Lan had silently thanked Emma for opening her senses. It had been a long time since she had felt these wings of affection fluttering inside.

The wintry silhouettes moved in graceful union. Lan Harding

91

had learned to dance. But more importantly, she had learned to live. She knew there was a crack in the shell where she had been hiding since Rachel had broken her heart. This woman, this contractor, had done it, had allowed Lan to peek out and see the blue skies and warm winds of compassion and tenderness. There would be hell to pay to close her back inside.

At that moment, no one's past was important. No problems could shatter this crystal moment. It was as if a perfect cocoon had been spun for them. And for the duration of the dance, no one else in the world existed.

Lan looked down at Emma and brushed back a lock of hair from her cheek. Her fingertips stroked Emma's face.

"Your face is cold," she said softly then cupped her hands to warm Emma's cheeks.

"It's funny. I don't feel cold. I know I should but I don't."

"Your lips are blue," Lan whispered, tracing her finger around the outline of Emma's lips.

The dancing had slowed to little more than mutual swaying.

"You look a little pale yourself," Emma said, her words spoken against Lan's fingertip.

Tiny clouds of breath rose from their nostrils and mixed between them.

"Nothing about me is cold right now," Lan replied firmly. "Especially my lips." Lan pulled Emma's face to hers and kissed her.

"No, I see they aren't." She gasped at the end of the brief kiss.

Lan felt Emma's smile melt through her as she held her face in her hands. Slowly she pressed her lips to Emma's and kissed her again, this time letting her lips part and drink in Emma's taste.

Emma pulled herself up on her toes and slipped her arms around Lan's neck, pressing into the kiss. Lan's arms encircled Emma's body and held her motionless. She tilted her head, finding that place where two people complete a kiss in flawless and nearly breathless union.

Chapter 9

"Good morning," Lan offered with a cautious smile. "You're here early."

"Morning," Emma replied with her usual chipper response. "The weatherman sure gave us a surprise last night, didn't he?"

"Sure did. I hear it bottomed out at twenty-seven."

Lan sipped her coffee and watched as Emma set her laptop on the table in the snack bar area she had adopted as her temporary office. She removed her coat and carefully hung it over the back of her chair. She turned on the computer and while she waited for it to boot up, she leafed through some invoices. Lan continued to study Emma, waiting for some sign she was ready for the normal chitchat that had become part of their mornings. But this morning, the gaping silence seemed to scream volumes. Lan leaned against the end of the fireplace and waited. Surely Emma would come around soon, she thought. Surely she would have something to say about last night, about the dancing, about the kiss. Lan had spent many sleepless hours wrestling with her guilt and embarrassment over letting the music, the moon, and the mood all conspire to melt her defenses. It would serve her right if Emma pulled Bishop Construction off the job and walked away. At the very least she expected to be raked over the coals about it. This waiting must be Emma's way of making her squirm. And it was working.

The one thing that kept haunting Lan was that, regardless of how much guilt she felt, she had enjoyed it, every tiny bit of it. It was more than just her animal instincts, more than just her pent-up emotions. It was far deeper than that. It was a statement of how she felt. It was an awakening of her soul. She swirled the last swallow of coffee in her cup and downed it. Emma still hadn't looked up. This was not a good sign, she decided. If Lan could kick herself in the butt by sheer mental will power, she would have a black and blue ass. It was time to take matters into her own hands, come what may. It was time to start some kind of conversation.

"How do you think the kiss, I mean, how do you think the concrete survived?" Lan stammered, quickly correcting her Freudian slip. She gave her butt another mental kick.

"I think we got it protected in time," Emma replied as she looked over at Lan. "But maybe we should go check it out."

"Okay," Lan agreed willingly, setting her cup on the counter.

Emma pulled on her jacket and headed for the side door.

"Aren't you going to wear a coat?" she inquired in a motherly tone.

"I'm fine. I've got thermals on," Lan replied as she reached in front of Emma and held the door open.

Emma stopped in the doorway and gave Lan a serious look.

"About last night," she started.

"Yes, I know," Lan said sheepishly. "I don't usually do that sort of thing. I'm really sorry, Emma."

"You're sorry?" Emma queried with a frown. "What are you sorry for? You didn't do anything. I was the one who . . ."

"You?" Lan blurted out. "You were perfect. I mean, it was me. I was the one who got carried away. I shouldn't have grabbed you like that and kissed you. It has been a long time since I did that. I don't know what came over me."

Emma smiled shyly. "You think you acted inappropriately. I think I did."

"So who gets to stake the claim on rudeness?" Lan asked.

"Oh, I wouldn't call it rude. Wishful, maybe, or forward. But not rude." Emma adjusted the collar on Lan's sweater then let her hand slide down and rest on Lan's chest between her breasts. "Are you really that sorry about last night?" she asked softly as she leaned into Lan.

"No," Lan murmured. "I'm only sorry . . ."

Before she could finish, Emma leaned up and kissed her deeply on the mouth. Lan continued to hold the door open with one hand while she pulled Emma to her with the other. Neither of them was going to be sorry for this kiss. It was long and wonderful, like something they had been practicing for years. Emma raised herself onto her tiptoes, eager for more of Lan's touch and taste. Her hands rushed up under the back of Lan's sweater. Her fingernails skated up and down her back.

Lan released the door and pulled Emma back inside. Her long fingers ran through Emma's hair, pushing aside the clips that held it neatly in place. She clutched handfuls of Emma's hair, artfully directing the choreography of their lips. This was not the frantic and demanding kiss they had shared last night, but controlled and expressive. The whole concept of maintaining a proper contractor-client relationship was coming apart at the seams. But at that moment, neither Emma nor Lan cared.

The sound of Max's pickup truck pulling into the parking lot was like a bucket of cold water thrown on them. They acted like teenagers necking on the front porch swing when the porch light comes on. Lan stepped back, wiped her hand across her mouth, and straightened her sweater. Emma scrambled to replace the clips in her ruffled hair.

"Timing is everything," Lan joked breathlessly.

"Uh-huh." Emma removed a small smear of her lipstick from Lan's lower lip then smiled tenderly. "We don't seem to be able to keep a professional distance between us. I hope this isn't going to be a problem. Are we okay here?" Emma asked warily.

"I think so. I hope so."

Lan realized Koji had been barking at the glass doors that led onto the deck. His angry bark told her he had spied something more than the normal birds roosting on the dock.

"All right, Koji," she said, stroking Emma's cheek once before she went to see what had him nervously pacing and yipping. "I'm coming."

She opened the door and followed the dog onto the deck. He ran to the railing, stuck his head between two balusters, and began barking as if pointing to something along the tree line. Lan squinted into the early morning sun. At first she didn't see it but then the brownish shape moved, its ears twitching back and forth.

"It's just a deer, Koj. Leave her alone. She wants to get a drink." Lan patted the dog's head reassuringly and continued to watch the deer as it first eyed the water near the boat dock then looked up at its audience. Lan stood motionless and gave Koji a quiet command to sit. "It's okay, girl," she cooed to the skittish deer. "You can get a drink. We won't hurt you."

Emma had followed Lan onto the deck. She too stood quietly watching the beautiful and delicate creature.

"Go ahead, girl," Lan coaxed again.

The deer stared up at Lan. Its ears flipped to the front. Then it looked back at the cove. It took an awkward crow-hop then tried to jump over a small downed tree, something any deer could manage easily. But there was no grace or agility to this animal. It stumbled then caught its balance, its hind legs stiff and clumsy. Its tail hung limp. Lan's forehead wrinkled with concern as she watched the deer trying to decide which way to turn.

"What's wrong with the poor thing? Is it lost?" Emma asked in a whisper.

Just then the deer lunged with an awkward hop to face the other direction. Its back legs seemed to do little more than try to support the fragile animal. As it turned, both Lan and Emma gasped in horror.

"Oh my God, Lan," Emma shrieked.

"Damn," Lan said, exhaling a heavy sympathetic sigh. Her hands clutched at the railing.

Halfway down its back, the smooth tan fur was ripped open. There was a jagged hole large enough for a fist just below the spine. Torn flesh protruded from the wound. The side of the deer was covered with dried and matted blood. The white bones of the spine poked out the gaping hole like polished knuckles.

"Oh Lan, it's been shot," Emma exclaimed as she grabbed Lan's arm in desperation. "Do something. Help that poor animal."

Lan fixed Emma with the look of helplessness. "There isn't much we can do for it," she said reluctantly.

"I'll get my cell phone. We can call a veterinarian or someone from the wildlife department, maybe."

"What's up?" Max asked as he joined them on the deck. "Oh hell," he groaned as he caught sight of what Lan and Emma were watching. He stood at the railing and watched the deer stumble through the brush.

"Can you help the poor thing?" Emma asked desperately.

"Looks like someone used a shotgun," he said with disgust. "It's chewed up pretty bad."

"It can't jump," Lan announced.

"Does the tail flag?" he asked Lan.

"No."

"Too bad." Max clenched his jaw and narrowed his eyes.

"Who should we call, Max?" Emma asked, looking at him expectantly.

Max turned to Lan. Their eyes met in a quick silent conversation. She nodded to him as if giving approval and instruction.

"I'll take care of it, Ms. Bishop," he replied before heading to the parking lot.

"Good. I hope the poor thing will be all right."

"Maybe we should go inside," Lan insisted.

"No. I want to watch."

"No, I don't think you do." Lan took Emma by the arm as if to usher her away from the railing.

"Sure I do. I love wild animals. They are so defenseless." Emma pulled away and went back to the railing. The deer was still stumbling helplessly through the thicket, its head now down. "We humans have to take care of them. Some animals are on the brink of extinction."

"Deer are not one of them."

"It doesn't matter. They are one of God's creatures." Emma grabbed the railing defiantly ready to watch first aid be administered to this animal.

An ear-splitting gunshot ran out. The deer's head snapped back and it dropped to the ground motionless. A flock of birds scattered out of the trees, the flap of their wings the only sound in the chilly morning air. Lan flinched then looked over at Emma. Emma's mouth dropped open. She stood at the railing in shock, unable to move. Her knuckles were white. The color instantly drained from her face.

"Are you okay?" Lan asked tentatively.

Emma's eyes remained fixed on the fallen deer.

"Emma?" Lan gently touched her arm. "Let's go inside."

One tear spilled out of Emma's eye and slowly rolled down her cheek. She swallowed hard then closed her eyes.

"It had to be done, Emma," Lan offered quietly. "The animal was suffering."

"He said he was going to help," Emma said with restrained anger.

"Stupid me. I thought he meant help the deer. Not kill it." She turned to Lan, her eyes narrowed and cutting. "What a heartless vicious thing to do," she said bitterly.

"It's hard to watch, I know," Lan started.

"Hard to watch?" Emma leered, crossing her arms. "Oh, I love watching people destroy defenseless animals. Let's do it again sometime. Maybe we can shoot some baby birds or drown some kittens." Emma brushed past Lan and hurried inside.

"Wait just a minute," Lan said, following her. "We are not monsters here."

"You could've fooled me." Emma turned back sharply. "That deer was hurt. It needed help. Some redneck fool with a shotgun put a hole in it and then left it to wander through the woods bleeding. That deer did nothing, nothing to deserve that." The color had returned to Emma's face and then some. Her blood pressure was rising by the second. "No wonder some animals are on the endangered species list. Man's answer to everything. Just shoot it."

"I told you, deer are not on the endangered species list," Lan said cautiously, realizing Emma was building up a head of steam and was not going to be denied her tirade.

"That isn't the point. He should have tried to help. He didn't even try. Maybe something could have been done. Bandages, antibiotics maybe. Why do humans always have to play God over the rest of the animal world?"

"That deer was going to die anyway. It had been shot in the spine. Its back legs were paralyzed. It couldn't even walk. And yes, whoever used a shotgun was stupid. That's why hunting with one is illegal. They do more harm than good. Just like this one, a shotgun wounds the animals, leaving them to wander off and die."

Emma started to agree, but Lan wasn't finished.

"But this is hunting season. And the fact remains that people with guns and bows are out there shooting deer. For whatever reason, for sport, for food, or just for the hell of it, thousands of deer are being shot. All over Oklahoma," she continued, gesturing broadly, "deer are being killed by young hunters with big guns and old hunters with old guns. And do you want to know why?"

Emma nodded, resigned to listening to Lan's side of the debate.

"Because that is the only way we have of humanely controlling the overpopulation. Society has killed off most of their natural predators, like coyotes and bear. Now there are nearly half a million deer in Oklahoma alone. Twenty-six million nationwide. That is too many. These animals are starving to death because there isn't enough food for them in the wild. They are so overpopulated, they have to come down out of the hills and the woods to find food. And they go looking right where we have put houses and strip malls and parking lots. They don't know they aren't supposed to eat vegetable gardens, or roses, or flower beds. And they leave behind ticks with Lyme disease. This particular deer was unlucky. If it had to die, I wish to God the hunter had used a rifle and put the bullet right through the heart, or better yet, through the brain."

Emma cringed at the thought. "So what's the answer? Slaughter them all?" she mocked.

"No," Lan shot back. "Deer are part of nature. Part of the balance of nature. But I would much rather see their numbers controlled by legalized responsible hunting than allowing them to starve to death, or even worse." Lan hesitated and looked away. "Causing accidents when they look for food along the highways." Lan went to the window to watch Max drag the deer toward his pickup.

"I didn't know you felt so strongly about it."

"The Cherokee have a reverence for all animals, especially the deer, which represent gentleness. It is a respect for the animal's spirit. It is more than just food. They use all of the deer. Nothing is wasted."

"I really don't want to hear this," Emma interrupted, raising her hands as a roadblock.

"Max's ancestors would use the hide for clothing, the bones for arrow tips and sewing utensils, and the antlers for knife handles,"

Lan continued as if the story was too important not to be told. "That deer will be butchered and in his freezer before the weekend. It'll help feed his family this winter. He has four married children and ten grandkids."

"Good for him. But it was still a terrible thing to watch. I wish I hadn't ask him to do anything."

"He didn't do it because you asked him. He did it because it had to be done. The only thing worse than watching an animal die is watching it suffer first."

"You and I don't see eye to eye on this," Emma said, returning to her work.

"So you would rather have it stumble around out there, bleeding, getting weaker and weaker until it falls down then flies start to gather over the carcass?" Lan instantly realized she was being insensitive.

"Oh, please," Emma smirked.

Lan rolled her eyes to the ceiling then back to Emma. "I'm sorry. Now *that* was rude, huh?"

"Yes, it was."

"It's just something happened a few years ago. A deer caused an accident near here," Lan related dispassionately.

"That's too bad. I don't remember hearing anything about it. Was anyone hurt?"

"Someone was killed." Lan's face remained expressionless.

Emma gasped. "Who was it? Someone you knew?" she inquired, trying to read Lan's face for clues.

"Yeah, someone I knew," she said, looking around for some task that urgently needed her assistance. "I think maybe we should get to work here. Maybe go check the cement. What do you think?"

"Wait a minute, Lan." Emma walked over to her and stared into her eyes. "Who was it? Who was killed?" Lan had her full attention, whether she wanted it or not.

"Someone . . . someone I . . . her name was Rachel, Rachel Greco." Lan's expression melted into reminiscence.

101

"Tell me what happened," she said softly, gently rubbing Lan's arm.

Lan shrugged her shoulders and looked away. "There isn't much to tell. It was a foggy night. She was on her way home. The highway patrol said she was going to fast too stop. When she hit the deer the car went up on two wheels then rolled over and down the embankment. She wasn't wearing her seat belt."

"And you blame the overpopulation for the accident?" Emma asked.

"No. Not really. It was Rachel's fault. She was speeding, no seat belt. It was just one of those things, I guess. But it was a time of year when deer are usually deep in the woods. Not down close to town. And it was very late at night. Only a very hungry deer would be foraging along the road at two in the morning."

"Was Rachel someone close to you?" she asked with concern and compassion.

"Yes, she was very close to me." Lan seemed relieved to have finally acknowledged the fact and dealt with it. It surprised her to be so open about her private life. This was a new experience for her.

"I'm so sorry, sweetheart." Emma took both of Lan's hands in hers. "How long were you two together?"

"Three years," Lan said with a reflective smile. "How did you know she and I were . . . ?"

"Lovers?" Emma inserted. "I didn't. But you had a painful faraway look when you talked about her. I bet you were devastated. I can't imagine losing someone that close to me."

Lan didn't say anything. Her mind was somewhere else.

"Hey kid," Max yelled up from the bottom of the steps loud enough to be heard inside. "Can you take care of the boat at the pump?" His rifle was slung over his shoulder. He was dragging the deer by the front legs he had tied together with his belt.

"Got it," she replied stiffly.

"Do you want any of this venison?" Max quipped as he continued toward his truck.

"No. I have plenty in the freezer. Enjoy it. Tell Leona I want a strip of jerky, though." She headed down the boardwalk for the dock.

Emma went out on the deck and watched as Max lowered the tailgate of his truck and heaved the deer up on it. She swallowed hard. She was never going to adjust to killing animals. They were God's creatures, too.

Max had begun the grisly task of field-dressing the deer. She asked herself why she was watching. It held all the interest of cleaning fish. No, more like witnessing her first autopsy. Her upper lip was strangely damp and her knees became rubbery. Snap out of it, she thought. Grow up. Be strong. Get a grip. She tugged at her sweater collar. Oklahoma must be having a heat wave. A burgundy liquid dripped from the deer's neck and pooled between Max's feet. The soft furry creature stared at the ground, its eyes fixed and glassy, its tongue hanging limp and swollen. Max wiped blood from the blade of his knife, then buried it into the abdomen of the deer near the tail and began drawing it up toward the neck.

Emma quickly closed her eyes and turned away. She leaned against the railing for a minute until her head cleared. Where was her laptop? Where was her schedule? Was it time for coffee yet? No, nothing to drink just now. It took all her concentration not to be sick to her stomach.

When Lan finished with the boat at the pump she spent a few minutes at the railing of the dock, collecting her thoughts and replacing her memories of Rachel's accident into the distant corner of her mind. She then returned to her office, thankful that time was softening the impact.

Chapter 10

The subject of the deer was left behind as work on the rebuilding moved into high gear. Thanksgiving week was strained by the shortened work week and Lan's sullen mood, something Emma didn't have time to pursue fully. Emma suspected it had something to do with Rachel because of the small picture of her taped to the bottom corner of the November page of the calendar in Lan's office. Lan had become withdrawn and quiet, always busy, always preoccupied with someone or something else. But Emma's inquiries about it were met with cheerful denials anything was wrong.

"Max," Emma asked as he was hosing out a bait tank. "Can I ask you something?"

"Sure," he replied as he continued with the task. "What do you need?"

"Is there some connection between Rachel and November?"

He turned off the hose and looked at Emma curiously.

"I know it may not be any of my business, but I was just wondering. Lan has been acting a little, shall we say, moody. When I asked her about it, she said nothing was wrong. Just busy with the marina. But I feel like there's something she isn't telling me."

Max turned on the hose and went back to cleaning out the tank.

"Yep," he replied. "November twenty-sixth."

"What is November twenty-sixth?"

"Rachel's birthday. She would have been thirty this year. Birthdays are tough on Lan. Always have been. Her folks pretty much ignored hers her whole life. They'd hand her a five-dollar bill and say 'Happy Birthday.' So she always made a big deal out of Rachel's. Big cake. Lots of presents. Usually had a party right here at the marina for her. This one probably hit her hard, being her thirtieth."

"She never said anything," Emma said with concern.

He smiled. "Yep. That's the kid, for you. She wouldn't tell you she broke her leg unless it was her gas-pedal foot."

"What can I do?"

He shrugged his shoulders. "Not much to do. The Christmas Regatta is coming up next week. That'll get her mind off Rachel."

"Thank you, Max. Thank you for telling me."

He nodded.

Lan filled the twin tanks on the big cruiser and pushed it off from the dock. Surprisingly, it had been a busy evening. The stiff northerly breeze and near-freezing temperatures hadn't deterred any of the usual Christmas Regatta participants. The tradition of stringing twinkle lights from the railings and masts then parading across the lake two weeks before Christmas was a time honored tradition on the lake. The locals said it separated the tourists from the natives. Lan had chosen to be one of the few marinas to open that afternoon for boaters to gas up and get ready for the sunset start of the festivities. It wasn't a big money-making day, but it showed her civic pride and hopefully reminded her customers she was still in business.

It was just before sunset when the last cumbersome pontoon boat eased into position to be filled. Lan leaned on the railing of the big barge to keep it from banging into the dock as the wake of the departing boat rolled past. Lan filled the gas tanks and handed out candy canes to the half dozen children on the boat then pushed the boat free of the dock, waving and laughing at the skipper wearing a Santa suit. She locked up the gas pumps and switched off the lights. With her hands shoved deep into her jacket pockets she headed up to the warmth of the marina.

Lan stopped halfway up the walk and looked up at the new sign welcoming customers to Shared Winds. She smiled to herself. Even though there was a lot of work still to be done, replacing this sign seemed like the marina's defiant statement of survival. Lan stood in the glow of sunset and basked in the satisfaction of this small triumph, ignoring the piles of building materials, tools, tarps, and debris.

The last few glowing embers in the fireplace dimly lit the big room. Lan stirred the coals and coaxed the last flickering flames from the nearly spent pile of ashes. She propped one foot up on the stone hearth and gazed into the crackling fire. She suddenly remembered what Emma had said on the way back from the Undercliff the day they stopped for cheeseburgers. Something about enjoying a cup of hot tea by a roaring fireplace. The details of the conversation were hazy but that part she did remember.

Lan pulled her cell phone from her jacket pocket and scanned through the memory list. There it was, *Emma Bishop—Cell #*. She punched the buttons and waited for Emma's voice to greet her.

"Hello," Emma's crisp business voice answered. "This is Emma Bishop. Sorry I'm not available right now but I will be glad to return your call if you'll leave your name and number."

Lan smirked and pushed the End button without leaving a message. There was no need. The impetuous idea of sharing a cup of hot tea and a roaring fireplace was dissolving rapidly.

"Guess she doesn't have her cell phone with her tonight," Lan thought as she replaced the phone in her pocket.

Lan absorbed the last long drag of enjoyment from the fireplace before turning on her heels and heading for the office. She locked up and turned off the lights, then gave a beckoning whistle for Koji. He was already waiting for her in the parking lot, wagging enthusiastically.

"How does pizza sound?" Lan opened the car door and waved him in. She buckled his seatbelt harness and gave him a pat. "What'll it be? Pepperoni? Sausage? How about veggie pizza?" She wrinkled her nose at the mutt. "Naw. Mushroom and Canadian bacon. Then it's home to work on the boat. That propeller shaft won't install itself."

Koji rested his head on the console for the ride to town.

"You need a bath, Koj. You don't smell like flowers." Lan ruffled the fur on the back of his neck. "Now Emma, there's someone who smells nice." Lan smiled to herself and the memory of her dance lesson.

Lan pulled into the parking lot at Giovan's Pizzeria and Pub. The owner, Bill Ramsey, was no more Italian than Lan but he liked the name. The fact remained: he made the best pizza in the county. No catsup on a cracker here, like most of the places in Grove.

Lan climbed out of the Jeep and looked back at the pup.

"You sit and behave or no pizza for you." Koji yipped once as if he understood then curled up on the seat for a nap.

Lan entered the darkened restaurant well after the dinner rush to find it still crowded and bustling. A bald-headed man behind the counter waved to Lan and pointed to a stool at the end of the counter.

"Park it over there and I'll be right with you." The man finished filling a pitcher of beer and delivered it to a booth. "I haven't seen you in months, Lan. Not since the storm. What'll it be tonight?"

"Hiya, Bill. Mushroom and Canadian bacon, I guess."

"Large?"

"Medium, to go."

"Anything to drink while you're waiting? Draft?" Bill wiped his hands on his apron and took out a receipt pad.

"How about a cup of coffee. Make it strong. I still have some work to do tonight."

"No rest for the wicked," he chuckled. "How's the marina coming? You find a contractor?"

"Yeah, I found one. It's coming along pretty well. We'll be ready for Welcome Back Weekend." From her mouth to God's ear, Lan thought.

"Good. Hate to lose another marina."

"Another marina?" she asked curiously.

"Didn't you hear? River Valley Marina closed down last week. The property has been put up for sale. Too much damage to repair. No one wanted to take it on. They said the only thing that would help that place was a match. Bet they bulldoze it to the ground and start over."

"I hadn't heard that. That's too bad. River Valley was a nice place. They had two hundred slips and a five-wide ramp." Lan hated to hear another business failed to recover even though it had been competition for Shared Winds. It seemed like a painful reminder of the vulnerability of her own marina.

"I'll get your order right in. Take about twenty minutes. With the regatta and all, we're really jammed up."

"No problem."

Lan sipped her coffee and jotted notes on a paper napkin while she waited. Even though she found it hard to turn off the demands of the business, she was trying. She forced her mind to the restoration of her boat. She imagined herself in her workshop, warmed from the woodburning stove, listening to the radio, content to tinker on whatever part she took a fancy to that evening.

She reached for the empty coffee cup and searched the room for a waitress she could flag down for a refill. The only one within sight was delivering a pizza to a booth in the corner. Lan watched her, ready to nab her attention as she returned to the kitchen. As she set the pizza on the table and turn to head back, Lan caught sight of the two shadowy figures at the table, both deeply engrossed in each other's company and conversation. It was Emma and a dark-haired woman in her thirties, stunningly dressed in a silk suit and dramatically perfect makeup. Lan quickly turned away, trying to reconcile what she had seen. Maybe it wasn't Emma, just someone who looked like her. Lan turned sideways on the stool so she could nonchalantly get another look at the corner booth without being obvious. It was Emma. She was dressed impeccably in a beautiful sweater and slacks, an outfit Lan hadn't seen before. One probably reserved for evening wear. Even across the room, Lan could see tiny diamond earrings dotting her earlobes. Her long golden hair was flowing softly over her shoulders in relaxed waves and curls. Emma tilted her head slightly, listening to the other woman intently, hanging on every word, smiling with concerned and sympathetic glances. Ms. Bishop looked ravishing, Lan thought. She seemed completely at ease with this person, cocooned in the world the booth provided.

Lan watched for a long minute then turned away, angry with herself for eavesdropping, even though she couldn't hear the conversation across the noisy restaurant. Lan couldn't help wondering who the mysterious woman was sitting with Emma. She wondered if this was a business client or perhaps an old high school friend she hadn't seen in years, just dropped by to show off the pictures of her husband and five kids. Lan sneaked another look at the table. That woman sure didn't look like the mother of five, not even the mother of one.

Lan watched as the two women sat there, transfixed with each other and their stories.

The woman tossed her hair and laughed discreetly, then took Emma's hand and held it across the table. Emma smiled back, and patted the woman's hand softly.

Lan quickly turned away again, studying the worn design on the coffee cup intently. Lan wanted to envision Emma pulling her hand away, or better yet, slapping the woman silly with it. But she had decided not to look back again. It was none of her business who Emma dated. After all, she was a grown woman. She could sit in a corner booth with anyone she wanted. Even hold their hand if she wanted. Of course Emma was seeing someone. Why shouldn't she be? She was attractive, intelligent, independent, charming, caring, witty.

"Your pizza is ready, Lan," Bill repeated.

"Thanks, Bill." Lan stopped her mental listing of Emma's attributes and came crashing back to reality. She quickly paid and grabbed the pizza box, glad she could finally leave.

Lan waited impatiently for the crowd around the door to dissolve. She wanted to get out of there, to go home, to throw herself into her work on the boat. Anything to take her mind off what she had seen. She couldn't help herself from taking one last glance at the booth. When she did, her eyes met Emma's, looking squarely at her with a frozen stare. Emma's hand was still in the grasp of the other woman. Slowly she pulled it back and placed it in her lap. She forced a smile at Lan. It wasn't a smile that beckoned her over or greeted an old friend. It was a small smile of forced acknowldgement.

Lan diverted her eyes and hurried outside. The fresh cold air felt good on her flushed face. She tossed the pizza box in the back seat and roared out of the parking lot, slinging chat on every car along the way.

She was down the street and out of sight by the time Emma hurried into the parking lot in search of her. Emma closed her eyes in disgust and threw her head back.

"Oh great," she yelled into the darkness.

Lan stoked the woodburning stove in her garage/workshop and stood in front of it, eating pizza and waiting for the room to warm up to work temperature. Koji sat near the stove, chewing on his pizza slice. Lan found it hard to concentrate on the boat, but she had made up her mind she was going to accomplish something, if only sorting through the box of parts. She was not going to dwell on Emma and the other woman. She was not.

Koji finished a second slice then curled up on his old sofa cushion to watch Lan work. Lan soon had the workshop shirtsleeve warm. She was down to her white T-shirt, wrist deep in greasing a propeller shaft bearing, when the door to the shop creaked open, allowing a brisk cloud of cold air to invade the warmth.

"Koji, you're letting in cold air," Lan yelled from the little stool where she sat behind the boat. "You need to learn to shut the door when you go out to potty."

The door closed.

"Sorry," Emma's voice replied.

Lan stopped what she was doing but didn't move. This was definitely the last person she expected to walk into her workshop tonight. Half of her wanted to look and see if Emma had that other woman with her, the other half was glad to hear her voice.

"Hello," Lan said finally, sticking her head out from behind the end of the boat.

"Hello. So this is the boat, huh?" Emma said, forcing a conversation.

"Yep," Lan replied, deciding whether or not she should finish installing the greasy bearing or sit and hold it.

"It is beautiful. I love it." Emma rubbed her hand along the smooth red mahogany hull. "You have to give me a ride in it someday. But when the weather is warmer. No more rides like that one to the wedding. I thought I never would warm up." Emma made a brrrrr sound then laughed artificially.

"Sure. Anytime." Lan realized she was being petulant. She dropped the part in the bucket of grease and stood up. "Did you need something?" Lan asked, wiping her hands on a rag. "Something about the marina?"

"No." Emma walked slowly along the side, tracing her fingers along the polished rim of the deck.

"What brings you all the way out here this late?" Lan checked her watch.

"Would you believe me if I said I just wanted to see the boat you are working on?"

"I doubt it." Lan pushed her hands into her pockets.

"Would you believe me if I said I wanted to see where you lived?"

"Um, probably not."

"Would you believe me if I said I wanted to explain about tonight?"

"Explain what? There's nothing you need to explain to me."

"Well, I do, want to explain, that is," Emma added.

"You mean that woman you were with? She seems very nice. And hey, it is none of my business what you were doing," Lan quickly inserted.

"It isn't?" Emma asked with a raised eyebrow.

"Nope." Lan began putting her tools away.

"Well, I guess you're right. Technically it isn't any of your business. But I want to explain anyway."

"Why do you think you need to justify anything to me?" Lan continued to keep busy. "You're a big girl. You can see whoever you want."

"Look, I know you saw me and Nicole together. I know you saw us holding hands." Emma followed Lan to the other side of the boat while she put tools in the cabinet. "And I saw that look on your face."

"Nicole?" Lan asked as she dropped a pair of pliers in a bin.

"Yes, Nicole Francis. She's a real estate agent from Tulsa and very successful. She's been a member of the million-dollar club for eight years. She really has a golden touch." Emma smiled reflectively.

"Yes, I saw the golden touch." There was the green monster wagging his ugly tongue again, Lan thought. "I'm very happy for you, Emma. Really." Lan gave Emma her most sincere look.

"Dammit! I don't want you to be happy for me. That is not why I came out here." Emma scowled.

"If you're out here to incite some kind of jealousy, it isn't working. Jealousy is for people who are already in a relationship. I'm not jealous. I'm just telling you what I saw. Me and everyone else in Giovan's. It was hard to miss."

"If you think I should be ashamed of holding her hand, you have another thing coming."

"Who said you should be ashamed? I just thought . . ." Lan's voice trailed off. She tossed another stick of wood in the stove and pulled her sweater on over her head.

"Thought what?" Emma asked with a puzzled look.

"Nothing," Lan replied ruefully, not sure exactly what she had meant to say.

"Oh yes, there was something you wanted to say, now say it," Emma demanded.

"Look, Emma. I know where we stand. You are the contractor and I'm the client. Our relationship is a professional one. We had a dance and a kiss, that's all."

"I think we had more than just one kiss," Emma added tenderly.

"Why do you care that I saw you out with someone?" Lan continued.

"I was not *out* with someone," Emma replied tersely.

Lan cocked an eyebrow at Emma.

"I mean, yes, you saw me out with someone but I wasn't *out* with her."

Lan smirked and poked another stick of wood in the stove.

"Wait. Let me explain this. Do you have any idea what you do to me, woman? You have me so flustered here." Emma ruffled her hands through her hair.

"You came all the way out here to tell me you and that woman weren't on a date?"

"Well, yes."

"So, you weren't on a date?" Lan looked up from her interest in keeping the stove going.

"No, we weren't on a date but yes, that is why I came out here. I saw that look on your face when you saw us holding hands. I suddenly wanted to crawl under the table and hide. I didn't want you to see me holding anyone's hand, regardless of the reason. I knew when you ran out I had let you down. I had let you think I wasn't serious about that kiss. I have never had a problem before keeping a professional distance between my clients and myself. I know I have a job to do. But we started something, Lan. We had taken the first step. I felt it. You felt it. I know you did."

"That's why I had to leave," Lan quickly added. "I couldn't watch you with that other woman. I thought if you are going to kiss one person, the way you kissed me, you should be honest about what that means. I thought when I kissed you, and you kissed me back, you were telling me something."

"Telling you what? What was that kiss telling you?" Emma asked softly.

"I don't know exactly. But I sure as heck didn't think it meant you were still holding hands across the table in a corner booth with someone else," Lan explained, ignoring the green monster and blustering on.

Like a cold slap in the face, the memory of the night Lan saw Rachel kissing another woman in the parking lot at Giovan's flashed across her mind. The vision of her lover's lips touching another woman's lips, her hands caressing another woman's body, had seared itself into Lan's soul. Now the image of Emma and Nicole holding hands in a corner booth at Giovan's was an even deeper pain.

"Is that why you ran out like that?"

"I didn't run out." Lan frowned.

"Oh, sure. You just hurried out the door like being shot out of a cannon so you could get home before the pizza got cold." Emma perched her hands on her hips defiantly.

"I saw the two of you together, looking at one another. Then you saw me. The look on your face gave me no reason to stay, Emma." Lan looked at her resolutely.

Now it was Emma's turn to fall silent. She looked up at Lan and searched her eyes for clarification. She saw pain etched in Lan's eyes, pain she had caused.

"Oh, Lan." Emma walked up to her and placed her hands on Lan's waist. "I didn't mean to hurt you. I really didn't. I didn't think you would jump to conclusions like this."

Lan narrowed her eyes and looked away.

"But you were right. Nicole and I were lovers."

Lan tried to pull away, but Emma held tight to her waist.

"We were together for three years. Three beautiful years." Emma squeezed Lan's waist. "But that is over. I needed to concentrate on my work. She wanted me to be a party girl and socialize with her. It just wasn't right for me. We both knew it would never work out between us. Now we are just friends. She and I have moved on with our lives, apart from one another."

"Emma, you and Nicole didn't look like two people apart from one another," Lan replied plaintively. "And besides, it isn't any of my business who you see."

"I'm going to kick you if you say that one more time, Lan Harding. It *is* your business who I see. I want it to be your business."

Lan looked at her innocently.

"Nicole called me and asked me to meet her for dinner tonight because she had something she wanted to tell me. Something too wonderful to tell me over the phone. So I said yes. I told her I would meet her for dinner, something we hadn't done in months. And my dumb luck, we picked the one place you had to go for pizza."

"Let me guess, she wants you back?" Lan offered stoically.

"Nope." Emma straightened the front of Lan's sweater and smoothed the sides. "She wanted to tell me all about her new romance. She wanted to tell me about this woman she is moving in with in Oklahoma City. She said this was the most wonderful woman she had ever met." Emma laughed. "This other woman sounds like a cheerleader, Girl Scout, superwoman, and movie star, all rolled into one." Emma looked up at Lan and smiled discreetly. "So you see, I wasn't there on a date with her, if that is what you thought."

"And the handholding thing?" Lan asked cautiously.

Emma tilted her head and smiled a cockeyed smile.

"Nicole always was one of those touchy, feeling kind. She has to hold your hand just to tell you she is cold and needs to turn up the thermostat."

Emma stopped explaining. She reached up and kissed Lan square on the mouth. Lan stood there deep in thought and allowed Emma to kiss her, without response.

"You know it is better if you participate," Emma mused, wiping her lipstick from Lan's lower lip.

"What do I do to you? You said I do something to you," Lan asked seriously.

"Well, I'm trying to show you. If you'd help a little, you might find out."

"You mean you do think about me, other than when we are working or teaching me to dance?"

"Oh, yes. A lot more than that," Emma replied.

Lan ran her finger up Emma's arm, slowly tracing a serpentine line along her sweater.

"How much more?" Lan began to move a finger up Emma's other sleeve.

"Oh, my dear Ms. Harding. You have no idea how much more," Emma declared. "I was so afraid I had messed it up tonight." Emma hugged Lan around the waist tightly. "I want to give us a chance. I *really* want to give us a chance. I know there are a lot of things working against us. But we have a lot more working for us."

Lan pressed her fingers on Emma's lips to stop her words. "I've had us on that road a long time ago. I tried to ignore it but I couldn't. Every time I see you, it is torture. Then tonight I saw you with Nicole and I told myself it was my own fault. I had made assumptions about us too soon. I blamed myself for the way I felt, seeing you there holding another woman's hand. I wanted that to be me, sitting across the table from you, holding your hand, sharing a pizza, smiling and talking about anything, nothing. I just wanted to be the one with you, that's all."

Lan slowly pulled Emma's lips to hers and kissed her fully, completely, holding her so tightly she could feel her heart racing beneath her sweater. Lan eased Emma back against the side of the boat, devouring her mouth and tongue with her own. She slid her hands down Emma's back and cupped them over her buttocks, cradling them firmly, pulling her closer, feeling Emma's hips and pubic bone against hers. Within moments, both were breathless with persistent tongues and eager groping hands. In their eagerness to find the perfect and comfortable position to touch and arouse the other, Lan whacked her elbow on the side of the boat and pulled back, causing Emma to smack her head on the boat railing. Both gasped and screamed at the same time. The comedy of their action was too much to take in stride. Lan laughed and rubbed the back of Emma's head while Emma giggled and gave Lan's elbow equal attention.

"Babe, do you think we could go inside? This isn't a very comfortable spot. And it is getting cold out here," Emma asked, kissing Lan on the chin.

"Come on," Lan said, taking her by the hand. "I'll make us some hot cocoa and start a big fire in the fireplace." Lan started for the door then turned back to Emma. "Thank you."

"For what?"

"Coming out here to explain what happened."

"Nothing happened."

"I know. Thank you for that, too."

"Be careful. It's hot," Emma warned, setting a cup of steaming cocoa on the coffee table. Lan was busy loading the fireplace with split logs.

Emma rubbed her hands on her arms, trying to stay warm.

"Sorry it is cold in here. The furnace takes forever to warm the house. I keep it turned back during the day while I'm gone. I'd rather sit by the fireplace anyway."

"I like your house, babe." Emma roamed around the living room, taking in all the markers of Lan's life. Pictures and blue-ribbon swimming medals framed behind glass, antique fishing poles hung in a rack over the front window, rich burgundy and pewter colored upholstery on the sofa and overstuffed chair, the rustic paneling, the candles grouped in random collections on the end tables and stereo cabinet, the absence of clutter, the artistic arrangement of antique balusters, spindles, and finials in the corners. It was a unique and pleasing combination of cabin-rustic and country-French.

"Who's the woman in the picture with you?" Emma asked, holding a small framed picture.

"Rachel," Lan answered without looking up. She knew what Emma was looking at.

"She looks very young in this picture."

"Yep, eight years younger than me." Lan finished lighting the fire. She sat on the sofa and sipped her cocoa.

"You look like you are in love with her."

"Was."

"Was she in love with you?" Emma asked gently.

"Good question. One I've asked myself many times." Lan set her cup on the table and rubbed the back of her neck. She shrugged her shoulders, trying to ease out the stiffness from carrying too much firewood.

"What's wrong with your neck?" Emma inquired as she moved to the couch.

"Nothing." Lan stopped. "How did you know there was something wrong with my neck?"

"I can see it on your face. And in the way you've been moving it. It must hurt pretty bad."

"Just a little. I noticed it after I carried in the firewood." She stretched her neck to one side then the other. "It'll be fine."

"Uh-huh," Emma said, narrowing her eyes at Lan. "I've seen how you carry wood for that huge fireplace at the marina. I bet you carried too much at a time."

Lan scowled at the thought.

"Sit down here in front of me," she ordered, pushing the table to the side and pointing to the floor between her legs.

"Why?"

"I'll fix your neck for you." Emma rubbed her hands together vigorously to warm them.

"I'll be fine tomorrow," Lan said reluctantly.

"Come on," Emma ordered quietly, patting the edge of the couch. "It won't hurt, I promise."

Lan hesitated then slid onto the floor and positioned herself in front of Emma. She pulled her legs up and rested her arms across her knees. Lan couldn't remember the last time someone offered to give her a massage.

"Relax," Emma said. "Relax," she repeated in a coaxing whisper.

"I am," Lan insisted, enjoying the magical touch of Emma's hands moving over her aching muscles.

"Your muscles are all in knots."

Usually Lan relied on a hot shower and a big blob of Ben-Gay to work out the kinks of overdoing it. As Emma's fingers pulled and pushed at the knotted tendons, Lan pushed back into the cushion of the couch, reaching for more and more of her touch. She closed her eyes and gave a small groan of approval.

"Am I hurting you?" Emma asked apologetically, pulling her hands away.

"No," Lan said reassuringly as she looked up at Emma. "It feels great. Thanks."

Emma looked down at her. "I can't do any more if you don't hold your head up." She ran her fingers through Lan's hair, making little curls at her temples. She then let her hands flow down over Lan's shoulders and encircled her. "Don't you want me to finish?"

Lan didn't reply with words. She reached up and pulled Emma down onto her lap then kissed her.

"I guess you do want me to finish," Emma gasped then returned the kiss.

"How about you? Do you want anything from me?" Lan asked as she ran her hands through Emma's hair, fluffing it out then letting it fall in soft cascades.

Emma looked longingly into Lan's eyes. She didn't have to say a word. The thoughts were already being shared. This moment had been coming since that first cool autumn evening when Emma roared into the parking lot and caught Lan in her headlights. It had only been a matter of time before their fight to remain mere professional associates crumbled into a passionate explosion of desire. At the same precise moment, they each were asking themselves the identical question. Why had they waited so long? With thorough kisses and inquisitive hands, the dance of intimacy had begun.

Lan pulled Emma's sweater over her head and tossed it aside. Emma soon had Lan's sweater off as well. Lan's mouth explored the valley between Emma's soft breasts as her hands felt the back of the bra for the hooks.

Emma traced her tongue up Lan's neck then stopped at her ear.

"It's in the front," she whispered through a gasp of anticipation.

Lan's fingers quickly obeyed and released the hook, peeling the bra over her shoulders. Emma arched her back as Lan's strong hands cradled her waiting breasts. Lan had considered herself awkward and unskilled at foreplay but with this woman she seemed amazingly at ease, even competent. As Emma cooed encouragement, Lan took first one breast then the other in her mouth, her tongue darting and teasing the nipples into hard erections. Lan released the button and zipper on Emma's slacks and slid them down over her hips. Emma helped Lan pull her jeans off; her undies came with them, then her bra, all pushed aside in a heap. Lan let a long slow stroke of her hand slip down Emma's black string bikini panties. Before laying her down onto the floor, Lan placed a sofa pillow under Emma's head.

"I sure hope the floor's clean," Lan grunted between kisses.

"Who gives a damn?" Emma pulled Lan on top of her.

Lan covered Emma's body with her own and kissed her deeply, their bodies sliding and massaging against each other. No part of Emma's beauty was off limits to Lan's curiosity. She wanted to touch and explore it all. She was almost frantic as she moved over the smooth skin, the soft curves, hands and mouth seeking out strange new worlds. Oh my God, she thought. Don't beam me up now, Scotty.

"Wait," Emma interrupted, pushing Lan's shoulders back. "Slow down." Emma rolled over and sat up, straddling Lan's waist. She looked down at her and ran her fingernails across Lan's chest, teasing little circles around each of her breasts. "Take it easy, babe. We have lots of time." She tenderly brushed Lan's face with the back of her hand. "I want you all night. Don't hurry."

"With a woman like you, it is hard to go slow. You are so beautiful." Lan reached up and stroked Emma's breasts then rested her hands on her thighs. "But I will try."

"My strong Indian woman," Emma sighed and blushed.

Lan playfully tugged at Emma's curly mass of dark pubic hair. "Be careful paleface. I haven't scalped anyone in a long time."

"Let it be me, oh please. Let it be me," Emma giggled and fell across Lan, hugging her and wiggling her hairy mound against Lan's.

Lan playfully swatted her tush like she was tapping on a war drum. She then rolled over on top of her and cuddled protectively close to her.

"I would never hurt you, my sweet woman," Lan whispered softly. "You are so special. Let me make love to you."

Emma closed her eyes and snuggled beneath Lan's warm body. Like the slowly growing intensity of Ravel's *Bolero*, Lan began again. With skillful hands and tender touch she awakened Emma's most intimate needs, needs Emma now welcomed back into her life. She floated in and out of each pleasurable area of Lan's exploration. Her nipples erect, her skin moist with desire, she arched and gasped as Lan moved down her body, teasingly closer and closer to her waiting valley of desire.

Coaxing Emma's legs apart, Lan cupped her hand over the entire pubic area, allowing her palm to gently massage the tiny clit. Her other hand caressed one of Emma's breasts.

"Yes, yes. Touch me, touch me," Emma cooed, reaching for Lan's hand, pressing it harder against her increasing need.

Lan placed kisses across Emma's tummy before moving her mouth down in slow steps to where her hand had awakened her lover's passion. Lan stretched out on the floor, cradling Emma's hips in her arms, her tender kisses tracing a wet trail up one inner thigh to the other. Finally, Lan's hot tongue plunged into Emma's wetness. Emma bit down on her lip. The pain of ecstasy was forcing her head back, her hands clutching at Lan's hair. Slowly at first, with delicate strokes and flicks, Lan's tongue pushed against the growing nub. Unable to speak, Emma urged her lover on with sighs and whimpers.

With tenderness she had almost forgotten, Lan brought Emma to the pinnacle of pleasure in repeated waves. Her mouth and tongue, like artist brushes, painted the perfect texture of love for Emma to enjoy. Gasping and moaning, her body covered in tiny beads of sweat, again and again Emma reached her peak, crashing and exploding like fireworks on a hot July night. Just as Emma shrieked from the intense rapture, the fireplace suddenly shot sparks into the air as if to celebrate the boundary that once existed between them and now had been removed.

Throughout the small hours of night Lan searched for Emma's most private needs and desires until each one was fulfilled completely. As the fire died to a golden ember, Lan took Emma by the hand and led her to the bedroom. They shared a single cup of herbal tea and cuddled under a down comforter until they fell asleep in each other's arms.

It was a peaceful sleep, full of wonderful dreams and soft memories. Emma woke early, protectively stroking Lan's hair, kissing her cheek, and cooing words of love to her sleeping warrior. The morning was a long way off, morning where work and business would once again divide them.

When Lan finally awoke, she reached for the soft touch of Emma's skin. Only her scent remained. Lan stretched and touched the pillow where Emma had slept, then folded her hands behind her head.

"I love you, Emma Bishop," she announced, her words echoing up through the rafters. "Where do we go from here?" she continued in a whisper.

Chapter 11

Lan was so engrossed in what she was doing she hadn't noticed Emma leaning on her office doorjamb, one arm behind her back, watching her work. Emma finally cleared her throat quietly. Lan sat back in her chair and smiled up at her.

"Hi," Lan said with a deep throaty flirt.

"Hi yourself," Emma replied, still leaning.

"Did you sleep well?" Lan asked. A devilish grin crept across her face.

"Oh yeah. And you?"

"Oh yeah," Lan replied, imitating Emma's inflection.

"Would you have any idea where this came from?" Emma asked, producing a single long-stemmed red rose from behind her back. "I found it on my table out there when I came in this morning."

"Oh, really?" Lan replied dramatically, playing along.

"Yes. There it was. A single red rose. No note, no message, no nothing." Emma held the rose to her nose as she watched Lan.

"Someone must have wanted you to have it, I guess." Lan leaned forward and crossed her hands on her desk. "They must have thought you liked red roses."

"I do. I love them. I just wish whoever left it for me, would have done it in person, or included a note so I could reply." Emma stared across at Lan with an alluring gaze.

"I wouldn't worry about it. It's probably just one of those gas station roses."

"I love gas station roses. They have more meaning than the ones from a florist."

Lan thought for a long moment, wrinkling her brow. "How do you figure that?" she asked finally.

"It means the person is thinking about you all the time, in kind of a constant state of contemplation."

Lan smiled wryly. "If you say so."

"It's very romantic too." Emma beamed at Lan. "Thank you."

Lan smiled back. "You're welcome."

"I had a wonderful time last night."

"Me too."

Emma walked around to Lan's side of the desk and leaned against it, her knee playing with the corner of Lan's chair.

"It will be hard but I hope we can keep this just between us. I want our private life, well, private." Emma spoke softly, with deep conviction in her voice.

"I know what you mean. We both have jobs to do here and that has to take precedence."

"I hope we can still find time for us. Time to be together." She looked at Lan for reassurance.

Lan brushed the outside of Emma's thigh with the back of her hand tenderly. "I hope so, too."

Outside the office, Jenny, the foreman and one of the best carpenters, male or female, to ever work for Bishop's, could be heard asking for Emma.

"In here, Jenny," Emma called out, putting a professional distance between herself and Lan.

"Hi there," she said, poking her head around the corner. "I need a couple decisions from the boss."

Emma and Lan pointed at each other.

"What kind of decisions?" Emma asked lightheartedly.

"For starters, I need to know if you want the cabins wired for indirect lighting, like they were. I thought it might be better to go with direct lighting and ceiling fixtures, rather than indirect and worry about where you want to put the wall fixtures or table lamps. The other thing is the windows and doors. The old ones were custom made and not a standard size. I can do it, remake them, but it would save some time and money to go with standard three-O doors and maybe two-six or three-O single-hung windows. You want to come take a look?"

"Sure. Come on, Ms. Harding. You get to help with these decisions." Emma waved Lan to follow her.

The threesome made their way to the campground where work on the cabins was well underway. The three foundations of the destroyed cabins had been cleared of every stick of lumber and rebuilt with fresh two-by-four framing, awaiting wiring and plumbing to be snaked through the studs, then enclosed with windows, doors, roofing, and rough-sawn cedar siding. The siding would be cut from the downed trees and kiln-dried at the local lumber mill. The partially damaged cabins had been pruned back to undamaged elements then rebuilt with matching siding, roofing, and windows.

From a stack of damaged cabin doors, Jenny had fashioned a distinctive Dutch door for the largest cabin. Lan had been the first to notice it and congratulate her on her resourcefulness and ingenuity. To celebrate the first major triumph of reclaiming storm damage to reusable material, Lan cut a strip of orange nylon material from one of the damaged water ski belts and drew a smiley face on it with a Sharpie. She safety-pinned it to Jenny's shirt as a reward for her attention to environmental details. As trivial as it seemed, the honor quickly circulated to the other workers and one by one other recycled contributions were conjured up and put into action. Lan used the same orange ski belt to make similar ribbons of honor, distributing them to anyone with a worthy suggestion.

Anyone who wore one was teased unmercifully but secretly they wouldn't trade it for a three-day paid vacation. It was as if the crew had become a family, a large group of big brothers and sisters protecting and nurturing Shared Winds back to life. Many workers had begun arriving early, working proudly, and staying later. Lan had unleashed a tidal wave of devotion with her comical strip of orange nylon.

Emma and Lan followed Jenny into one of the framed cabins.

"The door in this cabin was about a thirty-one-inch door, but they don't make that size. It would have to be special ordered. The other cabins all had something slightly different. No two were alike. The windows too. I would bet these cabins were built with whatever materials they had on hand. Nothing was a standard size. Looks like about Fifties or early Sixties from the wiring and plumbing," Jenny explained. "If you give the go ahead, I can make the headers and window frames for a standard size and save a lot of time and money."

Lan's mind was still toying with the memory of last night. She winked at Emma, being careful no one else saw her do it, then returned her attention to the window decision. Emma smiled to herself, admiring how striking Lan looked with the breeze stirring her hair and pinking her cheeks. The collar of Lan's jacket cuddled against her jawline, giving her face a portrait quality.

"So, what do you think, Ms. Bishop?" Jenny asked.

"Sounds okay to me," she replied, realizing she hadn't heard everything Jenny said. "What do you think, Lan?" Shifting the decision seemed like the smart thing to do since her mind was having trouble staying on task. Like steam on a bathroom mirror, the memory of Lan's gentle caress and tender touch were fogging her thoughts.

Lan knew Emma's mind was somewhere else. She had a pretty good idea where it was.

"I think changing to standard-size doors and windows is the smart choice here," she said to Jenny then looked over at Emma. "Don't you think that would be the best thing to do, Emma?" Lan asked then stroked the tip of her tongue across her upper lip.

Emma noticed the innuendo immediately and shifted her weight to her other foot. "Yes. I agree. I think it is a decision long overdue," Emma replied coquettishly.

"Good," Jenny said, frowning at the women's strange behavior. "I'll get right on it."

Emma started back for the marina. Lan held back, satisfied to follow several feet behind. Emma stopped and looked back at her, waiting for her to catch up.

"Why are you walking back there?" she asked as Lan approached. "You can walk with me. No one knows anything."

" 'Cause."

" 'Cause why?"

" 'Cause I like to watch you wiggle," Lan said, leaning closer and talking covertly. She then passed Emma and headed for the stairs.

Emma hurried to catch up and spoke in a whisper as she passed her. "You have a cute tush yourself."

Emma exaggerated her wiggle as she climbed the stairs, putting on a show for Lan.

Inside the crews were busy at work. Emma went to her table, took a sip from her coffee cup, and scanned her schedule on the laptop.

Lan collected a stack of mail and headed across the room toward her office. "Emma," Lan called out in her best business voice. "Will you see if you can schedule that inspection for later?"

Emma choked a bit on her coffee and glared back at her.

Both of them buried themselves in their own mountain of work, blocking out the noise and chaos.

It was nearly eleven when Emma refilled her coffee cup and went to see if Lan wanted one.

"How are you coming?" Emma asked, stretching and limbering up her back from hours at the computer.

"Is it too late to run away from home and join the circus?" Lan asked wistfully as she too stood up and stretched. She took Emma's coffee cup, downed a gulp, then handed it back.

"Yes, the deadline for that was the day you signed the contract to rebuild this marina."

"In that case, how about having some dinner with me tonight?" Lan asked.

Koji came scampering into the office, his tail wagging furiously. He stopped at Emma's side for a quick approval then circled Lan several times. She reached down and patted him on the head and scratched behind his ear.

"You're cold. Where've you been, Koj?" she asked with a frown.

Koji shook, broadcasting tiny bits of frost.

"That feels like ice," Emma said, wiping the moist droplets from her cheek.

Lan looked out her office window and heaved a long sigh. Huge snowflakes blanketed the parking lot and the grass. The first snowfall of the season was early, unexpected, and heavy. The air was thick with white. The clouds were low and ominous looking. A light snowfall usually started with gusty wind and small flakes. There was no wind and the flakes were enormous. Lan didn't like the looks of this and tried to conceal it, but Emma knew exactly what she was watching. This was the first sign that work outside was going to come to a screeching halt—and soon. The construction schedule for the next week quickly flashed before her, like flipping through a Rolodex. Suddenly she closed her eyes and leaned her head back as if she had just heard the worst possible news.

"What?" Lan asked, recognizing Emma's anguish.

"The ridge beam. We were going to set the ridge beam this week. The sawmill delivered it yesterday."

"Okay," Lan replied cautiously, not knowing why this was bad news.

"If we have much snow accumulation we won't be able to get the crane in here," Emma said, blowing out a mouthful of air. "The big crane I need to set the rafters is only available for three days this week. My father is taking it to Tulsa and it won't be back until March sometime."

"Surely there is another crane we can get, somewhere."

"With the angle of the slope next to the marina and the weight of the log, it is the only one tall enough to hoist that center beam into place."

Lan didn't say anything as she went to the window and slid her hands into her back pockets.

"Every other crane that can handle that much weight is in use. I've called as far away as St. Louis trying to locate one. If I use a smaller crane not rated for that much weight, we will do more damage than good. The center of gravity will be too high. It would tip over and drop that beam right through the roof," Emma continued disappointedly. "I was lucky to talk my father into letting me use it before he takes it out of town. He has three jobs waiting for it."

"Maybe it won't snow that much."

"Let's hope it stops soon." Emma stood next to Lan, both of them lost in silent prayer.

Lan and Emma went about their work, trying to remain optimistic. By noon, the carpenters had to shovel snow to find materials and supplies. Lan pushed papers around her desk, made phone calls, and answered e-mail requests for slip rentals. She occasionally paced the long path from her office through the marina, around the snack bar, out onto the deck then back again, running her hands through her hair as she made the turn. The snow didn't stop. It continued all day and into the evening. By six o'clock, Lan and Emma had watched the snow cover grow from a light dusting to a medium layer and on to a heavy blanketing.

"How many inches of snow?" Emma asked reluctantly as Lan shut the door and shook the snow from her hair.

"Eight, at least," Lan replied guardedly, not knowing how to soften the news. She decided not to add that it was still coming down as heavy as it was six hours earlier.

Emma looked away then back at Lan, tears welling up in her eyes. She held tight to her emotions, concealing the growing concern. She had been so careful, so precise in her planning. She had checked and double-checked everything. The materials list, the delivery schedule, every detail. Now she felt like she had been betrayed and not by anything she had expected. And certainly not by anything she could control.

It had been a long day, a frustrating day. The crews had done all they could outside. When it was no longer feasible or safe to keep them on the job, Emma sent them home. The cabins weren't finished, the dock wasn't finished, and now the biggest blow of all— the main building couldn't be finished until the beams were set. Emma felt like the air was rushing out of her like a slow leak in a bald tire. She went to the windows and stared out helplessly at the stark and bitter whiteness. How could this happen? How could the spirits that watched over Shared Winds do this to her, to Lan, to their hopes?

Lan stood next to her. She wanted to offer some words of comfort and support but she was grappling with her own anxiety about the weather delays.

"I don't think I'm up to dinner tonight, if that is okay with you?" Emma said quietly.

"This does kind of take the wind out of the sails, doesn't it?"

Emma nodded and said nothing, for fear the frightened little girl inside would come rushing out in agonizing screams and sobs. Even though each of them had her own agenda and list of concerns, both were trekking down the same road where reassurance was choked out by growing fear.

"Don't give up. You're a strong woman. I still have faith in you," Lan said, giving Emma a determined stare. "What would Quinn do?"

"He'd wait for the snow to melt in a week or two, assuming the weather returns to normal for this time of year. Then he would bring his big crane in and start over like nothing happened. He'd probably even give the crews a week off and tell them they'd be working overtime next month to make up for it."

"I'm sure we can work through this. You'll figure something out. Tell me what I can do."

"Well, for starters, you can tell me how I am getting home tonight. My house is on a steep hill. I don't know if my truck will get through that snow. It isn't four-wheel drive," Emma replied, looking out the window.

"Done. I know someone with a four-wheel drive Jeep," Lan said with a wink, trying to restore a measure of cheerfulness.

"Thank you, babe. I didn't need another problem tonight."

"How about you come home with me? We'll scrounge up something for dinner and we can talk about how to schedule around this snowstorm."

Emma hesitated for a second then nodded agreeably. "I think I'd like that."

It took nearly an hour to get through the deep snow and into Lan's driveway. The winding road from the highway up the hill to her house was like a fairyland of white. The trees along the road bowed down under the weight of the snow like court subjects before royalty.

Lan gunned the engine and plowed through the snow, stopping at the front porch of the long log cabin framed house. As soon as she turned off the engine and opened the door, Koji was out and bounding through the snow. He disappeared behind the garage, yipping and frolicking like a child with a new sled. Lan shuffled her feet through the deep snow from the Jeep up to the porch, smashing the snow and clearing a path for Emma to follow. Emma walked behind her, carefully staying in the blazed trail. Lan unlocked the door and swung it open for Emma.

"Go on in and make yourself at home. I'm going to get some wood for the fireplace." Lan headed around the corner of the porch where the dry wood was stacked.

Soon Lan had a fire warming the living room with the scent of pinecones and hickory filling the air.

Emma set her laptop on the kitchen table and went to work, trying to shuffle and guess at a new work schedule. Occasionally she would blurt out some frustrated remark, shake her head, and then start over. Lan looked over Emma's shoulder from time to time, but she too was worried and growing short tempered at the impending weather delays.

"How do you feel about an omelet?" Lan asked, staring into the refrigerator.

"Anything would be fine, babe. But I'm not very hungry."

"I know. But you have to eat something."

Lan fixed western omelets and cut up some apples and bananas for a salad. They each picked at it and pushed it around on the plate, preoccupied with the challenge of working around the snow. Lan did the dishes and worked on some fishing tournament applications while Emma called several equipment rental companies hoping a suitable crane had miraculously become available. Lan suggested she take a break and sit by the fire, enjoy the beautiful snow, and sip her tea. But Emma only scowled back, refusing to leave the computer and her resolve to conquer.

Lan finally gave up trying. She shoveled the front porch and steps. Then she watched the second half of the OU women's basketball game with the sound muted on the television. It was nearly midnight when she turned it off and went to take a shower. When she returned wrapped in her big terry cloth robe, Emma had leaned forward, resting her head on her arms. Emma quickly sat up and smiled a tired smile at Lan, then returned to her computer screen.

"That's enough for tonight," Lan ordered. She pulled Emma's chair back and scooped her up in her arms. "The office is closed."

"Wait a minute. I have some notes I need to finish," Emma snipped.

"It'll all be right here for you tomorrow."

"Could I at least turn off the computer?" Emma asked plaintively.

132

"Okay," she replied, sitting down in the chair with Emma on her lap. "Go ahead and shut it down."

Emma saved the files and turned it off. As soon as the screen went blank, Lan lifted her up again and started down the hall.

"And just what are you doing? Can't I walk for myself?"

"If I left it up to you, you'd be sitting there all night, trying to will the snow away."

Instead of turning into the bedroom, she pushed the bathroom door open with her foot and stepped inside. The lights were out but the room was aglow with a dozen flickering candles. The tub was filled to overflowing with bubbles. Lan had placed a fresh towel and clean robe near the tub. The room was warm and soothing.

"Is this for me?" Emma immediately forgot her displeasure at being plucked from her work. Lan's surprise was perfect.

Lan set her down and checked the water temperature.

"Just right," she said.

"Something smells wonderful. Is it the bubble bath?" Emma closed her eyes and breathed slowly and deeply.

"I put lavender oil in the water. It's a calming scent. It will relax you so you can sleep." Lan kissed her on the cheek. "You get in. I'm bringing you a cup of chamomile tea. It will give you sweet dreams."

"Thank you, babe. This is so nice. No one has ever made a bubble bath for me before. And the candles are so serene. Maybe we could put the candles outside and melt the snow," Emma said with chagrin.

"Tut tut," Lan quipped holding up a finger. "No talk about work."

"Okay." Emma was secretly glad to have the office door closed and locked, if only for the night.

"Be right back."

Lan closed the door behind her and went to make the tea. When she returned, Emma was in the tub, her chin just above the lush dome of bubbles. Her eyes were closed in peaceful relaxation. Lan placed the cup on the edge of the tub.

"You don't have to drink it all, just a sip or two."

"Can you take this tub to the marina so I can work from here?" Emma inquired, her eyes still comfortably closed.

"I have one there."

"You do?" Emma asked, opening one eye and looking at Lan.

"Yes. It's in the locker room downstairs. It's a whirlpool spa. Holds about six people. I just never think of using it. It has its own little redwood room. Has a timer on the jets." Lan looked as if she hadn't remembered it was there until that moment.

"Does it work?"

"I think so. I haven't filled it in a couple years."

"Well, when this is all finished, I want a good soak in it."

"You don't have to wait until the marina is finished. I'll clean it up and get it going. You can sit in it any time you want."

"Will you sit in it with me?" Emma asked innocently.

"I might be talked into it." Lan smiled then placed a handful of bubbles on Emma's head. "You take your time in here. I'm going to get Koji in—again. He loves to play in the snow."

"I'll be out shortly. I'm suddenly very tired." Emma smiled wearily.

Koji came at the first whistle. He shook, just inside the door, and then curled up on his mat. Lan turned out the lights and waited for Emma in bed. She folded her arms behind her head and stared up at the ceiling. She was tired but unable to block out the brutal truth. Time was not on their side. Shared Winds was now literally frozen in time.

Emma slipped into bed and tucked the comforter around Lan's shoulders, trying not to disturb her quiet snoring. She kissed her on the temple and cuddled next to her, ready for sleep.

134

Chapter 12

By the time Lan had awakened and found her senses, Emma was showered and dressed, once again sitting at her computer at the kitchen table. She sat staring at the screen. She knew there had to be a solution to her problem out there, just beyond her reach, just beyond the foggy confusion that seem to separate her from the answer she so desperately sought. She was a smart woman, an experienced contractor. She knew she could do this. But how? She refilled her coffee cup and leaned against the kitchen counter thinking.

"Good morning," Lan said, towel drying her hair. "You're at it again early." She gave Emma a kiss and filled a cup with coffee.

"I hope I didn't wake you, babe."

"No. But why didn't you? I could have gotten up with you."

"I just needed to do some thinking. It's as if the answer is out there, and I just can't see it. It's like it is covered in fog." Emma frowned at her coffee cup, struggling to formulate a plan.

"It'll come to you, sweetie. I trust you."

"I know this sounds silly, but I really want to get back to the marina as soon as we can. I feel like I can think better if I'm there where I can see the problem."

"I know what you mean. I had the same thoughts. Besides, I need to check for leaks. If it warms up above freezing, the snow will melt and leak through those tarps. I'll have an indoor waterfall."

They hurried through breakfast and began the trek back to the marina. The county snowplows had done little to clear the roads. The back roads were still untouched and nearly impassable. It took some doing but Lan was able to retrace their route through the deep powder back to the parking lot, where Emma's pickup was completely covered in white.

Max had already arrived and was shoveling a path to the front door.

"Morning, you two," he said, leaning on the shovel and grinning at them.

"Good morning, Max," Emma replied, realizing their arrival together made for an awkward scene.

"Morning," Lan added. She knew Max's imagination was off to the races. "Be careful shoveling that stuff, old man. I don't want my mechanic having a heart attack."

Max held out the snow shovel. "Here. You want to do it?" he teased.

"I thought I would," Lan argued.

"Oh, go play with your computer," he chided and went back to shoveling.

"Max, why don't you wait for some of my crew to do that? I'm sure some of them will trickle in soon. I can have an army of carpenters out here and they'll have that shoveled off in no time," Emma pleaded.

It was like a challenge now. Max was going to defend his ability and his age at any cost.

"I'm fine. I don't need any help. You two go on inside and make some coffee."

"Stubborn old goat," Lan muttered under her breath.

They tromped their way through the deep snowdrifts that surrounded and guarded the building. Lan was relieved to find the marina dry since the temperatures had remained cold enough to keep the snow from melting.

"Do you think any of your crew will come in today?"

"They'll try. They don't get paid if they don't show up. I have a few things to keep them busy inside but only for a few days. They need to be able to work outside."

"If they run out of things to do, we can send them out to shovel off the parking lot," Lan joked.

"If I had enough of them, they could shovel off the campground too," Emma added, joining in the joke. Her laughter was cut short and a stern look came over her face. She quickly looked away, her mind shifting into deep thought. She looked up at the ceiling, examining every detail of the damaged beams as her brain schemed and plotted some complex scenario.

"What?" Lan asked, noticing her intense concentration.

Emma held up her hand as if to stop Lan's inquiry until she had finished formulating her idea. She went to the center of the room, her hands on her hips, still staring up, her eyes narrowed and focused.

"It might work," she muttered to an invisible partner in her planning. "Yes. It just might work. But how many do I need?"

Lan opened her mouth to speak but again Emma held out her hand as a barrier. Lan decided to wait for a better opportunity to ask what she was doing.

Emma went out onto the deck and looked up both sides of the marina, taking note of the angle of the slope, the overhanging trees, and the amount of clearance along the building. She hurried back inside to her laptop, unaware her pant legs were covered with snow from the knees down. She made some quick calculations and notes in a file. She then looked up, allowing a cautious smile to crawl across her face.

"I have an idea on how to set the beams without the crane."

Lan looked curiously over the rim of her cup. "How's that?" she asking, blowing across the surface of the hot coffee. She hadn't heard anything yet that called for enthusiasm.

"We were joking about having the crews shovel out, well, I thought if we had enough manpower—"

"They could shovel out the entire grounds so the crane could get in here?" Lan asked knowing it sounded ridiculous.

Emma scowled at her. "No. The crane couldn't be driven in the snow or ice. It is hard enough to maneuver on dry pavement. But they could take the place of the crane."

"I don't think your guys can lift those huge beams all the way up there."

"They could if I had enough hands and used the right equipment."

"Equipment? What equipment?"

"Block and tackles, pulleys, rope—lots of rope—and sling hoists," Emma said, still formulating plans.

"And how many do you figure is enough?"

"With the crews I already have, maybe a hundred. No, make it a hundred twenty-five, just to be on the safe side."

"Is the coffee ready?" Max yelled as he stomped the snow from his boots and unzipped his coat.

"Yes," Lan replied, keeping her attention on Emma's developing idea.

"So, how do you like the snow?" he asked in Emma's direction as he crossed the room and filled a coffee cup.

"Not too much," Emma replied distractedly.

"The only crane big enough to lift the beams into place for the ceiling was only available for three days and now the snow is too deep to use it," Lan explained to Max.

"Can't you do other stuff and set the beams later?" Max asked, trying to come up to speed on what the problem was.

"The center beam has to be done first, then the rest of the trusses, before the ceiling can be finished. Then comes the window wall, then the kitchen and snack bar. Everything has to be done in order." Emma shook her head as she itemized the list.

"Like a row of dominoes," he mused. "One has to fall down before the next one."

Emma frowned at his analogy. She didn't want to think about anything falling.

"She has been telling me how she thought the job could be done without the crane, using manpower instead," Lan interjected. She suddenly set her cup down and looked intently at Emma as if some idea of her own was being hatched. "Tell Max about the extra hundred twenty-five people."

"I was just saying, if I had an extra one hundred to one hundred twenty-five people and enough rope, sling hoists, and pulleys, I think we could do it. We could use those big trees that overhang the roof to support the pulley system and pull the beams into place. Then my carpenters wearing safety harnesses could secure it. It's just a matter of physics. The pulleys transfer the work into vertical lift." Emma stopped the scientific explanation noticing it wasn't necessary. Lan and Max had taken on the look of comprehension and were both chewing on the idea themselves. "I just need to find one hundred twenty-five people who are willing to work one day for very little money."

"They don't have to be carpenters?" Max asked, deep in thought.

"No. I just need them to help string the ropes and pull. My crews will do the climbing and attaching."

"I think I know where you can find your help," he declared, looking at Lan then back at Emma, smiling confidently.

"Where?" Emma asked eagerly.

"I think there should be a special meeting of the Cherokee Tribal Council tonight," he announced proudly. "To discuss Shared Winds' roof."

"Do you mean . . ."

"Max used to be Tribal Chief. He can call a meeting of the tribal council whenever he wants," Lan said with approval. "I bet he's going to put the word out that we need one hundred twenty-five pairs of helping hands. Right, Max?"

"You got it, kid. What's the good of being on the council if you can't help your own?"

"But Max, I'm not Cherokee," Emma reminded him.

"Close enough," he replied kindly.

She kissed his cheek and gave him a hug. He blushed and frowned, uneasy with such expressions of affection, even if they were in the form of thanks.

"I'm just going to put the word out you need some folks with muscle to handle the ropes. It's up to you to make this work," he said.

"Thank you, Max. You are a prince." Emma smiled. "I guess you are more than a prince. You're a chief."

"It will be like the Amish farmers back in Pennsylvania who help each other build a barn. They get together and work as a big team to get the job done," Lan related.

"They'll work for free but they'll need food," he added. "And they'll be big eaters too."

"For this kind of help, I'll cook for them myself," Emma insisted enthusiastically.

"You won't have to. My wife will help. She knows how to cook for an army. She'll take over and have the whole thing organized in no time."

"We can use the kitchen and snack bar area for serving. We still have lots of paper plates and cups. The big pots and pans are back there somewhere. We can dig those out to use," Lan added.

"I'll get whatever they need. Just let me know." Emma felt a tremendous weight being lifted from her shoulders as Lan and Max helped iron out the details and offer encouragement.

"When do you want to do this?" he asked.

"Let's see. It will take two days to get the equipment and another day to clear the snow around the building so we have good footing. Let's say four days, just to be sure we have time to get everything ready."

"I'll put out the word there's a meeting tonight." Max slurped down the last of his coffee and went to Lan's office to use the phone.

When he was out of sight, Emma grinned happily at Lan and hugged her. Lan wrapped her arms around Emma and picked her up, swinging her around, laughing joyously.

"You did it, sweetie." Lan kissed Emma on one cheek then the other. "I knew you could do it."

Emma was red with excitement. "I hope it works, babe," she offered cautiously.

"It will. I have all the confidence in the world."

"Thank you for your help. And Max, too. You both were wonderful."

"Now all you need is about fifty miles of rope." Lan laughed again.

Lan's jest wasn't far off. By Emma's calculations, it would take a small mountain of rope and other gear to get the job done. She scavenged Bishop's warehouse and the marina's supplies and gathered tribal members, friends, and anyone else who would help to gather, rate, and tag rope. The smaller-gauge ropes were braided together to make one strong enough to support the main beam. Canvas slings and hoists were tested and measured as well. Emma devised a schematic drawing of the marina to simplify the stringing of the ropes and pulleys. It resembled the Lilliputians tying Gulliver down to the beach with a web of string.

When Leona heard the plans for feeding some one hundred twenty-five people plus Bishop's crews, she launched into high gear. She called her daughters and friends and put together a menu, shopping list, cooking schedule, and delivery strategy to rival General Eisenhower's troop movement.

Beam day, as it was jokingly called, started before dawn and was filled with apprehension and stress. Emma was completely consumed with the enormity of managing so many workers and so many details. Keeping the men and women all working together efficiently and safely was her paramount responsibility. She shuddered to think what OSHA would say about her work force. For that reason, no one was allowed to join a team unless he or she could hear the commands and run for safety if necessary. She and the two foremen each carried air horns that could be sounded in an emergency.

Max was made rope foreman. He divided the volunteers into two groups, north and south, one for each side of the building. These groups were subdivided into teams. Max divided the rope by color and each team was named for the corresponding color. The complex job of stringing and positioning the pulleys and hoists was left to Emma's workers.

A web of rope was strung over the marina like the rigging on a four-masted schooner. At Emma's request, Max set aside the heaviest rope to be used as a safety line for the beams, preventing the timbers from falling either through the roof or onto workers.

The parking lot was the gathering area for the volunteers. Men and women from all over the county rallied to the call for help. J.T. and Annie arrived with a caravan of cars filled with women eager to be front-line rope handlers. Even tribal elders came out to watch and offer advice. The snow and cold temperatures didn't keep the number from growing well past the one hundred twenty-five needed helpers. While they waited and watched the preparations, many offered a hand at shoveling the network of marina sidewalks that had not been cleared for the beam raising.

Leona and her crew of cooks arrived early in the morning to set up for lunch. The noon menu included roaster ovens filled with barbecued beef for sandwiches, cole slaw, potato chips, and apples and oranges for dessert, as well as gallons of hot steaming coffee. The evening meal, not to be served until the work was finished, included a choice of chili or venison stew, Cherokee fry bread, and dozens of fresh baked pies donated by friends and family members alike. Leona's helpers kept the roaster ovens stirred and seasoned throughout the day, the heavenly aroma wafting through the air and teasing the workers' hungry appetites.

"Allana Harding," Lan heard as she peeked under a lid and tasted the barbecue. "I'm going to cut me a switch and tan your backside, if you don't keep out of there," Leona admonished in a threatening voice.

"I'm just checking it." Lan quickly replaced the lid and licked her fingers. "It's doing fine."

Leona hurried over to make sure the lid was on good and tight. She gave Lan's cheek a pinch and smiled at her affectionately.

"Don't worry. Everything will be just fine. You go sit and relax. We have it all under control," she said with reassurance.

Sit and relax? That was a big no-can-do, if she ever heard one. Lan watched and paced as the crowd of volunteers buzzed around, waiting for the signal to start. Both the arriving rope crews and the food brigade reminded her of what it would be like to toss a sugar cube on an anthill.

"Koji," she called, noticing the dog racing in and out of the door, barking orders of his own. "Come here, you mutt." She signaled him into the office and gave the command to sit. "You stay in here and be quiet. Emma doesn't need your help today." Reluctantly he sat just inside the office door, watching the long parade of people streaming by.

The word was finally given and the crews and teams took their places. Emma handed the bullhorns over to her foremen. They had worked up a system of signals and commands that were passed to each side of the building where team captains led the pullers. Emma had propped open the door leading to the deck. She positioned herself just outside the door, watching the progress of the lift and placement in the ceiling. Lan felt like a general without an army. She couldn't decide where she could do the most good. She wore a path from the window to the door, chewing her nails and running her hands through her hair.

"You look like an expectant father," Emma teased as Lan nervously pulled at her collar.

"Does it show?" she mused.

"Just a little."

"Sorry, but I can't help it. I don't know what to do to help."

"I have a job for you," Emma said seriously. "If you see a big beam falling through the roof, yell TIMBER."

"Very funny."

"It will be fine. This kind of job takes a lot more planning than actual work. Don't worry." Emma smiled and returned her attention to the work at hand.

"Everybody keeps saying not to worry," Lan muttered to herself. "Who's worried?" She swallowed hard and went back to the window.

The tarps had been removed and the clear blue Oklahoma sky shone brightly through the hole in the ceiling. The large center beam was first. Slowly it was inched up the side of the building, with stops to check the angle and alignment. Six carpenters attached to safety harnesses awaited its arrival at the ridge. As the beam moved closer to its zenith, one of the carpenters leaned out and grabbed the rope, ready to guide it into place. At that same moment a kink in the canvas sling released, dropping the end of the huge timber to a precarious angle and pulling the carpenter off the roof. As he slid down the steep roof toward the edge and a long drop to the ground, he reached out and grabbed at the huge swaying beam with both hands. But the diameter of the log was much larger than his reach and his hands slipped down the freshly varnished wood, unable to grip onto anything to stop his fall. Just as his fingers slipped off the log he snatched onto the canvas sling. He held on with one hand while he frantically flailed with the other, trying to grab hold. His weight made the beam swing out from the roof. His legs dangled and kicked high above the ground workers. The safety harness Emma had insisted all the roof workers wear was slack and offering no support.

Jenny sounded a long blast on her air horn and screamed up at the other men on the roof, pointing at the dangling man.

"Grab his harness, Jim. Take up the slack," she yelled through the bullhorn. "Hold that beam steady. Level that end. Red team, slowly let out four feet of line. Slowly. Hold on, Mike. Hold on. We got you."

A palpable hush fell over the volunteers as they tightened their grip on the ropes. Three of the men on the roof pulled Mike's safety line up taut. Emma rushed to the railing and looked up at the man as he held on by just four fingers looped through one of the canvas straps. With his harness, tool belt, and insulated coveralls, he was too constricted and heavy to swing a leg over the swaying beam. She bit down on her lip and clutched the railing, terror-stricken eyes glued to the worker. It took all of her self-control not to scream out orders but Jenny had taken charge and was orchestrating the rescue. Emma didn't want unnecessary commands to confuse the process.

"Hold his line tight, Jim," Jenny commanded, reclaiming her composure. "Ease the beam up, slowly. That's it. Slow." The beam was raised, carefully bringing the dangling worker within a step of safety. "Slowly. Easy now. Hold on, Mike, hold on. Almost there."

As his strength and grasp gave out, Mike dropped, panic painted over his completely white face. But the beam had just passed over the edge of the roof and he landed onto the rafter framing with a thump and a scream. He quickly squatted down and grabbed on with a death grip, fear and relief sharing his glassy stare.

Emma waited until he had taken a few breaths before saying anything.

"You all right, Mike?" she called through the bullhorn.

He was still crouched down, recovering his senses. The other roof workers waved and nodded that he was okay.

"Mike?" she repeated, wanting to hear it from him.

He nodded, still holding tight to the roof. "I'm okay," he replied finally in a quiet and shaken voice.

"Good." She took a deep breath then continued. "What the hell do you guys think you are doing up there? Those safety harnesses are supposed to be adjusted so accidents like that don't happen. I don't care if you think they get in your way, tighten them up and do it now," she bellowed. "Any more crap like that and I will ground you. You can sit and sort the damn nails for all I care. No one works for me unless they wear their safety equipment and wear it right." Her voice echoed across the lake and back again. No one said a word as she yelled out her demands. The volunteers held tight to the ropes and listened, feeling like they were watching a trip to the woodshed. The men on the roof quickly adjusted their slack line and tugged on it to test its integrity.

"Mike, come on down," she added sternly.

"I'm okay, Ms. Bishop. I'll tighten up the slack." Mike resisted the embarrassment of being ordered to the ground.

"Down, Mike." She stared daggers at him. He reluctantly began lowering himself down from his perch while one hundred sixty-two pairs of eyes watched. He walked up on the deck where Emma stood beckoning him with one index finger.

"I'm sorry, Ms. Bishop," he apologized sheepishly. "That was pretty stupid of me. I guess I wasn't thinking."

Emma patted him on the back and gave him a small smile of compliance.

"Go get a cup of coffee and warm up," she said quietly. "We'll need you back up there after lunch."

Lan had been watching from farther down the railing. She had stayed back, quietly relegating the rescue and recovery to Emma and her skilled workers. Her confidence in Bishop professionalism had just been further reinforced by the coordinated effort and quick reaction. She was also impressed with Emma's attention to safety.

"Check the line on that beam, Jenny," Emma ordered. "Make sure there aren't any more loops in the sling. Do we need to bring it down and start over?"

"We're checking it, Ms. Bishop," Jenny replied as team captains examined their lines.

"You ropers? Do you need to bring it down?" Emma asked.

A resounding NO came back from the teams, eager to do the job right. She waited until all the teams gave the go-ahead before signaling the work to continue. Once again the beam began to move.

Slowly but steadily it crept up the side of the marina. With smooth gliding motion it swung into place. As the volunteers held it steady, the workers nailed, screwed, and pegged it to the undamaged side trusses. When the carpenters unhooked the hoists and swung them free, a loud victorious cheer rang out from the cold rope handlers.

Emma heaved a deep sigh and smiled over at Lan. "One down, six to go. But that was the hard one," Emma reported, taking off her hard hat and ruffling her hair.

"Lunch is ready if you want to feed them," Leona announced, noticing the break in the process. "It's past one."

"Lunch time," Emma called out the door to the crowd. This brought on another even louder cheer followed by a stampede of cold hungry workers.

Leona quickly got them into orderly lines. While the crews ate and warmed up, Emma checked some of the measurements one last time.

"Hey boss lady, you need to eat, too," Lan said, handing her a plate already filled with a sandwich and cole slaw. "Come on, sit and eat with me. I have a spot on the floor all picked out for us." Lan signaled her to follow.

"Thank you. Somehow lunch just didn't seem to be that important."

"I know. But we have to eat. Leona would never forgive us if we didn't."

Emma followed behind as Lan weaved her way through the people to a clearing where J.T. and Annie were sitting cross-legged on the floor.

"Great food, Em," Annie said, with barbecue sauce on her chin.

J.T. laughed at her and wiped it off with a paper napkin.

"Don't thank me. Leona's troops get all the credit for it. I understand dinner is going to be good, too. But the job has to be completed first," Emma admonished playfully.

"Slave driver," J.T. replied.

"Hey now," Lan added with a wink. "Don't be calling my boss lady names."

"How's married life treating you two?" Emma asked, trying to find the starting point to her drippy sandwich.

Both Annie and J.T. smiled and blushed. "Great."

"No details, please," Lan quipped.

All four laughed, keeping the joke to themselves as the surrounding diners stared at them curiously.

"And how about you two?" J.T. asked with a saucy grin.

Lan choked on her coffee and Emma dropped half the filling from her sandwich onto her plate. Both busied themselves with the sudden need to clean up the mess, as if to bury the question under a mountain of confusion.

"Oh, I see." J.T. laughed and returned to eating her sandwich.

Annie nudged her partner and shushed her, picking up on Lan's and Emma's body language. Annie looked down at her plate and smiled coyly, then peeked up at the two, giving a silent apology as well as consent.

Emma smiled to herself knowing Lan was truly embarrassed as a blush raced up across her face. Lan hurried through her lunch and was glad when there was a phone call she needed to take.

The afternoon was filled with slow but steady progress. One by one the side trusses were vaulted into place and attached to the side wall and the ridge beam. It was a cold tedious job, soothed by coffee and occasional rest periods to warm up inside by the roaring fireplace, which was working overtime to keep the marina warm while the doors seemed to be continually open.

Just before sunset, the last sling was released and swung free. The roof crew gave a tired wave and signaled the job was officially done. Sighs instead of the cheers rose up from the exhausted work crew while faces pinched with determination and concentration melted into smiles of relief.

As energetic as the first minute she set foot inside the marina, Leona put the evening meal in motion. The workers shed their coats, hats, and gloves in a big pile by the door and lined up, eager for warm food and a place to sit down. The ladies had arranged as many tables and chairs as could be found, providing seating for most of the workers. The rest found a spot on the hearth, on the counter-top, and in the easy chairs around the fireplace. It was a quiet meal. The sounds of good food and pleasant company filled the big room with warmth beyond what the fireplace could provide.

Lan and Emma meandered around the room, thanking each and every volunteer personally. Slowly the workers finished their meal and collected their gear, ready to head home. Emma continued to thank them as they waved goodbye, dragging themselves wearily out the door.

"Now that's the way I like to see people eat," Leona said with a satisfied smile, scraping the pots into storage containers. "There isn't enough left to make decent leftovers."

Emma swallowed back a tear and rushed over, hugging Leona around the neck.

"What's all this about?" Leona gasped.

"Thank you," Emma whispered. "I really appreciate everything you did."

Leona patted her on the back and returned the hug.

"Max tells me you are a good, hardworking woman. I like helping people who help themselves. Just like our Allana. She's a good egg, too." Leona smiled over at Lan.

"Thank you, Leona," Lan added with a warm glance. "We really do appreciate all the work you and your food crew did. And now"— she pointed to Max—"you and that old Indian are going home. I'm the boss now and I say you are finished. Take your roasters and aprons and get out of here."

"Thanks, sweetie, but we still have a lot of work to do. This place is a mess. There are foam cups and paper plates everywhere. And I'm certainly not coming back in the morning to clean it up."

"Nope, you aren't doing anything else tonight." Lan picked up Leona's coat from the counter and opened it for her to put on. "I'm the cleanup crew tonight. I need the exercise and you need to go home and put your feet up. You too, old man." She looked over at Max, who was sinking in the chair to a nap position.

The last of the pans, boxes, and trays were loaded in Max's truck and they begrudgingly headed home.

Lan heaved a deep sigh and pushed up the sleeves on her sweater, ready to begin the trash cleanup. Emma wheeled a trash barrel into the middle of the room and began collecting trash as well.

"Hey, what do you think you are doing?" Lan asked brusquely.

"I'm helping with the cleanup. What's it look like I'm doing?"

"Oh, no you don't." Lan stopped and stared at her sternly. "You are off the clock too, woman. You worked a fifteen-hour day today. You are through."

"So did you," Emma complained without stopping.

Lan walked over and took Emma by the hand and led her to the overstuffed chair by the fireplace. She set her down, folded her hands across her lap, and pointed up. "You sit here and admire your work. Let me do this," Lan admonished.

"Why can't I help, too," Emma asked with a childish whine.

" 'Cause I said so," Lan replied, walking back to the snack bar. She quickly went to work. She collected the trash and wiped off the tables, restacked the chairs, and rolled the trash barrel into the kitchen. "There. All done," she announced, unrolling her sleeves.

Emma had slid down and closed her eyes, her head leaned back against the chair. Lan let her sleep while she locked up, dampered down the fire, and turned off the lights. She knelt down next to the chair and gently placed her hand on Emma's arm. Emma stirred and opened her eyes.

"Did I fall asleep?" she asked through a yawn.

"Uh-huh." Lan brushed back her hair from her eyes and smiled at her adoringly. "You ready to go home?"

"I think so. I think I have done all the damage I can do here for one day."

Lan held out a hand and helped her up. They walked to the parking lot together. Lan waited while Emma started her truck and let it warm up.

"You drive carefully, Emma," she said sternly.

"You too, babe."

Emma pulled out and headed up the road toward the highway. Lan sat in her Jeep, watching until the taillights had disappeared. She adjusted her rearview mirror so she could see the roof of the marina. She sat quietly admiring it, grateful and relieved and tired. She tried not to think of all the work that still had to be done. She also tried not to think of the calendar, counting down all too fast.

Chapter 13

Lan finished her peanut butter and jelly sandwich for lunch and tossed the baggie in the trash. It didn't feel like Christmas Eve. It felt more like a suspended waiting game filled with unfinished projects and nervous anticipation. Christmas images of jingle bells and ho ho ho were fighting hard for a place on her priority list. The calendar was her enemy, scheming to sabotage and disrupt. She threw a paper clip at the calendar on the wall and smirked.

Emma knocked on the open door and walked in just in time to see Lan's face. "My, that is an ugly way to greet Christmas."

"I was wishing it was still November. Early November," Lan said with concern.

"We're coming along all right. We have time. With the roof repairs finished, things are moving along with the inside work." Emma leaned against the wall, her arms folded across her chest. "Take a deep breath and relax, Ms. Harding. This is your contractor talking."

Lan heaved a deep sigh and returned her look. "So, what are your plans for Christmas?" she asked innocently.

"The Bishop family tradition," Emma replied matter of factly. "Every year Dad flies the three of us up to Aspen for a Christmas ski trip. Actually, he skis and Mom and I sit by the fireplace in the lodge or go shopping. I don't ski." She made a dramatic cold-weather shudder.

"You go all the way to a fancy ski resort just to shop?"

"To tell the truth, I go to get away from work for a few days. The last time I didn't accept the invitation to go along, every client, foreman, supplier, sub, and inspector we had called about something or other. I learned my lesson. If I want a few days off, I have to go out of town."

"When are you leaving?" Lan asked, the disappointment becoming apparent in her voice.

"This afternoon. We fly out of Tulsa."

"Have a good time," Lan said, forcing encouragement. She had no idea why she thought it was any of her business where or what the Bishops did with their Christmas.

"What are you doing for Christmas?"

"Guess I'll head out to Max's for Christmas Eve. Leona fixes a big meal for the whole family. It's their family tradition. The first year I got invited to go out there for Christmas Eve was the year I graduated from OU and moved back to Grove. I had a little apartment over a garage, no money, and no one to spend Christmas with. Max's daughter Nancy and I were high school friends. She told her mom I would be spending Christmas alone. That afternoon Max came to town in a snowstorm and sat outside my apartment honking his horn until I came out and agreed to come spend Christmas Eve with them. So I did."

"That is wonderful they invite you to spend it with their family."

"One year, when Rachel and I were together, I told Max we weren't coming out. I was afraid I was wearing out my welcome. So I told him we had other plans."

"What did he say to that?"

153

"Nothing. In fact, he didn't speak to me for several days. When he finally got around to talking to me again, he told me I was family, not company. And families don't ignore families." Lan smiled. "I got the message. Now if I can't make it, I better have a good reason."

"That's nice to be included like that. You do have family," Emma added.

"Yes," Lan said, giving the idea some thought. "And I hear you've been invited out to the Battles' for Christmas Eve, too."

"I told him about our trip to Aspen. I think he expected me to say I'd cancel my trip and come anyway."

"You're going to miss a great meal. Leona and her daughters lay out a huge spread. Max smokes a turkey and they have ham and lots of wild game, salads and vegetables, and desserts to die for. And they even sing Christmas carols."

"Sounds wonderful, really. You tell Leona thank you for the invitation."

"Why not stay here and go with me?" Lan suggested.

"I can't," Emma replied apologetically. "You know how family things are."

"So this means I should give you this now." Lan took a small bundle from her top desk drawer and handed it to Emma, smoothing the wrinkled tissue paper as she walked around the desk.

"What's this?" Emma asked fondly.

"It's your Christmas present," she explained shyly. "You can open it now since I won't see you tomorrow."

"How sweet, babe. Thank you." Emma untied the red yarn bow and peeled back the paper. She took out a pair of buttery tan leather gloves. "Oh, Lan," she exclaimed genuinely. "These are wonderful." She quickly slipped them on and admired the fit. "How did you know I needed new gloves?" She rubbed the soft leather up and down her cheeks, cooing at the deliciously smooth feel. "I love them."

"Do they fit all right?" Lan asked reticently. "I can take them back if they don't fit."

"They're perfect." Emma clutched them against her chest as if she were coveting a prize.

"I told her your hands were this size," Lan said, holding up her hand and pointing to a spot not all the way to the end of her own fingers.

The thought of Lan judging her hand size by the way they had held hands gave Emma a warm feeling. She gave an approving smile.

"They were made just that size," Lan continued.

"You had them made specially for me?" Emma asked eagerly.

"Yes. Leona made them."

"Leona? Leona Battle? Max's wife made these?"

"Yes."

"Wow, I am impressed. Where did she get such wonderful leather? It is so soft." Emma continued to stroke and rub the gloves, admiring her present.

This was the moment Lan had nervously feared, the moment when Emma would ask about the gloves and where they came from. She knew she was going to have to explain the gloves weren't just any leather but were deerskin, from the deer she had seen Max kill. But how she was going to tell her was still up for grabs. It was going to be a complete surprise to both of them, as soon as she opened her mouth.

"You know how the Cherokee have a pride in reusing everything nature provides and not wasting anything," she began. So far, so good.

"Yeah," Emma replied, realizing a long story had just been hatched.

"You know, waste not, want not."

"Yes, I understand the concept."

"Well, Max and I agree that to help the environment and nature is to help ourselves as well. That's why he hunts and fishes responsibly. If the lake weren't fished regularly, it would become overwhelmed with fish and die. He helps feed his family and shows respect for a balance in nature. It's like the downed trees we used in the marina for the beams and firewood. A give-and-take."

Emma deliberately shifted her weight to her other foot as if to say you are stalling, get on with it before Christmas is over and the Easter bunny is hopping down the bunny trail.

"Yes." Emma repeated her understanding of the waste not, want not idea. "I think I have heard this one of your speeches before, Lan."

"When?" she asked defensively.

"Back when that poor deer was injured and Max shot it."

Lan didn't say anything. She just stared and waited.

"Oh my God," Emma whispered, looking at the gloves. "Are these deerskin gloves?"

"Uh-huh."

"Deerskin from my deer that Max shot?"

"Uh-huh," Lan repeated, bracing herself for something between getting the gloves thrown back in her face and a screaming match.

"These are from my deer?"

Lan nodded. Emma was silent a moment while the idea sank in. Lan watched her, ready to accept whatever punishment was about to come her way.

"These beautiful gloves, that fit so well and feel so good, came from my deer." Emma mulled it over, tasting the idea carefully.

"Your deer?"

"Yes, my deer. It was the first animal I ever saw hurt like that and then killed."

"You still don't understand why it had to be put out of its misery?"

Emma hesitated then pressed her gloved hands together. "Yes, I understand. It was just a shock."

"Max didn't shoot the deer just for the sport of it. He is very protective of all animals. It was an act of mercy, not murder."

"I know that now. Is that why you gave me these gloves? To remind me you were right?"

"No," Lan answered softly. "We Cherokee believe every animal has a spirit, a soul, a reason for being. To ignore the importance of this creature's life is to ignore a great gift. Deer represent good powers. They remind us to live a balanced life. I gave them to you out of respect for the deer's life."

Emma took Lan's hand in hers, allowing the soft deerskin to caress her skin. "I love to hear you talk about things you are passionate about. You don't do it very often but I want to know what you think, what you feel. I want to know everything about you."

At the sound of Emma's encouragement and prodding, Lan began to fidget, the threat of a nervous blush sending a homing signal to her brain.

"What are you doing?" Emma asked, watching as Lan grew more nervous. She smiled sympathetically. "You're embarrassed, aren't you?"

"No. I just have tight jeans on." Lan laughed artificially at the joke.

"You have trouble taking a compliment and hearing someone talk seriously to you."

Lan tried to ease her hand out of Emma's grip, but it was stuck. Emma smiled devilishly and shook her head. "If you want your hand back, you'll have to earn it."

Lan raised an eyebrow. "Earn it? What's the cost?"

"One kiss." Emma gave her most cheeky grin.

"Okay. I'm up to it." Lan leaned down and kissed her on the lips in a firm but brief dry kiss. She then pulled her hand from its hold.

"Oh, no you don't." Emma clamped down on her hand more tightly than before. "That was not a hand-freeing kiss. That was a how-are-you-today-Aunt-Edna kiss."

"Aunt Edna kiss?"

"Yes. That was one of those thin-lipped kisses you get on your birthday from an eighty-year-old aunt. I think you can do better." Emma moved closer, giving Lan a daring look. "Your reputation is at stake here."

"Never let it be said Lan Harding is an Aunt Edna kisser." Lan closed the last of the gap between them and pulled Emma to her with her free hand. She began her kiss slowly, softly. First with her lips closed, then open, allowing their tongues to swirl in a playful sultry dance. Emma released Lan's hand and folded her arms around her.

"Thank you for the beautiful gloves. I love them," Emma whispered after a long kiss.

"You're welcome." She kissed the end of her nose as a punctuation mark.

"Since we are giving out Christmas presents today, I have something for you, too." Emma led her by the hand out into the main room and positioned her in the middle of a blue plastic tarp stretched out over the floor between the fireplace and the door to the deck. It was taped down with a ribbon of silver duct tape all around the edge. "Your gift was a little hard to wrap." Emma pointed down at a small red bow stuck to the tarp. "Merry Christmas."

"Thanks sweetie," Lan replied, looking down at the bow. "I can always use another tarp."

"No, silly." Emma went to the corner of the tarp and pulled at the edge of the duct tape. "You have to unwrap your gift. Start here. And you have to unwrap it all."

Lan picked up the end and began pulling at the long sticky tape. Within a few feet, she had entangled both of her hands and one pant leg in the man-eating tape.

"I must say, you wrap presents better than you unwrap them," Emma mused while keeping her distance.

"Why aren't you helping me here?" Lan struggled to free one hand from the snarled sticky stuff.

"Not me. You aren't getting me in that mess. Looks like some kind of crude bondage ritual."

Lan continued wadding and rolling until she had released three sides of the tarp. "Can I just fold it back over that last side?"

Emma shook her head adamantly. Lan frowned and sized up the last edge. She pulled the umbilical line tight against the slack and gave a firm snap and tug. The last of the tape pulled free like a run down a pair of cheap pantyhose. Lan quickly rolled it up into a big ball and made a set-shot toward the wastebasket. It went long and stuck to the side of the counter like a wad of gum on a bedpost. Emma was standing in the middle of the tarp, straddling the red bow.

"Now, slowly pull back the tarp. Slowly," she admonished.

Lan picked up the edge and looked under. "Why? What's under here?"

"Hey. Come on. Pull it back slowly," Emma pleaded, moving off the tarp.

"Okay, okay." Lan did as she was told. When she reached the center, she stopped, speechless, staring at the six-foot-diameter circle embedded in the floor. It was a rich colorful mosaic of an eagle in flight, soaring over the treetops. A mixture of stones and ceramic chips, the tightly set pieces were polished and artistically arranged like a finely detailed painting. The eagle's eyes were piercing, focused on the horizon. His talons were sharp and clenched. His wings spread wide, in powerful strokes. Below his flight lay his wide forest dominion. In the distance, a secluded cove nestled between two hills. There were no people, no houses to litter his majestic sovereignty.

"Emma," Lan gasped breathlessly. "What have you done, woman?" Lan was awestruck.

"Do you like it?"

"Oh, yes I do." Lan moved around the perimeter of the circle, taking in every element. "This is"—she looked up and smiled broadly—"wonderful." She squatted and ran her fingers over the eagle's feathers. "This is beautiful, Emma."

"Do you recognize the ceramic pieces?"

"I don't know. Should I?"

"Remember that barrel of broken dishes?" Emma asked kneeling next to her.

"You mean this was made from the broken dishes from my snack bar?"

"Yes. And the river rocks were excavated from the ramp site and the campground. Everything in the mosaic was harvested from the marina."

"But it is so smooth. You'd think it would have rough edges. But it doesn't. It's like a painting or a sculpture."

"I can't take credit for that. Jenny did it. She is a heck of a tile setter, a real artisan. I drew up the design and she brought it to life. And that row of small stones around the tip of the feathers, each one of my crew set one of those stones, for good luck. When they heard what I was planning, everyone wanted to contribute. I thought maybe you had heard about it and weren't going to be surprised."

"No, I didn't hear a thing. How did you keep this a secret? It must have taken a long time to do all this tedious work."

"Jenny has been working on it for weeks. She'd roll back the tarp and work on it when you weren't around. Then lay a piece of plywood over it and cover it back up."

"You mean I have been walking on this all that time?"

"Yes, you have." Emma beamed proudly at carrying off the surprise. "But it was made to be walked on."

"I don't know if I want everybody walking all over this. It is too gorgeous to be stomped on with wet shoes and muddy boots." Lan frowned at the thought. "It will be like the painting on the bar room floor in that old saloon in Central City, Colorado. I'll have to put up a railing around it."

"No," Emma commanded. "It is part of the floor. Let it be here to touch everyone who steps inside Shared Winds. Let it be part of the experience."

Lan thought about it for a minute, continuing to rub the smooth stones. "Okay," she acknowledged finally. "But I'm not sure I like the idea of people walking on my Christmas present."

"I'm so glad you like it. I was afraid you might think it was too . . ." Her voice trailed off searching for the right word.

Lan took Emma's hand and kissed it. "I like it, more than you know. It says so much. It's like the gloves."

"Uh-huh," Emma agreed instantly. "Both of the gifts are a kind of rebirth."

"The eagle represents protection, strength, and a powerful wisdom. This will protect everyone who comes here." Lan leaned over and placed both of her hands flat on the mosaic. "This is exactly what Shared Winds means to me. Freedom, beauty, and protection."

"And I like my gift, too, sweetheart. They are the perfect gift. They are like a lesson in culture. Thank you." They looked at each other, understanding unfolding between their gazes. "You really are a sentimental soul, aren't you, Allana Harding?"

"Naw, not me." Lan grinned sheepishly.

"Oh yes, you are. I like that. It's your softer side you keep hidden. You make jokes and laugh to stay at a distance."

Lan said nothing. She didn't know whether to argue with Emma or just admit she was right.

"Can I drive you to the airport?" Lan asked, helping her to her feet.

"Thanks, babe. But Mom and Dad are picking me up at my house at three. And I'm going to have to leave soon. I still have some packing to do. The crews only worked until noon today. I gave them this afternoon off."

Emma checked her watch and frowned.

"I'm sorry." She patted Lan's cheek. "I have to go. I'll barely have time to get ready as it is. Come, walk me out to my truck." She slipped her hand in Lan's and led her to the parking lot. "Tell Leona and Max merry Christmas for me," she said, buckling her seat belt. "And merry Christmas to you, babe."

Lan leaned in the truck and kissed her, a stoic expression on her face.

"Merry Christmas, Emma." A strange emptiness consumed her as Emma closed the door and started the engine. They gave each other a last long look as Emma slowly pulled the shifter into drive.

Lan watched as Emma pulled out of the parking lot, leaving her alone with an empty marina and an even emptier Christmas. She tried to focus on the dinner at Max's, crowded with close friends, a house full of laughing children, and their unconditional acceptance. But part of her was leaving with Emma for Aspen, Colorado, a long cold and hollow distance away.

"Have fun," she called after her. She stood in the parking lot after Emma's taillights turned onto the highway, listening as the faint sound of her engine shifting through the gears faded into silence.

"She's going skiing, Koji." She squatted and ruffled his ears affectionately. "She's going to Aspen for Christmas." Koji wagged and wiggled at Lan's touch. "Aspen fucking Colorado." There was that word she didn't approve of but it slipped out anyway. She patted Koji on the back and headed for her Jeep. "Let's go home."

Chapter 14

Lan drove home to the sound of Christmas music on the Jeep radio but her mind was on Emma's trip. She turned off the road and stopped at the mailbox to collect her mail—a marina supply catalog, a water bill, an ad for a new car dealership in Grove, and a red envelope that looked very much like a Christmas card. There was no return address on it, but the postmark was from Halstead, Montana. Lan sat staring at the carefully swirled lettering of her name and address. It was the same precise penmanship she remembered signing her grade cards and field trip permission slips. It was also the same handwriting that explained her mother's new life with Robert and their plans to move to Montana to try ranching.

Lan wanted to rip it open. She wanted to feel the exhilaration of hearing from her mother but she knew what this was. It wasn't a long newsy letter. It wasn't a warm, comforting card from *Mom*. It was a dutiful card. One sent out of ritual, not compassion. She knew she would put it with the other cards just like it in the shoebox on the top shelf of her closet.

Lan carefully pulled the envelope flap open and slid the card out. She opened it, gave a quick glance inside then slid it back in the envelope. She ruffled Koji's fur then roared up to the house, her eyes narrowed and moist.

Lan changed into a pair of black pants and her red Christmas sweater with a row of snowflakes down the sleeves. She stepped into her freshly polished black boots and gave them an extra buff on the back of her pants legs. With the presents loaded into the backseat and Koji buckled in the front, she headed out for the twenty-minute drive to the Battle house. It was a 1960s ranch-style house with little curb appeal other than the meandering long driveway through a thickly wooded lot. Max had bought it because it was more than remote—it was obscure, deep in the Oklahoma backwoods, where hunting, fishing, and an appreciation for nature and their Cherokee culture could be taught to his children. Leona knew it meant long drives to school, stores, and just about anywhere else she needed to go, but she, too, enjoyed the open spaces and secluded location. Max and Leona spent many an evening after the dinner dishes were done walking hand in hand through their woods, planning their future, enjoying each other's company and allowing the innocence of just being flood their souls.

Lan pulled into the driveway already lined with cars. All the married children had arrived. Nancy with her husband and two kids; Stacy with her husband and three kids; Beth and her new husband, two kids, and her very pregnant belly; and Max Jr., or MJ as he was known, with his wife, three kids, and one on the way. The Battle family joke was that as long as Wal-Mart sold folding chairs and card tables, the family could continue to grow. Lan was godmother to Nancy's oldest and Beth's youngest. She wasn't sure what responsibilities that involved, but she agreed anyway. How hard could raising kids be, she thought.

She turned off the engine, opened the door, and nodded to Koji.

"We're here." She unhooked him and waved him out. At the exact moment she stepped out and slammed the door, three snowballs zeroed in on her head, followed by giggles and squeals of achievement. Lan hunched her shoulders to keep the cold snow from falling inside her sweater, but it was too late. She shook her head and brushed the snow off. "Hey," she yelled trying to sound mad. "What the . . ."

Three more missiles were launched followed by three heads popping up from behind a crude snow fort. Lan ducked and all three flew over her head and smashed into the Jeep. Max smiled broadly and threw another one that got her in the leg as she jumped out of the way. Nathan and Lucy, the outdoorsy pair of eight-year-old grandchildren, giggled and tossed a relentless barrage of snowballs from their pre-made stockpile. Most of them fell short or sailed over the car.

"No fair making them ahead," Lan scolded as she scooped up a handful and began her retaliation.

"All's fair in snowball fights. Grandpa said so," Lucy chirped.

"That's right, Lucy. Keep throwing. We've got her now." Max cheered, looking over the rim of the fort. Just as he did, Lan let a zinger go which whistled past his ear. "Ha! You throw like a girl, missy."

Incited to defend her gender identity, Lan smirked and reloaded. She carefully formed two snowballs and closed one eye, fixing her target in her sights. She lofted the first in a high arc to drop on the top of Max's head. He watched as it descended and, at the last second, he moved to the right to avoid it. At that precise moment, Lan threw the second snowball at his new position and struck him square on the chin.

"Uh-huh," she answered. "We girls throw pretty well."

Max wiped off the snow and sneered wickedly. "I should have never taught you to throw a ball."

"You didn't teach me how. If I had learned from you, I'd still be throwing at the ground," she laughed.

Max threw one and Lan replied with another. Then Max, then

Lan. Most missed their target. The kids chimed in with their best efforts. Lan tossed high floaters in their direction—the kinds that are easily avoided but let them know they were included in the fun. Nathan giggled at every one he tossed. Lucy narrowed her eyes and spent a lot of time doing reconnaissance about the target. Max and Lan continued throwing and laughing until the laughing affected their aim. Koji had returned from his romp and joined the mayhem by chasing and retrieving stray snowballs.

"Did you remember the Cool Whip, Allana?" Leona yelled from the front door.

"Yes, I did," she replied as she heaved another one. "I brought presents, too."

"Presents?" Nathan asked wildly, standing up straight like a turkey behind a log. "Do I get one?"

Lan arched a soft snowball that struck him on his tummy. "Yes, you get one, Nathan."

"Me, too?" Lucy asked, showing more restraint.

"Yes," she answered with an affectionate grin. "Everybody gets one."

"Even Grandpa?" Nathan inquired. "Grandma said he had been bad this year and Santa is only bringing him a pinecone and a meadow muffin."

Lan gave a belly laugh and nodded in agreement.

"Brush off that snow before you set one foot in this house." Leona nodded emphatically.

"Yes, ma'am," they all said at once.

The four gladiators brushed and stomped as much snow from their clothing as they could as they marched to the back door. Whatever snow pellets were still clinging to their coats and shoes seemed to have earned a right to come inside. Each member of the procession stomped at the threshold and dropped a hat and gloves on the chair in the mudroom. Lan put three containers of Cool Whip on the bottom shelf in the refrigerator then dug her fingertip into the Jell-O salad.

"Hmm, cherry?" she asked, licking it off.

"Strawberry," Nancy replied from her post at the stove stirring whatever needed stirring.

"It's good. But it doesn't taste like strawberry."

"I used 7UP instead of the cold water," Leona announced.

"You've been reading *Better Homes and Gardens* again." Lan, Nancy, and Stacy all laughed and nodded.

"Is Miss Bishop coming for dinner, Lan?" Leona asked, wiping her hands on her apron.

"She said to tell you Merry Christmas and thank you for the invitation, but she went with her parents to Colorado skiing."

"Skiing in Colorado. Now there's *my* idea of a Christmas present," Stacy said. "A cabin in the mountains or sitting around a huge fireplace in a lodge, eggnog served by a cute guy with a tight ass. Yep, I could get used to that real easy."

"Your kids would have a great time, too," Nancy added.

"Oh, no! My fantasy trip does not include kids," she said deviously then batted her eyelashes.

"You're right, Stacy. You could leave the kids here. Lan would be glad to babysit while you are gone, wouldn't you, Lan?" Nancy teased, grabbing Lan by the arm.

Nancy and Stacy laughed hilariously at the thought of Lan babysitting the brood.

"What's the big deal about going to Colorado to tramp around in the snow? You can do that right here," Lan argued lightly.

"That isn't the same. Just think, a warm fire, a down comforter, no kids, gorgeous view." Stacy gazed off mesmerized by the idea.

Lan was glad they couldn't read her mind. She envisioned the warm fire, down comforter, and a gorgeous view of Emma Bishop. And she didn't have to go off to Colorado or anywhere else to find it. She had that right in her own living room.

"Hey, kid," Max called, sticking his head in the back door. "Can you bring me some water for the smoker? It's almost dry."

"Sure," Lan replied, taking the two-liter pop bottle from the counter that was earmarked for the job.

"Smells good," she said, handing him the bottle.

He raised the domed lid and aromatic smoke billowed up around them. He carefully poured the water beside the large turkey into the water tray that sat just above the smoldering coals.

"I used hickory and apple wood this year. Wish I had some more of the mesquite wood we used last year. Had a good flavor." He poked the turkey with a fork. A trail of juice leaked out and sizzled as it hit the coals.

"There's some wild cherry in the brush pile at the marina. Try some of that next time you smoke something," she offered. She watched as he tended the coals, her hands stuffed deep inside her jacket pockets.

"Good idea." He narrowed his eyes, keeping them on the smoker. "Too bad she couldn't make it, kid," he said quietly.

"Yep," Lan replied dryly, knowing he meant Emma.

"Yep," he echoed.

They were silent for a while, as if watching the turkey cook needed their attention.

"Yep," Max repeated, stomping a glob of snow from the tip of his boot.

Lan knew Max wanted to say something but didn't know how to start. He could have just as easily gotten the water bottle himself, but he asked her to do it so she would come outside and they could talk. She could tell he was wrestling with one of those fatherly-type chats they had when serious matters grew too intense or too important for jokes. It was this pre-discussion dance that was awkward for both of them. It usually involved throat clearing, diverted eyes, and lots of silence as they closed in on the substance of the conversation.

"So, you like her?" Max asked after clearing his throat.

Lan thought a moment. She didn't realize her feelings for Emma were that transparent.

"Yeah, I do," she replied peacefully.

"She like you?" he also asked, still squinting at the cooker.

"I think so." Lan raised her shoulders so her collar could hug her cold ears.

"Good," he replied with a satisfied nod.

Lan smiled slightly. Max seemed to be finished with their talk. He had the information he needed and gave his opinion. It wasn't in his nature to offer small talk just the sake of talking.

"You'll have to bring her out next year," he said then headed for the house.

Lan followed, reveling in that idea.

After the plates had been filled and refilled, tummies patted, and dishes done, the mayhem of passing around and opening presents began. The adults tried to keep track of what child got what and from whom, but it wasn't easy. Lan gave each of the kids a toy and one of the new Shared Winds T-shirts with their name printed over the pocket. She gave each married couple a gift certificate for their favorite restaurant in Grove. Lan didn't dare challenge tradition and like every year, she gave Max and Leona a pair of tickets for the *Cherokee Queen* dinner cruise on the triple-decked sternwheeler. Leona made the night they would go into an event. It was her favorite thing to do that didn't involve her family.

"Where's Koji?" Lucy asked, searching the room and holding what looked like a tennis ball with tissue paper wadded around it behind her back. "I have a present for him." She came to Lan and pulled at her arm.

"Come on, Luce. Let's go see if he's outside," Lan said, taking her by the hand. She opened the back door and Koji came running in, shaking and wagging his tail in gratitude. "Sit, you mutt." Lan snapped her fingers and pointed to the floor in the kitchen. He obliged impatiently.

"Koji, here's your present." Lucy placed it on the floor in front of him and squatted to watch him. He looked at her and wagged. "Tell him to open it, Lan." She looked up at Lan with eager brown eyes.

"Tap your finger on the ball, Lucy. He will open it."

"How did you know it was a ball?" Lucy frowned with deep disappointment.

"I just guessed, sweet pea." Lan grinned and squatted next to her. She touched the package and scratched the paper. "Open it, Koj. Lucy wrapped it especially for you."

Koji did as he was told, biting off the wrapping and leaving a pile of paper bits. He picked up the ball and stood waiting for someone to play with him. Lucy sat on the floor and patted her lap, hoping he would give her the ball so she could toss it, but he wasn't ready to give it up.

"Lan?" Leona called from the living room. "Come in here. This heavy one has your name on it."

Lan ruffled Lucy's hair and gave Koji a pat, too, before going to see what heavy package Leona was talking about.

"What's this?" she asked, eyeing the box. "Is this one of the stumps you caught last time you went fishing?" The whole room laughed uproariously at Leona.

"No, it is not." She feigned a scowl. "It's one of Max's." Everyone laughed even harder. Leona smiled tenderly over at Max. "Go on, Lan. Open it. And I will have you know I went along when he got this. So this year, I even know what your present is."

Lan sat down on the floor next to the suitcase-size box and began ripping and peeling paper. She opened the lid and dug down through the newspaper for her prize. Her eyes widened and she laughed wickedly as she took out a camshaft for her 1948 Chris-Craft.

"Oh man, is this for my forty-eight?" she asked with a childish glow. She studied it up and down, running her hand over the smooth shiny metal. She couldn't say anything else. The lump in her throat was rising.

"Yep," Max answered, unable to say anything else himself, as he saw Lan's delight over the gift.

"You two sure get excited about the strangest things. It's a boat part, for God's sake," Nancy said, eyeing her father warmly.

"I don't know where you found this, but I sure appreciate it." Lan spent a long time fondling her gift. "Thank you, Max. Thank you, Leona. This is great." She grinned uncontrollably.

"Merry Christmas, kid," Max said gruffly. Then he smiled.

"Merry Christmas, everybody," Lan replied.

Chapter 15

Lan had decided she would sleep late Christmas morning. There was no reason not to. But her eyes popped open early, her body forgetting she had the day off. After fifteen minutes of blanket thrashing, she climbed out of bed, showered, and went about her normal morning routine. Koji was fed, the newspaper was added to the stack waiting in the basket to be read, and breakfast was eaten standing at the sink. The cereal bowl was washed, shaken dry, and replaced in the cabinet. All through breakfast and the morning chores, Lan felt the urge growing to call Emma and wish her a Merry Christmas. It seemed strange and lonely that she was so far away. She hoped Emma was at least having a good time. The image of Emma Bishop in a ski outfit, trudging through the mountains of snow to shop for a turtleneck or pair of earrings was amusing to Lan. She imagined herself trudging along ahead of her, blazing a trail through the snow, or sitting across from her in a quiet Aspen café, or better yet, keeping her warm all through a long snowy night. Lan usually didn't indulge in frivolous fantasies, but it was Christmas. She owed it to herself. Merry Christmas.

She made a small fire in the fireplace and milked a cup of coffee for thirty minutes, deciding what was next in her day. She went out to the shop, walked around the boat, and then returned to the house, unable to find the interest in working on it. She cleaned the bathroom and kitchen floors to Christmas music. She could almost hear Emma's beautiful voice singing along. Koji came to the edge of the kitchen and sat down watching Lan crawl along on her hands and knees, sponging the corners.

"Why aren't you helping, Koj?" she asked, sitting back on her heels. "Most of this looks like your canine dirt to me."

He rested his muzzle on his front paws and looked up innocently. She finished the floor then pulled a big package wrapped in brown paper from the corner behind the small Christmas tree.

"Do you want to open your present?"

She set the package in the middle of the floor and tapped the paper with her fingers. Koji came to investigate with a measure of prudence.

"You'll have to open it yourself." She tapped it again.

He sniffed then began to wag his tail. After repeated reassurances, he pawed at the paper then bit at it, tearing off pieces and making a pile of shredded wet paper on the floor. As he picked at the package, Lan fed the fireplace with the scraps of paper. Once all the covering had been accounted for, he examined the new corduroy-covered cushion. It was plump and clean, something he would spend the rest of the day correcting.

"Merry Christmas, you old hound you," she said, ruffling his fur with both her hands.

She was bored. She strained at the thought of going to the marina. No one was there and nothing needed her that desperately. This was her day of rest, relaxation, to do whatever she wanted to do.

But what she wanted was in Aspen. She put on her coat and gloves and wrapped a scarf around her neck.

"I'm going for a walk," she announced to Koji from the doorway. "You coming?"

Koji had just trampled a good dent in the new cushion and was ready to test its napping qualities. He pulled himself to his feet, stretched, but remained on the cushion.

"Okay, but you're going to be a couch potato."

She headed through the woods, her boots crunching through the crusty top layer of the snow. Little clouds of breath circled her head and rose into the cold quiet afternoon air. The trees stood like frozen statues lining her route. She meandered several miles deeper into the woods. Occasionally she stopped to watch a squirrel scamper up a tree or a bird moving from one branch to another. The deep forest was serenely silent, a fortress she often visited to find peaceful thoughts. Here she could clear her mind, free herself from stress, return to a balanced existence. But wherever she turned, she saw just one image. Emma. With her eyes so bright and caring, her skin so soft and radiant, her touch so warm and alluring.

Lan scooped up a handful of snow and formed a snowball. Her hands molded around it, feeling the firm contours of a perfect snowball. The memory of Emma's firm round breasts popped into her mind, as if nothing she could see or do today was going to escape some resemblance to Emma Bishop. Angry at herself for not being able to conquer this obsession, she threw the snowball, smashing it against a tree. She heaved a deep sigh and headed back to the house. The sun was out of sight over the edge of the horizon as she stepped onto her property and crossed the field to the porch. Normally returning from a walk in the woods brought her back refreshed and calmed. This one brought her back only frustrated and cold.

Lan stirred the fireplace and added a log, the warmth flowing over her face. She stared into the flames, remembering the night she and Emma made love in front of the fire. She clenched her jaw and tossed another log in for good measure. She wished Emma were there. She tossed in another log, this one to dispel the urge to feel sorry for herself.

She stood at the opened refrigerator door, looking for something she could call Christmas dinner. Nothing sounded good. Maybe later she would be hungry. Just as she had gotten comfortable on the couch with a novel she had been meaning to start, she could hear the distant sound of a car pulling up her road. When it stopped in front of the house, she went to turn on the porch lights and opened the front door.

Lan's heart flew into her throat and pounded ecstatically as the driver's door opened and Emma stepped out, her face bright and beaming in the moonlight.

"Merry Christmas," Emma said with a proud grin.

"Merry Christmas, yourself," Lan replied, almost breathless with surprise.

"I wasn't sure you'd be home." Emma headed for the stairs where Lan waited in stocking feet.

"What happened to Aspen?"

"Oh, it was great. Lots of snow. Very crowded," she related, eyeing Lan's expression. "Several inches of new powder so the skiing was super, or so they said."

"If it was that great, why are you here?" Lan was desperately trying to remain calm and reserved.

"I forgot something, so I had to fly back this afternoon," Emma replied as she reached the porch.

"What did you forget?"

Emma's gaze started at Lan's sock feet and moved up slowly until she reached her eyes. A seductive smile crawled across Emma's face.

"I forgot where I really wanted to be on Christmas."

Lan nodded, her eyes swimming deep in Emma's, revealing her delight at this unexpected change of plans.

"And where is that?" Lan hooked her finger inside the front of Emma's coat and rubbed up and down on the camel-colored wool.

Emma stepped closer. She took Lan's hand and placed it on her cheek, closing her eyes and enjoying Lan's touch.

Lan pulled her other hand through Emma's hair, allowing it to fall in soft cascades.

"Can I interest you in a cup of tea by the fireplace?" Lan whispered, stroking Emma's cheek with the back of her hand.

"Yes," Emma replied, turning her lips up to meet Lan's kiss.

Lan heated water in the microwave and prepared two cups of tea while Emma leaned against the counter in the kitchen.

"Have you had dinner?" Lan inquired, handing Emma her cup.

"I didn't but I'm not hungry."

"Are you sure? I can whip up something. I didn't have much either."

Emma wrinkled her nose and looked pensively at Lan, as if to say she might be talked into something light.

"What do you have?" she asked, joining Lan to stare into the opened refrigerator.

"Wait." Lan shut the refrigerator door and took Emma by the hand, leading her to the couch. "You sit here for a minute. Let me surprise you, okay?"

"Oh, I love surprises."

Lan went back into the kitchen. Emma could hear drawers and doors opening and closing and the clatter of dishes and glasses being stacked and unstacked. After a few minutes, Lan reappeared carrying a tray. She flipped off the lights with her elbow, allowing the glow of the fireplace to light the room. She placed the tray on the coffee table in front of Emma. It was covered with a towel so Emma's curiosity was piqued. Lan slid the table to the side and spread a red checkered tablecloth on the carpet in front of the fireplace. Then she signaled for Emma to take her place on the tablecloth.

"It looks like a picnic." Emma grinned and sat down on the makeshift picnic blanket.

"That's exactly what it is. A Christmas picnic." Lan sat down across from Emma, placing the tray between them. She peeked under the towel and pulled out a small round cutting board arranged with slices of cheese and salami. Then she pulled out a plate filled with apple slices, celery sticks, and green olives. Next she brought out a Kaiser roll, cut into wedges. Finally she dramatically produced a bottle of wine and two wine glasses. She opened the wine and handed Emma a glass of the dark red something or other from the grocery store, and poured one for herself. It wasn't wonderful wine, but it was a perfect dinner.

"Oh babe, how wonderful. A picnic in the snow. I love it." Emma smiled tenderly and leaned over, giving Lan a kiss of appreciation.

They enjoyed the fun, eating and sipping wine, sharing an occasional kiss, and feeding each other tidbits. Even without a big turkey or ham, they were sharing a memorable Christmas dinner. Emma insisted on clearing away the dishes when they finished then sat on the couch next to Lan, leaning against her as they watched the fire burn down.

"That was so nice. Thank you, babe." Emma pulled her feet up and curled up next to Lan, snuggling close.

Lan leaned back and wrapped her arm around Emma's shoulder, stroking her softly, allowing her touch to take the place of needless words. Emma sighed and nuzzled closer.

"I'm glad you came back."

"Me, too."

"What did you tell your parents the reason was you were leaving?"

"I told Mom I had some unfinished business to attend to."

"And she believed that?"

"She asked if the important business had a name. I told her yes. She ask if her initials were LH." Emma looked up at Lan and smiled. " I told her yes."

"You told her about us?" Lan asked skeptically.

"No. She seemed to know. She is a very perceptive woman."

"And your dad, what did he say?"

"Not much. He smiled, kissed me goodbye, and wished us a

Merry Christmas. And they know I'm a big girl. I make my own decisions."

"You are very lucky to have loving understanding parents," Lan said, kissing her on the temple.

"Did you hear from your mother for Christmas?" Emma asked cautiously.

"I got a Christmas card from her yesterday."

Emma sat up and smiled at Lan. "That is great. What did she say? Anything about a visit?"

"Nope. Mom and Robert's names were imprinted on the card. She didn't write anything inside. And there was no return address on it," Lan related matter of factly. She pulled away and went to stir the fading fire. She busied herself with another log to hide her pain. This Christmas tradition wasn't new. Lan was resigned to this annual empty hope for some word or recognition from her mother. She accepted it and considered that surviving it had made her strong.

"I'm sorry, sweetie." Emma wanted to say more, but somehow her words seemed inadequate against so large a heartache. "Maybe next year she will write something inside." Emma wished she hadn't said that. It sounded shallow and cold. She wanted to hug Lan tight enough to block out the heartless way her mother was treating her. Emma had never met the woman, but she hated her.

"Yeah, maybe next year she will put her return address on it, too." Lan gave her last bit of interest to that thought and turned back to Emma with a smile. "But this year, I have you. And you, sweet woman, are the perfect Christmas present." Lan sat down on the couch just as Emma stood up.

"I should go out and get my suitcase from the car. Where did I leave my shoes?"

Lan hopped up and stepped into her boots. "I'll get it." She hurried out into the cold night air before Emma could give her the car keys. Emma took her keys from her coat pocket and waited in the open doorway for Lan to notice the doors were locked.

"Hey," Lan yelled from the driveway.

"Yes?" Emma teased. "Did you need something?"

"It's locked," Lan said sheepishly, shuddering from the cold.

"Oh, that." Emma held up the remote entry and clicked the button. The lights flashed and the doors unlocked. "You know I'm not helpless. I could have gotten it myself," she announced into the darkness.

"I know. Next time you can go," Lan replied, scurrying back up the steps with the suitcase. She kissed Emma on the nose then carried the suitcase down the hall.

Emma clicked the door locks then followed her into the bedroom.

"I had a present for you but I'm not sure you deserve it. Have you been good this year, little girl?"

"Heck no," Lan quipped, stretching out on the bed, her arms folded behind her head. "What'd you bring me?" she asked in a sassy voice.

Emma dug around in the suitcase then pulled out a plastic shopping bag.

"Here it is," she declared, holding up the bag. "But you have to wait a minute. I will be right back." Emma disappeared down the hall. Lan could hear the bathroom door close then the faint sounds of Emma singing "Jingle Bells." A minute later the bathroom door opened again. Emma reappeared in the bedroom doorway in a long, red and sheer Christmas negligee set. The nightgown had spaghetti straps and hugged her hips, showing a shadowy triangle of dark hair. The robe was trimmed in red lace and was iridescent in the pale bedroom light.

Emma made a slow dramatic turn, holding out the robe so the sheerness of both pieces could be fully appreciated. Lan sat up and watched. Her mouth dropped open. Emma turned again, as if practicing for a fashion show.

"What do you think? Do you like what I got you?"

"All that's for me?" Lan stared at Emma, watching her body move under the thin red cloud.

"Well, I thought I could wear it," she said in a low throaty voice as she spun and waltzed closer to the bed. "And you could unwrap it." She stood next to the bed looking down at Lan. She draped one side of the robe over Lan's head and slowly pulled it down, the folds floating across her face.

It had been a long time since anyone had gone to such elaborate efforts to seduce her, but Emma was doing an excellent job of it.

"I like this idea—a lot." Lan held the filmy robe out so she could see the nightgown. Emma's breasts were visible beneath the silky fabric, her nipples small and dark. Lan sat on the side of the bed, Emma standing between her legs. She ran her hands down Emma's body, feeling the thin veil that stood between her and the soft supple skin. She buried her face in Emma's breasts, kissing and caressing them through the nightgown. Emma ruffled Lan's hair, gasping and pressing her tighter against her hardening nipples. Lan slid the robe over her shoulders and let it drop. She found the bottom of the nightgown with her hands and slipped them up underneath, stroking upward from the ankles, calves, knees, then moving slowly over Emma's thighs. She continued to nuzzle against her breasts as her hands cupped at Emma's buttocks. Lan's mouth moved down across her stomach, her tongue flicking at her skin through the fabric. Her hands inched their way between her thighs, her nails skating down Emma's skin in little circles, teasingly closer and closer to the moist dark valley that awaited her touch. Emma gasped and arched her back, leaning into the tantalizing touch of her lover's skillful hands. Finally Lan raised the nightgown and pulled it over Emma's head. She then folded her arms around Emma and brought her onto the bed. She tenderly laid Emma back on the pillow and spread her long golden hair around her head like a halo. She sat back on her heels and admired her beauty. Emma smiled up at her. This was the image Lan had seen in her mind all day. This beautiful woman, her eyes filled with such softness and love.

Lan slipped out of her clothes and stretched out, carefully covering Emma's body with her own. She moved slowly and tenderly.

Emma moaned and gasped as Lan's body moved over hers in passionate rhythms, her hands and mouth probing and caressing every secret spot, bringing wave after wave of exquisite rapture. Beads of sweat traced across Emma's body as Lan delved deeper and deeper.

"Oh yes, yes. Don't stop, please don't stop." Emma groaned, her nails digging into the sheets. She arched her body and strained against Lan's tongue. With one powerful crescendo, Emma screamed in ecstasy and sank back into the bed, breathless. Lan hesitated and looked up at Emma's satisfied expression. She started again. And again Emma rode the waves of passion and exploded in a cascade of delight until she lay happily exhausted.

Emma rested and held her lover close to her. She had every intention of reciprocating Lan's thrilling expressions of love and passion, but before either one could begin, they both had fallen asleep, still wrapped in each other's embrace.

Chapter 16

Lan awoke first, and reached over to see if Emma was still next to her. She was. Her long hair tangled and matted from their night of sweaty passion. Her makeup a faded memory. Her lipstick long kissed away. But she was still the most radiantly beautiful woman Lan had ever seen. She inched her way closer to the sleeping woman and gently wrapped her arms over her body. She was warm and soft. Lan kissed her temple softly and drifted back to sleep.

When Lan opened her eyes again, Emma was sitting next to her, watching her sleep. Her hair was brushed, her body scrubbed and fresh, a look of devotion on her face.

"Good morning," Emma said softly, kissing Lan awake.

"Hmm," Lan groaned and stretched, a smile creeping across her sleepy face. "Morning."

"I'm sorry about last night, sweetheart." Emma slowly eased on top of Lan, kissing her shoulders and neck.

"What are you sorry about?" Lan stroked Emma's back as she slid her body gently against hers. "You were wonderful."

"I mean, I'm sorry I fell asleep before I could let you know how special you are." Emma slid her hands down Lan's thighs and let her nails skitter back up to her waist.

"It's okay. You're still here. Did you have anyplace to rush off to?" Lan pressed her hips up against Emma's pubic bone, their curly mounds of hair brushing against each other in a tantalizing caress.

"I'm right where I need to be," Emma whispered as she nibbled at Lan's ear then traced her tongue down her neck.

Emma began slowly, teasingly so. They had all day and Emma planned on keeping Lan busy for much of it. She caressed Lan's body and kissed her, passionately touching and raising Lan's desire. Lan moved back and forth beneath Emma's soft body, gasping and urging her on. Lan relaxed, surrendering under Emma's advances, eager to accept the fire of her passion. This long-awaited explosion of desire had been a delightful craving she had nearly forgotten. She closed her eyes, swimming in a sea of tingling pleasure.

Emma made love to Lan. And again and again.

Chapter 17

With less than three weeks left before the grand opening week-end, nerves were beginning to show some wear. There were no huge problems in the final repair schedules, but small aggravations, much like a mosquito bite under a watchband, popped up almost daily. Emma found herself returning, exchanging, and reordering every-thing from mismatched tile to defective sprayer valves to plumbing fittings. It was as if the last possible details were determined to offer some resistance to the job completion. But she gritted her teeth and worked her way through them, one at a time.

Lan was wrestling with her own share of last-minute frustrations. Her distributors and suppliers had the same nit-picky problems that she used to laugh about and ignore but with time growing short, each reorder and cancellation was an agonizing grate to her nerves. It was the moments she and Emma could steal together, if only for a quick cup of coffee as they moved from one crisis to another, that made these frenzied final work days tolerable.

"You look like the cat that swallowed the mouse," Emma said guardedly, as she entered the office.

"Who, me?"

"Yes, you. What's up?"

Lan rolled her desk chair back and took out the plastic sack she had been hiding on her lap. "Happy Valentine's Day," she announced, unable to keep her secret another second. She removed the sack and handed Emma a large red velvet heart-shaped box. It had a ruffled pink satin trim and a red silk rosebud on the top. It had all the earmarks of a box of candy, a three-pounder, at least.

Emma laughed at the lavish gift. "Sweetheart, thank you. What a huge box of candy. You are so thoughtful."

Lan beamed with pride. "You're welcome."

"I have to admit, this is my first box of candy like this." Emma came around to Lan's side of the desk and gave her a kiss.

"You're kidding. You've never gotten a box of candy before?" Lan asked incredulously.

"Oh, I've gotten candy before but never one like this. Thank you. I love it." She sat on the arm of Lan's chair and removed the plastic wrapper. She lifted the lid and peeked inside gleefully. "Yum. My favorites. Dark chocolate." She took a bite of one then offered Lan a nibble. "These are wonderful, babe. I will have to ration myself."

"I know it isn't very imaginative or original but I wanted our first Valentine's Day together to be memorable. So, I got the biggest box of candy I could find," Lan explained as she walked her fingers up Emma's thigh. "Sweets for my sweet woman."

"So I'm your little bon-bon?" Emma asked with a seductive glance.

Lan gave a chuckle. "We sound like J.T. and Annie."

"You're right. First thing you know we'll be calling each other jelly bean."

They both wrinkled their noses and shook their heads in a resounding no.

"You don't get your Valentine's present until later."

"How much later?" Lan asked in a breathy voice, dropping a saucy innuendo.

"I am taking you to dinner tonight for your Valentine's present," Emma replied with a grin.

"But I, for one, am hungry now," Lan teased as she walked her fingers higher up on Emma's thigh.

"Now stop that," she scolded, pushing her hand down. "Restrain yourself, woman."

"I am showing restraint. If there weren't twenty guys out in the other room, I'd be having Bishop hors d'oeuvres right now," she leered in a lusty voice.

"You are such a tease." Emma picked up Lan's fingers and bit them playfully.

"Dinner, eh?" Lan flashed her big grin. "Are you going to tell me where we are going?"

"Nope. I want it to be a surprise."

"Is it someplace fancy or just Happy Meals to go? I need to know what to wear."

"Anything is fine. It's casual."

"Ms. Bishop?" Mike called, hurrying into the office with a box of pipe fittings. "These are the wrong size PVC joints. They're all half inch, and we need three-quarter for the sinks."

Emma rolled her eyes at Lan and groaned. "Okay, Mike. Let me check the invoice and see what happened," she said heavily. "Six-thirty," she said, looking back at Lan as she followed Mike out of the office.

"Later."

Emma stuck her head back in the office and pointed to the box of candy she had left on the desk. "Don't eat all my candy, woman." She smiled, knowing Lan would love to make some suggestive reply to that statement.

It was a long and busy day. It was after six when they each wrapped up their work and called it a day. The marina was quiet, empty of all workers. Emma slid down in her chair and extended her legs out under the table. She raised her arms high above her head, yawning and stretching.

"There'll be none of that," Lan ordered as she crossed the room and stood behind Emma's chair. She began massaging her shoulders with tender fingers.

"Oh, that feels so good," Emma replied, closing her eyes and melting back into her strong hands.

"Tough day?"

"Just a long day."

"Are you sure you want to do dinner tonight? If you are tired, we can do it another time."

"Yes, I'm sure." Emma reached back and pulled Lan's hands around her. "But we will have to go from here, if that's okay with you." She looked at Lan's watch. "I made the reservation for seven and we'll have just enough time to make it."

"Wow. Dinner reservations. I'm impressed."

"Nothing is too good for my baby." Emma leaned her cheek against Lan's arm as it enfolded her.

Emma headed for Grove with Lan quizzing her about the destination for most of the way. She pulled into the parking lot at Giovan's Pizzeria and took the first available parking space. Lan smiled broadly and took Emma's hand as they walked to the door. The restaurant was packed and several groups were waiting for a table.

"Hi, Lan. Hi, Emma," Bill Ramsey said, signaling them to follow him. "Here you go, Emma," he announced as he motioned them toward the corner booth, the same booth Emma and Nicole had shared.

Emma turned around to see Lan's expression. She was grinning happily.

"Enjoy your dinner," he declared then returned to the front.

They slid in the booth across from one another. "Happy Valentine's Day, sweetheart," Emma said softly, leaning over and taking Lan's hand in hers. She puckered her lips and blew Lan a kiss.

"And you said I was sentimental," Lan replied, squeezing her hands. "This is the best Valentine's present you could have given me. Thank you, sweetie." Lan looked longingly into Emma's eyes, speaking volumes of silent love to her special lady.

"I'm so glad you think so." Emma's face beamed with devotion and contentment.

"Hello, ladies," a young waitress said, placing water glasses on the table. "I'll be right back to take your order."

"What kind of pizza do you want?" Emma asked, still holding Lan's hands and swimming in her eyes.

"Whatever you want is fine with me."

"I would like to just sit here and look at you."

When the waitress returned, Emma still couldn't decide so Lan ordered for them.

"We'll have mushroom, sausage, and black olive," she said, raising her eyebrows at Emma for approval.

"Sounds good," Emma agreed.

"Do you want the Valentine's Special?" the waitress asked as she wrote on her pad.

"What's that?" Lan inquired.

"You can have the pizza in the shape of a heart, if you want."

"Absolutely," Emma added quickly.

The waitress hurried off to turn in the order. Bill came to the table with a bottle of red wine and two glasses. "Is this okay, Emma?" he asked, showing the bottle. "You asked for something to go with pizza." He waited for Emma's nod then set the bottle on the table.

"Here's to Valentine's Day," Lan said, holding up her wine glass for Emma to clink. "A wonderful reason to be with someone special." They sipped then Lan continued. "To be with the one you love," she added quietly.

They sipped again, their eyes glued to one another.

"After dinner, will you come home with me tonight?" Emma asked in a wishful whisper.

Lan sipped her wine and winked. They ate pizza, drank wine, gazed at each other, and occasionally held hands. Lan's dream had come true. The corner booth now belonged to them. And with careful, pleasing, and passionate hours spent together, the night belonged to them as well.

Chapter 18

"Phone's for you," Max mumbled through a mouthful of dough-nut, as he stuck his head around the office door.

"Where's my maple doughnut?" Lan asked as she fished through the papers on her desk for the phone.

"You get chocolate today. No maple." Max set a napkin-wrapped doughnut on the corner of the desk.

"Shared Winds. Can I help you?" she said into the receiver as she used her boardinghouse reach to retrieve her pastry. "Hey John. How are things in KC?"

Max rolled his eyes and belched loudly. Lan shook her head harshly and silently shushed him.

"When did you get in?" Lan set the doughnut down and leaned back in her chair to listen. "He has it about finished. Just needs to adjust the timing and do an oil change." She raised her eyebrows to Max, as if asking for his agreement. Max smirked and rolled his eyes but finally nodded. "I left a sixteen-foot fiberglass outboard in your boathouse when I picked up your cruiser so I'd have a ride back. How about I bring it over tomorrow?" Lan frowned into the receiver and listened more. "John, if it absolutely has to be today, it'll be later this afternoon. And that's if Max doesn't find any more problems. He'll have to give it a test run. Max won't sign off on it until he tests it, John. You know that."

Max shook his head adamantly then pointed to his watch and signaled five hours.

"Okay, John. Tell you what. I'll bring it over this afternoon before dark."

Max frowned at Lan, telling her she had made a promise she might not be able to keep.

"Oh sure, I'll have your baby back in your boathouse tonight. You'll have it for your party tomorrow, I promise."

Max was ready to argue the moment Lan hung up.

"What the hell you mean you'll have it back in his boathouse tonight. I need four or five hours just to put the motor back together."

"He has some VIPs coming down in the morning and needs it back ASAP. Besides, you have all day to work on it. I'll give you a hand."

"Then I'd need eight hours to finish it," Max quipped. "It's cold and windy out there on the lake today so if I do get it finished, you'll need to get over and back before dark."

"No problem. That big day cruiser rides like sitting in your living room."

"Yeah, but that little skiff you left over there doesn't."

"Then quit dropping doughnut crumbs on my desk and go finish it," Lan teased and returned to her doughnut.

Max muttered to himself all the way down to the dock where a forty-foot cabin cruiser was tied to the last slip. He scanned the water, watching the gently rolling waves lap at the hull of the big boat. As of now, it looked okay. But the forecast was questionable.

189

Lan occasionally left her work to check on his progress. By early afternoon the engine was assembled and was just an oil change away from a timing check and test run.

Max stood in the office doorway, wiping the last of the grease from his hands on a rag.

"I gave her a test run around the cove. She's all set to go." Max seemed tired and cold but anxious for Lan to get going. "You almost ready to head back with it? It's getting windy, kid. Are you sure you couldn't take it back tomorrow?"

"I'll be fine." Lan checked her watch. "Is Emma back yet?"

"Haven't seen her." Max started out of the office then turned back with a puzzled look. "How about me taking it back this time?"

"Nope," Lan said matter-of-factly, turning off her computer. "You fix them, I deliver them."

"She's all gassed up and ready to go."

Lan hunched her shoulders to the late February wind as she waited for the big cruiser to lumber through its warmup. A belch of smoke from the exhaust was followed by a slow chugging of the twin engines. She tapped the gauges with her knuckles until she was satisfied they were true readings.

"How's the oil pressure?" Max yelled from the dock.

"Sixty, maybe sixty-five. Tach, good. Charge, good."

"Don't push it over three thousand RPM. Let the rings and seals have a chance to seat," he ordered. "Tell that clown to take it easy with her for a week or so. And tell him to do himself a favor and let her warm up before he stands on the throttle."

"Heck, no." Lan scowled devilishly. "I like his repeat business. Having to rebuild his motor every year because he's too stubborn to take care of it is like money in the bank."

Max frowned at her, shaking his head with disapproval.

"I know, I know," she complained. "I'll tell him. I always tell him and he always says sure, he'll do that. And every fall he burns a valve or blows a head."

Lan nudged the throttle forward and inched away from the dock.

"When Emma gets back, tell her I shouldn't be more than an hour. Tell her I'll be back before dark," she yelled.

"You take care of that new valve job or I ain't telling her squat," Max bellowed then headed toward the marina. "And be careful," he added under his breath.

The cruiser cleared the cove and was out of sight by the time he tossed another log on the fire and gave it a stir. He filled the log crib next to the stone hearth and swept up the wood chips. He unpacked a box of parts and stacked them on shelves in the ship's store then sat at the counter, sorting through some marine parts catalogs and slurping on a mug of strong coffee.

"Hi Max," Emma said cheerfully as she crossed the room. "Even though the furnace is working again, I sure like this fireplace." She warmed her back in front of the roaring blaze. "Have you seen Lan? She isn't in her office but her Jeep is still here."

"She took the Taylors' cruiser back. Left about an hour ago. Said to tell you she'd be back by dark."

"I hope she wore a warm coat. I thought we were finished with this cold windy winter, but it is giving us one last hurrah I guess." She combed her fingers through her wind-blown hair.

"Don't need to worry. There's a heater in that big boat."

"How about the boat she's bringing back. Does it have a heater, too?"

"No," Max replied hesitantly. "But she'll be okay. She'll probably open her up and fly back. Never knew her to pass up an opportunity to fling a rooster tail."

They both laughed. It was true more times than not. Lan would surely deliver the repaired boat and be back in her home cove in no time. At least that's what Emma and Max each told themselves.

Max went to the door to the deck and looked out into the waning evening light. There was nothing but emptiness and black water striped with ruffled whitecaps. He discreetly checked his watch so as not to alarm Emma. It had been over an hour since Lan had headed across the lake, way over an hour. Max knew full well Lan had had time to get to Grove and back again more than once. He poked at the fireplace, trying to remain calm.

"I'd put more wood on the fire, but she'll be back pretty quick now. I'll just let this die down."

The buzzer from the gas pump dock sounded, followed by the blast from a boat horn. Max snapped on the floodlights and started down to the dock. Emma followed along behind, using this as an excuse to see if Lan was in sight yet.

"Give me ten gallons, Max." A gray-haired man in a heavy parka and an Evinrude cap was tying his bowline to the dock. His big boat rocked back and forth as the waves heaved relentlessly. A smaller boat bobbed like a bathtub toy behind his boat, straining at the tow cable.

"Why are you buying gas from me, Charlie? Don't you have a pump?" Max unlocked the pump and began filling the tank.

"I thought I had enough to do this tow job, but steering into the wind killed my gas mileage. I didn't want to get stuck out on the lake with a dry tank."

"That windy, huh?" Max asked nonchalantly.

"That ain't the worst of it. The lake level is way up with all this runoff we've had. It has floated a bunch of widow-makers off the shore and is pushing them downwind. I nearly hit a couple big ones. That'll be enough, Max. I wanted to get back before dark. You can't see them at night. Hell, you almost can't see them in daylight." He handed Max a wad of money and pulled his bowline in, then chugged out of the cove.

"What's a widow-maker, Max?" Emma asked tentatively.

"Submerged floating tree. The storm downed lots of them. They're all along the shoreline. We've cleaned ours up, cut them up for firewood. But some folks just leave them. When the water level goes up, some float off the bank and drift across the lake just under the waterline. It's hard to see them. If you hit one with a boat . . ." Max didn't want to finish that thought.

Emma looked at her watch then twisted it on her wrist. She

stared plaintively at Max, her eyes searching his face for comfort and reassurance. He offered an uneasy smile.

"How long has she been gone, Max?" Emma asked in a business voice, expecting no less than the truth. The wind stirred her hair around her face, flicking at her eyes. She took her stocking cap from her coat pocket and pulled it on, both for warmth and to restrain her wind-blown hair.

"About an hour," he said, sounding like a teenager reporting how long he had been out past curfew. He instantly felt the need to be honest. He looked at his watch. "In three minutes, it will be two hours."

"Does she have her cell phone with her?" she asked, taking hers from her coat pocket.

Max dug in his shirt pocket and held up Lan's red cell phone.

"She had me call the Taylors just before she left to let them know she was on the way. She said she wouldn't need it."

"Push the redial button," she ordered.

Max quietly fumbled the tiny buttons with his big weathered hands.

"Damn," he muttered. "Gotta do it again. Damn buttons are too small."

Emma took the phone from him and pressed the buttons.

"Mr. Taylor?" she asked poignantly. "Yes, this is Emma Bishop. Has Lan Harding delivered your boat yet this evening?" She nodded to Max to let him know.

"Can you tell me how long ago she left? No, no problem. Just checking to see when to expect her." Emma's face suddenly lost its color and her eyes widened. "That long? Did she say if she was stopping anywhere on her way back? I know. There isn't much open on the lake yet. If you happen to hear from her, will you have her call the marina or her cell number? Yes, you too. Thank you."

Emma pushed the End button and stared at the phone.

"He said she dropped off the boat an hour and a half ago, then headed right back. She wanted to get back before the wind got any worse." Emma sounded stunned and worried.

"Okay," Max said, reconciling the news to himself. He searched the blackened distance where the cove opened into the lake. "I think I'm going to go have a look. Maybe she's having trouble finding the cove."

"I'm going with you," Emma declared.

"You don't need to. It'll be pretty cold out in the middle of the lake and windier, too. Why don't you stay—"

"Don't even bother saying it, Max. I *am* going with you. Which boat are we taking?"

"We'll take the pontoon boat. It isn't as fast but it's more stable in the wind."

"Let's go," she ordered, following him to the slip where a silver-colored metal pontoon boat was suspended on a hydro hoist several feet above the water. He engaged the hoist and lowered the wide barge into the water. He quickly hopped on board and checked the gas tanks. Like a one-man pit crew, Max started the engine, untied both ends of the boat, and pushed off. Emma stood next to him holding on to the canopy frame. He headed for the mouth of the cove, the bow lights carving a white tunnel in the darkness. As they cleared the protection of the cove, the wind began pushing the boat sideways, whitecaps splashing against the side. It was a cold wind. But a different kind of cold from that October ride to Two Tree Island. This was a wet stinging cold, a nasty venomous cold. Emma blocked it out. Her whole being was focused on the empty cloud of ink they were charging into. She was concentrating on an image, any image, somewhere in the night. A boat, a person, anything that meant Lan was out there, safe.

"Maybe she ran out of gas," Emma offered.

"Maybe." Max checked his compass and headed for Grove. "Hold the wheel on this heading," he said, pointing at the compass. "I want to adjust the lights out front."

Emma did as she was told, stiffly guiding the big barge into the night. Max turned the floodlights on and adjusted them to paint a broad arc of light out ahead of the boat. He peered into the empty waters; his hawk-like vision searched while he listened for the high-pitched scream of Lan's Mercury outboard above the low rumble of their own engine.

"Anything?" Emma yelled.

With nothing to offer, he shook his head and kept searching. Cautiously they made their way across the lake toward Grove. Several times Max had Emma shut off the engines. As the boat swayed in the wind, rocking back and forth through the whitecaps, they stood silently, straining to hear the sounds of another boat.

"Do you think she put in someplace because of the weather? Maybe she decided to call for a ride or something." Emma spoke wishfully, as if she could make it true by saying it.

"Maybe," he replied half-heartedly. Inside he knew Lan would never give in like that. She would laugh her big laugh and race across the lake, defiantly sending a spray to the winds.

"Of course, where could she put in? You can't see the shore at night." Emma peered into the night, trying to prove herself wrong.

"She has a light on the boat and she has a flashlight in the tool box. She'll be all right." Max sounded like he was trying to convince himself as well as Emma.

"Sure she will. But I bet she is cold. She'll want some coffee. I should have brought some nice hot coffee in a thermos. And maybe a sandwich. She'll be hungry, too. She hasn't had dinner yet, I'll bet." Emma realized she was rambling. Her eyes met Max's in desperation. "Where is she, Max?"

He took a deep breath, closed his eyes, and bellowed into the darkness, "Allana!"

"LAN!" Emma added in a frantic but demanding voice.

They called out again then listened to the silence. The waves continued to roll the boat from side to side. Max locked his feet between two railing posts and cupped his hands to his mouth, yelling out Lan's name in deep low blasts.

They continued on across the lake, circling the inlet near the

Taylors' boathouse. There was no sign of Lan or her boat. Reluctantly they started back, retracing the route she had to have taken. Again, Max periodically cut the engine and listened, hoping to hear some sound of life, some sound of anything other than the relentlessly whistling wind and the angry waves. Just as he shut down the motor and listened to the painful emptiness, a large wave slapped at the boat and knocked Emma into the side. She grabbed the railing to avoid falling overboard.

"You all right, Ms. Bishop?" he asked, hurrying to help.

"I'm okay. That one caught me off guard."

"Maybe you should sit down," he said, patting the captain's chair.

"No," she quickly replied. "I can't see when I'm sitting down."

She returned to her post, her gloved hands gripping the steering wheel, ready to do her duty.

"Max!" she gasped in horror, unable to scream. A large tree branch grew out of the darkness and eerily moved toward them like a giant jousting spear. Then another. Then a shadowy shape of a truck-sized rock loomed over the port side of the boat. The screeching sound of metal on rock scraped along under their feet. The boat pitched sharply, throwing them to the floor. Max grabbed the steering wheel with one hand and Emma's arm with the other, stopping her from a headlong collision with the gunwale. The boat skidded along at a precarious angle, scraping hideously the entire length of the hull, before dropping back into the water with a splash.

"What the hell?" he cursed as he scrambled to his feet and peered over the side to check for damage.

"What was that? Did something hit us?"

"No, I think we hit something."

"What?" Emma pulled herself up into the captain's chair.

"I'd say Cherokee Island," Max offered as he moved along the length of the boat, checking for punctures.

"How did we hit an island? I kept the compass heading just where you told me."

"It's not your fault. It's mine." He finished checking the hull then pointed his flashlight at the engines to see if they were still in the down position and the props intact. "I didn't take into account the drift." He tried the engines. They faithfully turned over, chugging like nothing had happened.

"You mean we drifted into Cherokee Island?"

"Yep. Each time we stopped and shut down the engines, this wind and the waves pushed us sideways. We zigzagged our way right into it. Are you okay?"

"I think so."

Max stood up straight, his eyes narrowed, his forehead furrowed in thought.

"It couldn't be?" he muttered under his breath.

"What? What couldn't be?"

"The wind. Yeah. The wind." His expression grew intense.

"The wind pushed Lan off course," Emma said as if it were a blinding revelation.

"We're searching on the wrong side of the island. The wind probably pushed that little sixteen-footer like a cork. I bet she's on the downwind side of the island."

He spun the steering wheel and maneuvered around the end of the island. They both felt a renewed urgency and a bitter guilt for the time already wasted searching in the wrong place.

"Where do we look?" Emma asked, shining her flashlights across the bow.

"I bet she got pushed a good half mile downwind. She got her bearings and started back but by the time she reached the middle of the lake, she was being rolled and blown right for Cherokee Island and she didn't even know it."

"Stop, Max," Emma yelled, the flashlight capturing the bow of a partially submerged boat. "What's that?"

Max shut off the engines and allowed the boat to drift over to the bobbing tip of the small boat. He reached down and snagged the rope that was floating like a dead snake. It pulled heavy, like a whole boat was on the other end.

"This is hers," he announced, kneeling to pull it close enough to check for damage. As he eased it over to one side, the submerged damage rose out of the water like the gaping jaws of a hungry shark. There was no need to soften the news for Emma. She had already seen it for herself—a hole big enough to push an outboard motor through was ripped in the side. The outboard motor was twisted sideways, the propeller suspended above the motor mount. Max shone a flashlight into the hole.

"What's that, hooked on the prop?" he asked, holding the boat steady with one hand and training the light on a dark blue object tangled around the propeller with the other.

Emma knelt down next to him and pulled the boat around to retrieve whatever it was.

"It's a pair of jeans. Lan's jeans," she said, trying to untangle them through a veil of tears. "Oh no. It can't be." She pulled the jeans free then clutched them to her chest, tears streaming down her face. "We have to find her. Please," she pleaded. She fumbled her flashlight back into action, wiping the tears from her face with the back of her glove.

"It's okay, Emma. She'd take her jeans off if she were in the water. They would be too heavy. She'd can't swim with them on." Max took the anchor from the storage bin and tied it to the wreckage then slipped it into the water.

"Why are you bothering to anchor that boat? You are wasting time."

"I don't want it to drift over the dam or be sucked into the turbines. If I don't anchor it here, by morning it will be over the spillway." As soon as he said it, he knew he had added another piece of gory detail Emma didn't need to hear. He pushed the wrecked boat back with his foot. He joined her in sweeping the surface of the water with his flashlight, stopping at every whitecap, hoping it was Lan. Emma blinked back the tears that clouded her vision. She gripped the light in both hands, as if it would perform better if she were in complete control of it.

Max released the lock and lowered the trolling motor over the side. With a flashlight in one hand, the other guiding the trolling motor and a foot on the throttle, he began a zigzag search pattern. Emma never took her eyes off the water. The wind that usually subsided after dark, continued to increase, whipping relentlessly at their faces, splashing cold, stinging water over the deck, wetting their shoes and pant cuffs. Back and forth, in ever-expanding arcs he steered.

"Lan," Emma continued to call out, her voice cracking from the cold and fear.

She didn't seem to notice her face and ears were red from the spray, her lips blue from the cold. Max's ponytail flailed at his neck, the cold wind slapping at the leather toughness of his face.

"It is so cold, Max. How can she survive when it is so cold and windy?"

"She is a good swimmer. She will be all right. The beaver and otter will protect her. The spirits of survival will be with her," he said confidently. "Be with Allana, oh great spirits," he called, raising his voice to the sky. "Warm her, guide her, give her strength."

Emma added a silent prayer, as deep and full of love as she could muster.

"Listen," he gasped, releasing the throttle on the trolling motor.

They both strained to hear whatever it was but there was only the sound of wind.

"I don't hear anything," she whispered.

"Wait." He turned his head and listened. "There it is again."

A faint garbled whistle cut the cold night wind. Then another.

"A whistle! I hear a whistle," she declared ecstatically.

"That is Lan. That is her whistle." Max pointed his light in the direction of the sound. He wet his lips and blew a loud reply then listened intently. Nothing. He whistled again and waited. Three distant chirps floated back across the water. He nodded to Emma, a twinkle in his eye signaling his relief.

Emma smiled broadly, the tears once again rolling down her cheeks. This time they were tears of joy and relief.

He quickly adjusted their course and headed for the sound.

"Over here," Lan's tired voice gurgled.

"Lan, we're coming. Hold on," Emma called back, desperately fanning the water ahead of them with her light.

"Do you see her?" Max asked as he corrected his course toward her voice.

"Not yet."

"Over here." The voice was growing closer but weaker.

"There she is," Emma shouted as the spotlight captured Lan's head and shoulders, bobbing through the waves, her arms frantically fighting the rising swells.

Max carefully steered alongside as Emma knelt down and extended her hand for Lan to grab.

"Take my hand, babe," she commanded. Just as she was about to make a rescue, the wind rolled a whitecapped wave between them, pushing Lan out of reach, dunking her.

"Lan!" Emma reached down into the cold water, groping for anything she could pull up. For an agonizingly long minute Lan remained beneath the surface. Max quickly unlaced his boots and pulled off his jacket. Just as he was ready to dive in, Lan popped up spitting and coughing out parts of Grand Lake.

"There she is, over there. Can you get closer?"

Max returned to the trolling motor and eased the big barge alongside again. Emma lay on her stomach, reached down, grabbed Lan by her shirt collar, and pulled. With one hand on the controls to keep the boat steady, Max tossed a length of rope in front of Lan.

"Grab on," he shouted.

Lan obeyed, her cold and numb hands making a feeble attempt at gripping the line. Max pulled but the rope slipped through her hands. He lowered the rope again.

"Wrap it around you and make a knot. I'll pull you up."

Lan struggled with the rope, the cold water and hypothermia robbing her of rational thought. Emma held tight to her collar as the wind rolled the boat up one wave then down the other side, slapping water in her face, threatening to pull her overboard. Max did his best to keep the boat on a steady course so Lan wouldn't be run over.

"Grab the rope, Lan," Emma grunted through clenched teeth. "Don't you dare go under again, do you hear me?"

Max wrapped the rope around his hand several times and braced himself, ready to pull Lan to safety as soon as she secured the knot. Emma leaned over as far as she could, taking the end of the rope with her free hand and pulling it through the loop Lan was fumbling with. She quickly looped it around and pulled it through again, tugging it down tight.

"I've got you now," Emma whispered, taking Lan's cold hand in hers. "Pull her up, Max. Easy."

Soon Lan's limp, colorless body lay on the deck, clothed only in underpants and a shirt. Emma covered her with her coat. Max tucked his jacket around her shivering legs. No one spoke. It was as if the effort for words was better spent tending to Lan.

"I'm sorry." Lan spoke faintly, her jaw shaking involuntarily from the cold, her lips blue and thin. She looked up at Emma, her eyes full of guilt and vulnerability. "I misjudged the wind."

"Shh . . ." Emma cooed, wiping Lan's face and brushing back her wet hair.

"Wrap this around her." Max tossed a beach towel from the storage box under the seat. "It's not very heavy but it is dry." He cranked up the big engines, checked his compass, and headed for the cove, pressing the throttle all the way open.

Emma held Lan's quivering body close to hers, shielding her from the cold wind. She closed her eyes and hummed quietly, remembering that cold windy boat ride to Two Tree Island and how Lan's body felt so warm and reassuring that day.

"We'll be there soon," she whispered, rocking Lan gently. "Hold on, babe. I've got you."

"I can't stop shaking," Lan stuttered through the violent trembling.

Emma tucked the towel and jacket tightly around her then rubbed Lan's arms vigorously. Her fierce concentration on protecting and warming Lan's nearly lifeless body kept Emma from realizing she was equally cold.

Max roared into the cove and headed for the dock. A few yards from the slip, he put the engine into neutral and waited a few seconds then threw the props into reverse. The boat heaved up over the wake then stopped and settled against the dock. Max killed the engines, hopped ashore, and tied the stern and bowlines securely.

"Can you walk?" Emma asked.

Lan opened her eyes.

"I think so," she replied after taking stock of her still partially numb legs.

"Need some help?" Max bellowed.

"No," Emma and Lan said in unison, Lan's voice growing stronger but still not fully recovered.

Emma helped Lan to her feet. With wobbly legs beneath her strong sense of self-reliance, she grabbed the railing and stepped onto the dock. Lan wasn't a prude, but she wasn't an exhibitionist either. If she had been her normal independently mobile and mentally aware self, she would have wrapped the towel around her waist, or at the very least pulled her wet shirt down over her exposed wet and transparent underpants.

Max took his jacket from Emma and hurried ahead up the steps to the marina.

"I'll get a fire going," he announced.

Lan steadied herself on the guardrail and handed Emma her coat.

"Put this on before you catch cold," Lan said, holding the coat up by one cuff. A shiver ran down her body and back up again.

Emma took the coat and held it open for Lan.

"I'm all right. You put it on," Emma insisted.

Lan ignored the offer and started up the boardwalk.

"Lan Harding, you are one thick-headed woman," she yelled after her.

Lan climbed the two flights of stairs with cautious steps instead of her usual athletic two-at-a-time strides. Emma positioned herself a step behind as a makeshift safety net. By the time they reached the warmth and safety of the marina door, Lan was out of breath and pale. Emma opened the door and helped her inside. Max had restarted the fireplace and it was roaring a much needed welcome.

"Get over here and warm up," he shouted gruffly.

Lan shuddered and shivered her way to the fireplace, Emma supporting her until she sat down on the warm stone hearth. Max poured the last of the coffee in a mug and handed it to Lan.

"There isn't much left and it is pretty strong, but drink it anyway."

It took both hands for her to hold it. She sipped carefully, shaking and spilling half of it.

"Do you need me any more?" he asked, tossing another log on the fire for good measure.

Lan shook her head.

"Then I'll see you tomorrow. I'll lock up the dock before I go." Max stood halfway out the door and looked back at Lan. "I can handle things tomorrow. Why don't you take the day off, rest up?" Max was trying to be coy, suggesting she couldn't possibly be able to work in her weakened condition. After all, she just survived succumbing to hypothermia by the narrowest of margins.

Lan didn't look up. She waved him out the door leaving no doubt she didn't want to discuss it and she wasn't going to be coddled.

"He sounds mad," Lan said, listening to his boots stomp across the wooden deck.

"He's not mad. He was just worried. Like I was."

Lan didn't want to argue. She didn't have the strength. It was taking every bit of energy she had left just to hold her head up and keep from collapsing into a puddle of spent skin and bones.

"You sit here on the hearth," Emma said sternly. "I'll be right back."

Lan nodded. She crossed her arms over her knees and rested her head on her arms. The warm fire flowed over her back and around her. She closed her eyes, too tired to fight the need to rest as her mind forced her to relive the moments after she was thrown into the water.

All she could see was black and cold endless water splashing up at her neck, numbing her arms and legs, squeezing the breath from her lungs and stinging her eyes. She pulled stroke after stroke against the waves, but she felt her efforts were miserably futile against the wind-driven whitecaps. No matter which way she turned to gasp for breath, a wave was waiting to flood her mouth and lungs with frigid water. She turned onto her back, driving powerful leg kicks through the water only to have swell after swell pummel her head and push her under. Beneath the surface, it was impossible to tell up from down. She fought the underwater turbulence as it held her down and confused her senses, her lungs burning, aching for air in the hellish black void. Her legs, numb and weak, kicked wildly. Her head broke through the surface at last, her mouth open and gasping for air. There were no lights, no stars, no sounds. Only those of the rolling angry water and the whistling wind. The inborn sense of direction Lan relied on for stability and confidence was muddled. With nothing to base her location on and her body rapidly surrendering to hypothermia, pure survival seemed a monumental task. She pushed and pulled her legs in a clumsy frog kick, her arms swirling at her side.

"Head up," she told herself. "Eyes open."

Which way was north? The wind was out of the north, she remembered that. Blowing straight toward the dam—the spillway—the turbines. The huge, open, spinning, body-eating turbines.

With deliberate kicks, she turned until her face felt the direct full force of the wind. North. That was north. She had to keep heading north. The dam was behind her. Everything was growing thick and garbled, and she was unable to think clearly. But she had to move into the wind—away from the dam. That much she knew. If she let the wind push her south she would go straight over the dam or worse, be sucked into the turbines—being spit out as 110 watts, powering a television set or helping to microwave someone's popcorn. She didn't like popcorn. It always got stuck in her teeth. Nachos, she liked nachos. Microwaved nacho cheese. Kick, keep kicking. She would be sucked through the turbines, her body spent to generate the power to microwave nacho cheese. Warm cheese. Cheese to dip in. She wanted to dip her legs and arms in warm cheese. Just for a minute. She promised she would come right back to the cold water. North, swim north. Kick. Head up.

Her legs were so cold. Numb. No. They had fallen off. She couldn't feel them anymore. Her legs were gone. She wanted to reach down and touch where they had been, but she couldn't make her arms obey. They kept swirling, stirring the water. Doggy paddle. Head up. A cramp from her right calf muscle shot up to her hip. She jerked, her face dipped below the waterline. She craned her neck to bring her nose up above the surface. Her legs hadn't fallen off. They were still there—painfully cramped—but still there. The charley horse stiffened her muscles, sending electric needles up and down her leg. She could no longer tread water with just one numb leg and two tiring arms. She threw her head back and gasped for breath, her mouth and nose breaking the surface of the water like a baby bird hungry for sustenance. She gulped in what seemed like a gallon of dirty lake water then choked and coughed it back out. Head up. Kick. Tread water. North. Move north. Cold. So cold. Numb. Legs are numb. Her head was spinning, unable to formulate clear thoughts, unable to pull her body to the surface and float. Both legs now cramped, locking her body in constant cold numbing pain. With her legs hanging beneath her stiff and useless, she swirled her arms frantically to maintain buoyancy. Moving into the wind was no longer important. Now sheer survival was even in doubt. Sucking in water with every breath was adding to the hypothermia. Would she drown or freeze to death first? She wanted to cry out, to scream at the top of her lungs. Ask the spirits of her ancestors to guide her, warm her, and protect her. With garbled pleas, she called into the darkness. Plaintively, she begged for help. How much longer could she hold out before she disappeared below the surface of Grand Lake? How long?

Lan opened her eyes and raised her head. Emma was draping a blanket around her shoulders and stroking her fingers through Lan's damp hair. Emma saw the memory of fear etched deep into Lan's eyes. Without unnecessary words to clutter the stillness, she knelt in front of Lan and took her trembling hands in hers. A reassuringly warm smile communicated everything Emma couldn't say. As if letting her touch and expression do her bidding for her, Emma could keep her fear, relief, and anger from screaming out in long strings of profanity.

Emma wanted to say, Goddammit, Lan, what the hell were you

thinking! She wanted to scream at her, tell her that she shaved ten years off her life tonight with her reckless and foolhardy antics. Why didn't she wait? Why was she so driven to perfection? Goddamn superwoman. Emma said nothing, though. It was all in her eyes and her smile.

"I'm sorry," Lan whispered as she pressed her cold lips against Emma's forehead. "I didn't mean to scare you. I had no idea the weather was going sour so fast. I thought I could get back before all hell broke loose."

Emma began to speak, but whatever it was she intended to say was washed away by an uncontrollable flood of tears. Lan opened her arms and pulled Emma to her, rocking back and forth as her lover poured herself out in body-shaking sobs.

"I'm okay," Lan continued, hugging her tightly. "I'm safe here with you now, my sweet woman."

Emma laid her head on Lan's lap and wrapped her arms around her legs, her tears spilling out and wetting Lan's legs all over again. She couldn't stop crying if she wanted to. Lan cradled her for a long time, realizing how much pain she had caused for both Emma and Max.

Chapter 19

Within two days, Lan had regained her strength from the near drowning and was once again totally consumed with the last-minute details before Welcome Back Weekend. The last week of work was crunch time for both Emma and Lan, leaving little time for themselves.

"Why are you sitting out here in the parking lot?" Emma asked, sticking her head in the Jeep window, startling Lan out of a daydream. "Tomorrow is your big day. Welcome Back Weekend and grand reopening."

"Just thinking and enjoying the morning," she said, taking a deep breath. "You're here early. It isn't even seven o'clock yet."

"I wanted to get an early start on the final walk-through. Jenny and I have been here since five." Emma tried to stifle a yawn.

"So, whose last-minute to-do list is longer?" Lan asked, climbing out of the Jeep.

"Yours," Emma replied staunchly.

"The one you had yesterday sounded pretty long, too."

"Not me," Emma gloated proudly.

"How about the paint touch-up in the kitchen?"

"Done."

"Well, how about extra sets of cabin keys?"

"Done."

"The missing switch plates?"

"Done."

"Or the broken pane in the French door or the towel dispensers in the restrooms?"

"Done, all of it." Emma grinned smugly.

"Damn, woman. You did get here early."

"I was worried we'd find some problem that required extra work, but we didn't. Everything went very smoothly. I was pleasantly surprised." Emma pulled two certificates from a large envelope and handed them to Lan. "Here, these are for you. Your health department permit and the fire department certificate. You are now rated for one hundred twenty-five in the snack bar and three hundred in the rest of the marina. Those extra extinguishers and kitchen sprayers raised your ratings. It should help on your insurance premium."

"Thanks. I'm sure glad you thought of that." Lan read her certificates proudly, a wide grin spreading across her face. "Does this mean I am back in business?"

"Yes, ma'am. It most certainly does." Emma smiled, sharing in Lan's delight.

Lan couldn't say anything with the lump in her throat. Instead, she handed the certificates back to Emma and signaled for her to replace them in the manila envelope. When it was done, she grabbed Emma around the waist, picked her up, and spun her around, laughing loudly.

"Hurray," she shouted. "Oh my God! It's done. It's done." She kissed Emma's cheeks and continued to spin her in celebration.

"Thank you, Emma. Thank you, thank you." She set her down and rushed to the edge of the parking lot. She perched her hands on her hips and looked at her officially completed marina. "All right," she announced victoriously. She turned to Emma, still grinning wildly. "You did it. You rebuilt my marina."

"Are you happy with it, sweetheart?" she asked.

"Yes. I am more than happy with it. You have given me back my business. I couldn't be more pleased." Lan returned to Emma's side and took her hand. "You did everything you promised and more."

"I'm glad you are pleased. I wanted to make you happy. I wanted you to have your business back just the way it was, or even better. You deserve it. You deserve only the best."

"Thank you." Lan squeezed Emma's hand tenderly. "And now, sweet woman, I have some things to take care of if I want Shared Winds to be ready for tomorrow."

"I have a huge stack of paperwork at the office to finish up, too. I'll be back this evening and we can celebrate." Emma gave Lan an adoring smile.

Lan kissed Emma's hand and stroked her cheek before going inside. The frantic but joyous last-minute preparations for the big day kept Lan's rehired employees busy until mid-afternoon. She sent them home early, knowing the weekend would be exhausting for all of them. Lan had one more detail she wanted to take care of as well. She headed home to hitch up her boat trailer.

Lan backed the Jeep carefully, guiding the boat trailer down the ramp with its precious cargo. Even in the waning evening light, the polished brass railing of the fully restored Chris-Craft shone brightly and the Jeep's taillights danced in the freshly varnished mahogany. When the trailer axles were completed submerged, she turned off the Jeep, set the emergency brake, and climbed out. She released the towrope from the winch and climbed onboard, easing into the driver's seat. She grasped the steering wheel with both hands, rubbing her palms around the wheel, getting a feel for it as if she had never touched it before. But then, she had never before sat behind the wheel of her boat as a seaworthy craft. This was a whole new experience and she wanted to savor it. She blew the road dust off the dashboard and polished the gauge covers with her fingers. There was nothing left to do but start it up. She took a deep preparatory breath and turned the key. It responded instantly with a solid churning of motor and water. She eased the throttle into reverse and backed off the trailer guides. She allowed the boat to idle near the ramp, watching the gauges intently. Oil pressure, good. RPMs, good. Battery charge, good. Personal exhilaration, high.

She nudged the throttle forward and moved out into the middle of the cove. She was surprised at how effortlessly it handled, even smoother than she had hoped. With a strong protective instinct for her newly rebuilt engine, she ignored the urge to head out of the cove for open water and high speeds. Instead, she settled for touring the cove in lazy circles and figure eights, moving from one side to the other. Like a child with a new bicycle, she hated to stop. She was having too much fun to call it a night, even on this restricted course. Finally she accepted that it was time to pull into the slip and turn it off. Playtime was over. She headed for the slip but at the last possible moment, she spun the wheel and went back out for one more go-around, a playful grin on her face. She finally parked it in its spot and turned off the engine. She leaned back and draped her arm over the back of the seat, her hand massaging the new upholstery, smiling contentedly.

Lan felt her world coming into a new and comforting balance. The marina was finished and ready for Welcome Back Weekend. Her boat was rebuilt and running like the day it was new. And best of all, Emma Bishop was in her life. She stepped onto the dock and engaged the hoist, locking the boat safely out of the water. Lan patted it lovingly, pride swelling her chest.

"There you are," Emma declared, walking toward the dock. She spied the Chris-Craft and hurried to get a better look. "Oh, Lan. It is beautiful. I didn't know you were bringing it to the marina today." She fawned over the boat, rubbing the side with long strokes. "This is the most gorgeous boat I have ever seen. You should be very proud of yourself, sweetheart. Your hard work shows. It is wonderful."

"Tomorrow, if I have time, we'll go for a ride," Lan replied. "The first day of Welcome Back Weekend is pretty hectic sometimes."

"That's okay. We'll get around to it soon. Tomorrow is Shared Winds' day to shine." Emma wiped some water droplets from the shiny brass railing. "It's great you have your boat all finished and back at the marina for the grand reopening."

"I thought it was only fitting to have her here at the dock." Lan watched as Emma walked the length of the boat, admiring the pristine beauty and graceful elegance. When she reached the stern, Emma stopped, staring at the name freshly painted on the end in gold script lettering. She turned her eyes to Lan and smiled.

"*Dancer*. I like that." Emma boasted, "It is a perfect name for such a graceful creature. Just like its owner."

Lan blushed. "I named her for the teacher."

"Oh, sweetheart, thank you."

Lan leaned back against a post and looked at Emma proudly.

"What?" Emma asked at her pensive grin.

"I was just thinking about that first time you came down here. Do you remember?"

"Yes, I do. It was at night," Emma reflected.

"You stepped in a hole, right over there."

"And you rescued me," she added softly.

"I didn't rescue you. I just kept you from falling through."

"I wasn't talking about the hole. I was talking about rescuing my business for me. You trusted me when I desperately needed someone to trust me."

"Has Quinn said anything yet about you and the company?" Lan asked hopefully. She knew it was weighing on Emma's mind even though she tried to hide it.

"No, not yet," she replied, trying to mask her disappointment. She took a deep slow breath then forced an acceptable smile.

Lan knew Emma was both concerned about her future and fighting self-doubt about her abilities.

"I just let you do what you do best, take care of the details. From what I have heard, we beat the odds. According to the experts, Shared Winds had too much damage, too little time, and too inexperienced a contractor." Lan looked up at her beautifully repaired marina.

"I heard that, too," Emma replied, sharing in the accomplishment.

"Fortunately, I'm not a gambler," Lan said.

"You gambled on me."

"That was no gamble." Lan reached out and gathered Emma in. "Just an investment."

"I'm so glad you think so." Emma leaned into her, wrapping her arms around her waist. "If things don't work out with the construction company, you can hire me to grill hot dogs or pump gas."

"Do you have a resume? How about references?" Lan teased.

"My resume is impeccable. On my last job, I worked for this very stubborn and independent part-Cherokee woman who owned a marina that was damaged by a tornado. She expected miracles and accepted nothing less than best efforts."

"Oh, really?"

"Yes. She is very much like you." Emma poked Lan in the ribs.

"Maybe I need someone like that. You could introduce me." Lan arched her brow wickedly.

"Oh, no you don't. You don't need to be introduced to anyone. You are taken, woman." Emma grabbed Lan's butt with both of her hands. "You are mine."

"Good." Lan held Emma in her arms and swayed back and forth.

"I'm looking forward to a long, long relationship. One filled with quiet nights by the fireplace and long walks in the woods. And maybe a picnic or two."

"How about boat rides?"

"If it's all right with you, can we save those for warm weather?" Emma suggested with a wink.

"Emma. Emma Bishop." Quinn stood at the railing on the deck looking out over the dock.

"Down here, Dad," she called back. She gave Lan a quick kiss and swatted her on the butt as Quinn started down the stairs.

"Hi, Quinn," Lan said as he approached.

"Hi, Dad," Emma added. "How's Mom?"

"Hello, Lan. And hello daughter of mine." Emma gave him a welcoming kiss. "Your mother is fine and wondering why we haven't seen much of you lately. When are you coming out for dinner?"

"Tell her I'm sorry but you know how hectic the final few weeks can be."

"That's what I told her you'd say." They smiled at each other in mutual understanding of frantic last-minute corrections and additions.

"So you're all finished?" he asked guardedly.

"All finished. Not a speck of paint or a loose screw unaccounted for," Emma boasted.

Lan nodded her head in agreement. "Inspections and certificates even framed and hung on the wall."

"I'll bet you are glad to have the mess gone," he joked.

"I have a whole new respect for a freshly swept floor."

He reached in the brown grocery sack he was carrying and took out a bottle.

"I brought you something," he said, handing Lan a bottle of champagne with a bow stuck on the top. "But it isn't for drinking."

"Thank you," Lan replied skeptically, not sure what else he thought she should do with it.

"It's for the christening," he added, noticing Lan's apprehensive stare. "Big events like this usually have ribbon cutting. I thought it would be more appropriate to have a launching, being by the water and all. If Shared Winds was a ship, you would break the bottle over the bow. But I think you can find something to whack it on. Consider it launching your newly repaired marina into service."

"Thank you, Quinn. I appreciate this." Lan offered her hand. He shook it, accepting her heartfelt thanks.

"I hope it brings you good luck, Lan," he said sincerely.

Emma, surprised and gratified, smiled proudly at her father's gesture.

"And I hope to see more of you," he added then looked over at his daughter. "Maybe the two of you could come out for dinner soon."

"I'd like that," Lan offered gladly.

"Are you and Mom coming out tomorrow for the grand reopening? Lan promised you a hot dog, you know," Emma asked, putting her arm around her father.

"We can't, honey. We're flying out to Vegas for the weekend. We're leaving at seven-thirty in the morning. That's why I came out this evening."

Emma's face melted into disappointment.

"I know I said we'd be here, honey. But you can blame it on your Uncle Ross. He and Shirley are going with us and he made the reservations."

"I should be furious with you. This is my first big job and I finished on time and under budget." Emma scowled.

He gave her a hug and kissed her on the cheek. "You did a great job. You conquered all the problems like a true professional. I'm very proud of you, Emma."

He turned and gave a long slow look around. "It's a first-rate job. I couldn't have done better myself."

Lan stopped herself before reminding him he hadn't wanted the job, but Emma did. She wanted to tell him how great Emma was, how well she could handle the business. She wanted to go to bat for her and explain how he should trust her enough to take over Bishop Construction. But it wasn't Lan's place to do that. This was a business matter between father and daughter, owner and employee. It was up to Emma to demonstrate her ability and up to Quinn to accept it. Lan just smiled and nodded in agreement that yes, she had done a great job.

Quinn checked his watch. "Honey, I'm sorry but I have to go. I'm meeting your mother at La Varone's for dinner and I'm going to be late as it is. By the way, I left you two a little something up on the deck. Break that bottle over the dock then go up and toast your completed marina with the other bottle I left up there." He patted Emma's back and turned to head up the boardwalk.

"I still owe you that hot dog, Quinn," Lan called after him.

"Mustard and onions," he replied, looking back with a grin.

"You bet."

Lan and Emma watched as he climbed the stairs to the parking lot. They waited until he had pulled out and the sound of his truck engine faded into the night.

"That was nice of him to bring this," Lan said, reading the label on the bottle. "This isn't cheap stuff, you know."

"This isn't a cheap marina," Emma added.

"True," Lan replied with a raised eyebrow.

"So, are you going to christen it?"

"Seems like a waste of good champagne, but I think Shared Winds deserves a good send-off."

"Definitely."

Lan went to the end of the dock, held the bottle up to the night stars, and offered a silent prayer to God and to the spirits for their help in giving Shared Winds back to her. She also gave thanks for Emma Bishop in her life. She held the bottle by the neck and whacked it hard against the dock, just above the waterline. The bottle exploded and fell into the water, showering champagne over the flooring. With a satisfied grin, Lan raised her arms in victory. Emma applauded and cheered, like a witness to an Olympic champion.

"How does it feel to be back in business, Ms. Harding?" she asked in her best reporter voice.

"Great!" Lan beamed. "I am truly pleased."

"Come on. Let's go toast a completed job."

They hurried up to the deck, arm in arm. Quinn had left an ice bucket with a bottle of chilled champagne and two champagne glasses on the railing. Beside it was a small package, with a red bow and a card that read, To Emma, From a proud father.

Emma examined the little box, deciding if she wanted to open it before the toast or wait until later.

"Open it," Lan admonished as she fumbled with the cork.

"Okay," Emma agreed. "I wonder what it is. Dad isn't much on gifts."

She unwrapped it and opened the little box carefully. She took out one of the fresh new business cards from the package and read it. Her mouth opened and her eyes immediately filled with tears. Unable to speak, she handed the card to Lan to read.

It said: Bishop Construction. Emma Bishop, Owner.

About the Author

Kenna White lives in a small town nestled in the Ozarks where she enjoys her writing, traveling, making dollhouse miniatures, and life's simpler pleasures.